Rafael Sabatini, creator of s
was born in Italy in 1875
Switzerland.. He eventually seuucu in England in 1892, by which
time he was fluent in a total of five languages. He chose to write in
English, claiming that 'all the best stories are written in English'.

His writing career was launched in the 1890s with a collection of
short stories, and it was not until 1902 that his first novel was
published. His fame, however, came with *Scaramouche*, the much-
loved story of the French Revolution, which became an international
bestseller. *Captain Blood* followed soon after, which resulted in a
renewed enthusiasm for his earlier work.

For many years a prolific writer, he was forced to abandon writing
in the 1940s through illness and he eventually died in 1950.

Sabatini is best-remembered for his heroic characters and high-
spirited novels, many of which have been adapted into classic films,
including *Scaramouche, Captain Blood* and *The Sea Hawk* starring
Errol Flynn.

Gerr,

The Hounds of God

Rafael Sabatini

I hope that you, also, will one day be "Sir Gervase"! Happy birthday!

HOUSE OF STRATUS

love x kisses,
Billy x Mags

This edition published in 2001 by House of Stratus, an imprint of
Stratus Books Ltd., 21 Beeching Park, Kelly Bray,
Cornwall, PL17 8QS, UK.

www.houseofstratus.com

Typeset, printed and bound by House of Stratus.

A catalogue record for this book is available from the British Library
and the Library of Congress.

ISBN 07551-153-9-2

Contents

Contents (contd)

Chapter 1

The Misanthrope

It was Walsingham who said of Roger Trevanion, Earl of Garth, that he preferred the company of the dead to that of the living.

This was a sneering allusion to the recluse, studious habits of his lordship. His lordship, no doubt, would have regarded the sneer as a thunderbolt of lath; that is, if he regarded it as a thunderbolt at all. It is much more likely that he would have accepted the statement in its literal sense, admitted the preference and justified it by answering that the only good men were dead men. This because, being dead, they could no longer work any evil.

You conceive that the experience of life which brings a man to such a conclusion cannot have been pleasant. His misanthropy dated from his adolescence, arose out of his close friendship for the gallant Thomas Seymour, who was brother to one queen and husband to another, and who, under the spur of ambition and perhaps indeed of love, would, upon the death of Katharine Parr, have married the Princess Elizabeth. As Seymour's devoted and admiring friend, he had seen at close quarters the slimy web of intrigue in which the Lord Admiral was taken, and he had narrowly escaped being taken with him and with him sent to the block. He had witnessed the evil working of the envious ambition of the Protector Somerset, who, fearful lest fruition of the affair between the Lord Admiral and the Princess should lead to his own ultimate supersession, had not scrupled to bring his brother to the scaffold upon a fabricated charge of high treason.

It was pretended that the Admiral was already the lover of the Princess and that he conspired with her to overthrow the established regency and to seize the reins of power with his own hands. Indeed, the full pretence was that his courtship of the Princess was no more than a step in the promotion of his schemes. The two offences were made so interdependent that either might be established upon evidence of the other.

Young Trevanion suffered arrest, together with all the principal persons in the household of the Princess Elizabeth, and all who were in close relations with the Admiral, whether as servants or as friends. Because he was at once a member of the household of the Princess and probably more in Seymour's confidence than any other man, he became the subject of assiduous attention on the part of the Council of Regency. He was brought repeatedly before that Council, examined and re-examined, questioned and probed *ad nauseam*, with the object of tricking him into incriminating his friend by admissions of what he had seen at Hatfield whilst living there and of what confidences his friend might have reposed in him.

Although, years later, when the admission could do no harm to any, his lordship is known to have confessed that the Admiral's passion for the young Princess was very real and deep, with roots in other than ambition, and that once at Hatfield he had surprised her in the Admiral's arms – from which it may reasonably be concluded that she was not indifferent to his passion – yet before the Council, young Trevanion could remember nothing that might hurt his friend. Not only did he stubbornly and stoutly deny knowledge, direct or indirect, of any plot in which Seymour was engaged; but, on the contrary, he had much to say that was calculated to prove that there was no substance whatever behind this shadow of treason cast upon the Admiral. By his demeanour he put the members of the Council in a rage with him on more occasions than one. It was an education to him of the lengths to which human spite can be carried. The Protector, himself, went so far once as to warn him savagely that his own head was none so safe on his shoulders that by pertness of words and conduct he should himself unsettle it further. Their malevolence, begotten as he perceived of jealous fear, made these men, whom he had accounted among the noblest in England, appear despicable, mean and paltry.

Under the shadow of that malevolence Trevanion was sent to the Tower, and kept there until the day of Seymour's execution. On that blustering March morning he was granted a favour which he had not ventured to solicit; he was conducted to the chamber in which his doomed friend was imprisoned and left alone with him to take his leave.

He was one-and-twenty at the time, an age in which life is so strong in a man and death so abhorrent that it is almost terrifying to look upon another who is about to die. He found the Admiral in a state of composure which he could not understand; for the Admiral too was still young, scarcely more than thirty, tall, vigorous, well made and handsome. He sprang up to greet Trevanion almost gladly. He talked volubly for the few moments they were together, scarcely allowing the younger man to interject a word. He touched almost tenderly upon their friendship, and whilst moved by Garth's sorrow, desired him to be less glum, assured him that death was no great matter once you had brought yourself to look it in the face. He had taken a full leave, he announced, of the Lady Elizabeth, in a letter which he had spent most of the night in writing to her; for although denied pen and ink by the Lords of the Council, he had plucked an aglet from his hose and contrived to write with that, and with the ink supplied by his own veins. This letter, he told Trevanion, speaking boldly and loudly, was concealed within the sole of his shoe, and a person of trust would see to its safe delivery after he was gone. There was an odd smile on his lips as he made the announcement, a singular slyness in his fine eyes, which puzzled Trevanion at the time.

They embraced and parted, and Trevanion returned to his own prison to pray for his friend and to resolve the riddle of that unnecessary and indeed incautious confidence touching the letter in his shoe. Later he understood.

With the knowledge of men which the Admiral possessed, he had been quick to conclude that it was out of no kindly feelings Trevanion had been permitted to pay him this last visit. It was the hope of the Lords of the Council that Seymour might seize the opportunity to send some message to the Princess which would be incriminating in character, and their spies were posted to overhear and report. But Seymour, guessing this, had taken full advantage of it to inform them of the existence of letters which he desired them to find, letters which had been written so that they might be found, couched in such terms that their publication must completely vindicate the Princess.

That was the last act of Seymour's devotion. Although the letters were never published, they may have done their work by limiting the persecution to which the Lady Elizabeth was thereafter subject. But the jealous spite which had spilled Seymour's blood left the honour of the Princess besmirched by the foul tales that were current of her relations with the Admiral.

It was Trevanion, himself, some months later, after his release and when about to withdraw from the scene of events which had killed his faith in men, who, in going to take his leave of the Princess Elizabeth, informed her of the letter. And that slim girl of sixteen, with a sigh and a sad smile that would have been old on a woman twice her years, had repeated, perhaps in a different tone, the cautious words she had used of the Admiral on an earlier occasion.

"He was a man of much wit but very little judgement. God rest him!"

It was perhaps because Trevanion accounted this requiem so inadequate that when she would have had him resume his place in her household, he was glad to be able to answer her that this the Lords of the Council had already expressly denied him. Besides, his one desire was to remove himself from the neighbourhood of the Court. He had been through the valley of the shadow, and he had been permitted to perceive the vile realities, the unscrupulous ambitions, the evil greed, the unworthy passions festering under the fair surface of court life. It had filled him with loathing and disgust, and had put a definite end to all courtly aspirations in himself.

He withdrew to his remote Cornish estates, there to devote himself to husbandry and to the care of his people, matters which his father and grandfather had entrusted to their stewards. Nor was he to be lured thence by an invitation from the Princess Elizabeth when she became queen and desired to reward those who had served her in her time of tribulation.

He married, some ten years later, one of the Godolphins, a lady of whom repute says that she was so beautiful that to behold her was to love her. If that is true of her it would appear to be the only commendation she possessed. She was destined to carry the disillusioning of the Earl of Garth yet a stage further. A foolish, empty, petulant creature, she made him realize once again that the fairest skin may cover the sourest fruit, whereafter she departed this life of a puerperal fever within a fortnight of the birth of their only child, some five years after their ill-matched union.

Just as his one glimpse below the surface of Court life had sufficed him, so his one experience of matrimony surfeited him. And although only thirty-six at the time of her ladyship's death he undertook no further adventures in wedlock, nor indeed adventures of any kind. He was soul-weary, a distemper that not infrequently attacks the thoughtful and introspective. He took to books, by which he had always been attracted; he amassed at Trevanion Chase a prodigious library, and as the years slipped by he became more and more interested in the things that had been and the things which philosophy taught him might be, and less in those that actually were. He sought by study to probe the meaning, purpose and ultimate object of life, than which there is no pursuit more likely to alienate a man from the business of living. He became more and more aloof, took less and ever less heed of events about him. The religious dissensions by which England was riven left him unmoved. Not even when the menace of Spain hung like a black cloud over the land, and everywhere men were arming and drilling against the day of invasion, did the Earl of Garth, now well advanced in years, awaken to interest in the world in which he lived.

His daughter, who had been left more or less to bring herself up as she chose, and who by a miracle had accomplished the task very creditably, was the only living person who really understood him, certainly the only one who loved him, for you conceive that he did not invite affection. She had inherited a considerable portion of her mother's good looks, and most of the good sense and good feeling that had distinguished her father in his youth, with just enough of her mother's perversity to give a spice to the mixture. If she reached – as she eventually did – the age of twenty-five unmarried the fault was entirely her own. There had been suitors to spare at any time after her seventeenth year, and their comings and goings at times had driven his Lordship to the verge of exasperation. She was credited with having broken several hearts. Or, to put it more happily, since that untruly implies an undesirable activity on her part, several hearts had been broken by her rejection of their infatuated owners. She had remained as impassive as one of the rocks of that Cornish coast against which ships might break themselves if hard-driven by weather or ill-handled.

She loved her liberty too well to relinquish it. Thus she informed her suitors. Like the queen, she was so well satisfied with her maiden estate that she accounted it the best estate in the world and was of no mind to change it for any other.

This was no mere pretext upon which mercifully to dismiss those wooers who did not commend themselves. It was, there is every reason to believe, the actual truth. The Lady Margaret Trevanion had been reared, as a result of her father's idiosyncrasies, in masculine freedom. Hers from the age of fifteen or sixteen to come and go unquestioned; horses and dogs and hawks had engrossed her days; she was as one of the lads of her own age with whom she associated; her frank boyishness kept her relations with them on exactly the same plane as that which marked the association of those boys with one another. If the advent of her first suitor when she had reached the age of seventeen produced the result of setting a check upon her hoydenishness, arousing her to certain realities and imposing upon her thereafter a certain introspection, she did not on that account abandon her earlier pursuits or the love of personal liberty which their free indulgence had engendered in her. The odd thing is that she was nowise coarsened by the masculinity with which her unusual rearing had invested her. Just as the free and constant exercises of her tall supple body appeared but to have enriched it in feminine grace, so the freedom of mental outlook upon which she had insisted had given her a breadth and poise of mind from which she gathered a dignity entirely feminine, as well as command over herself and others. She afforded perhaps a remarkable instance of the persistence of inbred traits and how they will assert themselves and dominate a character in spite of environment and experience.

At the time at which I present her to you she had reached her twenty-third year firmly entrenched in her maidenhood; and, with the plainly asserted intention of remaining in that estate, she had so far successfully discouraged all suitors but one. This one was an amiable lad named Gervase Crosby, of a considerable Devon family, a kinsman to Lord Garth's neighbour, Sir John Killigrew of Arwenack, and a persistent fellow who could not take "no" for an answer. He was a younger son with his way to make in the world, and Killigrew, a bachelor, with no children of his own, had taken an interest in him and desired to promote his fortunes. As a result of this the boy had been much at Arwenack, that stately castellated house above the estuary of the Fal. Killigrew was closely connected with the Godolphins and therefore looked upon the Earl of Garth as a kinsman by marriage and upon Margaret as a still closer kinswoman on the maternal side. He was one of the few among the surrounding gentry who ventured freely to break through the seclusion in which the old earl hedged himself about, and who was not to be discouraged by the indifference of his welcome at his lordship's hands. It was under his aegis that young Crosby was first brought to Trevanion Chase, when a well-grown handsome lad of sixteen. Margaret liked him and used him with frank boyish friendliness which encouraged him to come there often. They were much of an age, and they discovered a similarity in tastes and an interest in the same pursuits which made them fast friends.

Killigrew, after much deliberation, had resolved that his young kinsman should study law, with a view to a political career. He argued that if young Crosby's brains were any match for his long comely body there should be a brilliant future for him at the Court of a queen who was ever ready to promote the fortunes of a handsome man. Therefore he brought tutors to Arwenack and set about the lad's education. But, as often happens, the views of young and old did not here coincide. Crosby was of a romantic temperament, and he could perceive no romance in the law, however much Killigrew might labour to demonstrate it for him. He liked a life of adventure; to live dangerously was in his view the only way to be really alive. The world was still ringing with the echoes of the epic of Drake's voyage round the globe. The sea and the sailor's opportunity to probe the mysteries of the earth, penetrating uncharted oceans, discovering fabulous lands, called him; and finally Killigrew yielded, being wise enough to perceive that no man will make a success of a career in which his heart is not engaged.

Sir John took the boy to London. That was in 1584, just after his twentieth birthday. Before setting out upon that voyage of adventure, Gervase had desired to establish moorings at home against his return, and he had offered himself, heart and. hand and the fortune which he was to make, to the Lady Margaret.

If the offer did not dazzle her ladyship, it certainly startled her. From their fairly constant association, she had come to regard him almost as a brother, had come to permit him those familiarities which a sister may permit, had even upon occasion allowed a kiss or two to pass between them with no more than sisterly enthusiasm. That, unsuspected by her, there should have been anything more than brotherliness on his part seemed ludicrous. She said so, and brought down upon herself a storm of reproaches, pleadings and protestations which soared in moments to heights of terrifying vehemence.

The Lady Margaret was not terrified. She remained calm. The self-reliance which her rearing had imposed upon her had taught her self-control. She took refuge in that phrase of hers about her preference for a maiden estate. What was good enough for the Queen, she announced, was good enough for her, as if making of virginity a point of loyalty.

Shocked and dejected, Gervase went to take his leave of her father. His lordship, who had just discovered Plato and was absorbed in that philosopher's conception of the cosmos, desired to cut these valedictions short. But Gervase deemed it incumbent upon him to enlighten the earl on the subject of his daughter's unnatural views of life. No doubt he hoped, with the irrepressible optimism of the young, to enlist his lordship's aid in bringing her ladyship to a proper frame of mind. But his lordship, irritated perhaps by the interruption, had stared at him from under shaggy eyebrows.

"If she chooses to lead apes in hell, what affair is that of yours?"

If Master Crosby had been shocked already by the daughter's attitude towards what he accounted the most important thing in life, he was far more deeply shocked by her sire's. This, he thought, was a nettle to be grasped. So he grasped it.

"It is my affair, because I want to marry her."

The earl maintained his disconcerting level stare. He did not even blink.

"And what does Margaret want?" he asked.

"I have told your lordship what she says she wants."

"Since she says what you say she says, I wonder that you think it worth while to trouble me."

This would have discouraged any young man but Gervase Crosby. He drew a swift shrewd inference favourable to himself. I suspect that Killigrew had good reasons besides the lad's looks and inches for intending him for the law, just as I suspect that a good lawyer was lost in him when he took to the sea.

"Your lordship means that I deserve your approval, and that if I can bring Margaret to a change of views… "

"I mean," his lordship interrupted him, "that if you bring Margaret to a change of views I will then consider the situation. It is not my habit to deal with more than I find before me, or to plague myself over possibilities which may never become realities. It is a habit which I commend to you now that you are about to go forth into the world. Too much good human energy is wasted in providing for contingencies that never arise. I make you, in these words, if you will trouble to bear them in your memory, a parting gift of more value than you may at present discern. I shall hope to hear of your good fortune, sir."

Thus the misanthrope dismissed the lover.

Chapter 2

The Lover

Mr Crosby's bearing was marked upon his departure from Arwenack by none of that exultation proper to the setting out of a young man who regards the world as his oyster. Too much that he valued was being left behind unsecured; and the earl, he could not help admitting to himself, had not been encouraging. But what youth desires it believes that it will ultimately possess. His confidence in himself and in his star was restored and his natural buoyancy re-established long before the journey was accomplished.

Travelling by roads which were obstacles to, rather than means of progress, Sir John Killigrew and his young cousin reached London exactly a week after setting out. There no time was lost. Sir John was a person of considerable consequence, wielding great influence in the West and therefore to be well-received at Court. Moreover some personal friendship existed between himself and the Lord Admiral Howard of Effingham. To the Admiral he took his young cousin. The Admiral was disposed to be friendly. Recruits for the navy at such a time, especially if they happened to be gentlemen of family, were more than welcome. The difficulty was to find immediate employment for Mr Crosby. The Admiral took the young man to Deptford and presented him to the manager of Her Majesty's dockyards, that old-time slaver and hardy seaman, Sir John Hawkins. Sir John talked to the lad, liked him, admired his clean length of limb and read promise in his resolute young countenance and frank steady blue eyes. If he was in haste for adventure, Sir John thought he could put him in the way of it. He gave him a letter to his young kinsman, Sir Francis Drake, who was about to put to sea from Plymouth, though on the object of that seagoing Sir John seemed singularly – perhaps wilfully – ignorant.

Back to the West went Gervase, once more in the charge of Killigrew. At Plymouth they sought and duly found Sir Francis. He paid heed to the strong recommendation of Hawkins' letter, still greater heed to the personality of the tall lad who stood before him, some heed also, no doubt, to the fact that the lad was a kinsman of Sir John Killigrew, who was a considerable power in Cornwall. Young Crosby was obviously eager and intelligent, knew already at least enough of the sea to be able to sail a fore-and-aft rig, and was fired by a proper righteous indignation at the evil deeds of Spain.

Drake offered him employment, the scope of which he could not disclose. A fleet of twenty-five privateers was about to sail. They had no royal warrant, and in what they went to do they might afterwards be disowned. It was dangerous work, but it was righteous. Gervase accepted the offer without seeking to know more, took leave of his kinsman, and went on board Drake's own ship. That was on the 10th September. Four mornings later Drake's maintop was flying the signal "up anchor and away".

If none knew, perhaps not even Drake himself, exactly what he went to do, at the least all England, simmering just then with indignation, knew why he went to do it, whatever it might prove to be. There was a bitter wrong to be avenged, and private hands must do the work since the hands of authority were bound by too many political considerations.

In the North of Spain that year the harvest had failed and there was famine. Despite the hostile undercurrent between Spain and England, which at any moment might blaze into open war, despite Spanish intrigues in which Philip II was spurred on by the Pope to exert the secular arm against the excommunicate bastard heretic who occupied the English throne, yet officially at least, on the surface, there was peace between the two nations. England had more corn than she required for her own consumption and was willing to trade it to the famine-stricken Galician districts. But because of certain recent barbarous activities of the Holy Office upon English seamen seized in Spanish ports, no merchant ships would venture into Spanish waters without guarantees. These guarantees had ultimately been forthcoming in the shape of a special undertaking from King Philip that the crews of the grain ships should suffer no molestation.

Into the Northern harbours of Corunna, Bilbao and Santander sailed the ships of the English corn-fleet, there to be seized, in despite of the royal safe-conduct, their cargoes confiscated, their crews imprisoned. The pretext was that England was lending aid to the Netherlands, then in rebellion against Spain.

Diplomatic representations were of no avail. King Philip disclaimed responsibility. The English seamen, he said, were no longer in his hands. As heretics they had been claimed by the Holy Office. To purge them of their heresy, some were left to languish in prison, some sent as slaves to the galleys, and some were burnt in fool's coats at the *autos-de-fé*.

To rescue even those who survived from the talons of the Holy Office was beyond hope. It remained only to avenge them, to read Spain a punitive lesson which she should remember, a lesson which, it was hoped, would teach her to curb in future her zeal of salvation where English heretics were concerned.

The Queen could not act in her own name. For all her high stomach and for all the indignation which it is not to be doubted now consumed her, prudence still dictated that she should avoid with mighty Spain an open war for which England could not account herself prepared. But she was willing enough to give a free hand to adventurers, whom at need she could afterwards disown.

That was the reason of Drake's setting forth with his twenty-five privateer ships. That was the voyage on which Gervase Crosby went to win his spurs in this new order of chivalry whose tilting-yard was the wide ocean. It was a voyage that lasted ten months; but so eventful, adventurous and instructive did it prove that not in as many years of ordinary sailing could it have offered a man a more generous schooling in fighting seamanship.

They sailed first of all into the beautiful Galician port of Vigo at a time when the grapes were being gathered for the vintage, labours which their sudden appearance interrupted. And here Drake published, as it were, his cartel; he made known, inferentially at least, the aim and purpose of that imposing fleet of his. Of the Governor, who sent in alarm to know who and what they were who came thus in force and what they sought at Vigo, Drake asked to be informed whether the King of Spain was at war with the Queen of England. When he was fearfully assured that this was not the case, he asked further to be informed how it happened, then, that English ships which had sailed into Spanish harbour under the safe-conduct of King Philip's word had been seized and their owners, officers and crews imprisoned, maltreated and slain. To this he received no proper answer. He did not press for one unduly; he contented himself with inviting the Governor to consider that English seamen could not suffer that such things should happen to their brethren. After that he demanded water and fresh provisions. There was also a little plundering, a mere ensample this of what might be done. Whereafter, with refurnished ships, Sir Francis sailed away, leaving Spain to conjecture in dismay and rage whither he was going and to concert measures for forestalling and destroying so endemonized an Englishman – *inglez tan endemoniado*.

November saw him at Cape Verde, where he missed the plate fleet upon which no doubt he had intentions. Its capture would have indemnified England for the loss of the confiscated corn. He turned his attention, instead, to the handsome town of Santiago, possessed it, sacked it, and might have been content with that but for the barbarous murder and mutilation of a poor ship-boy, which revived memories of some Plymouth sailors lately murdered there. The town was fired, and Sir Francis sailed away, leaving behind him a heap of ashes to show King Philip that barbarity was not the prerogative of Spain and that talion law existed upon earth and always would exist as long as there were men to enforce it. Let his Most Catholic Majesty learn that Christianity, whose particular champion he accounted himself, had for corner-stone the precept that men should do unto their neighbours as they would have their neighbours do unto them, and, conversely, not do unto their neighbours what was detestable when suffered in their own persons. Lest this King, who was so passionately concerned in the eternal salvation of others, should himself miss salvation through an inadequate appreciation of that great principle, Sir Francis meant to bring it strongly to his notice by further illustration.

The fleet spent Christmas at St Kitts, and having there refreshed itself, went to pay its respects to San Domingo, that magnificent city of Hispaniola, where as a monument to the greatness of Spain the grandeurs of the old world were reproduced in palaces, castles and cathedrals. Here things, without being difficult, were not quite so easy as at Santiago. The Spaniards turned out horse and foot to resist the landing of the English. There was some fighting; some cannonading, in the course of which the Spaniards killed the officer commanding the particular landing-party of which Gervase Crosby was a member. Gervase, eager and audacious, acting upon impulse and without any sort of authority, took his place, and skilfully brought up his men to join the vanguard under Christopher Carlile which carried the gate and cut its way into the town.

For his part in this, Gervase was afterwards commended by Carlile to Drake, and by Drake confirmed in the command which he had so opportunely usurped.

The castle meanwhile had surrendered, and the English put the city to ransom. Its treasure had already been removed out of it, and all that Drake could extract from the Governor was twenty-five thousand ducats, nor did he succeed in extracting this until he had reduced nearly all its marble splendours to ruins.

After San Domingo came Cartagena, where a tougher resistance was encountered, but subdued, and where again young Gervase Crosby showed his mettle when he led the men of his recent command to scale the parapets and engaged the Spanish infantry at point of pike. The captured city saved itself from the fate of Santiago and San Domingo by a promptly forthcoming ransom of thirty thousand ducats.

That was enough for the purpose; enough to show King Philip that the activities of the Holy Office were not meekly to be suffered by English seamen. Destroying in passing a Spanish fort in Florida, Drake's fleet set sail for home and was back in Plymouth by the end of July, having proved to all humanity that the mightiest empire of the world was by no means invulnerable, and having apparently made war inevitable by throwing down a gauntlet which the hesitating King of Spain could hardly ignore.

The Gervase Crosby who came back to Arwenack was a very different person from the Gervase Crosby who had gone forth a year ago. Adventure and experience had ripened him, dangers faced and conquered, and an increase of general knowledge, which included a fair command of Spanish, had given him a calmer self-assurance. Also he was bronzed and bearded. He came in confidence to Trevanion Chase, conceiving that the capture of the Lady Margaret would prove now a trifling matter to one who had been at the capturing of Spanish cities. But the Lady Margaret manifested no enthusiasm for his deeds, when, for her benefit and in her presence, he recounted them to the earl, who had no wish to hear them. When his lordship had heard them despite himself, he curtly pronounced Drake a shameless pirate, and, in the matter of the hanging of some monks at San Domingo, a murderer. His daughter agreeing with him, Master Gervase departed in a dudgeon too deep for expression that his glorious deeds upon the Spanish Main should be so contemptuously dismissed.

The explanation lies in the fact that the Earl of Garth had been brought up in the Catholic Faith. He had long since ceased to practise the Christian religion in any of its forms. The narrow intolerance of priestcraft of whatever denomination had revolted him, and study and brooding, and Plato in particular, had brought him to demand a nobler and wider conception of God than he could discover in any creed alleged to have been revealed. But underneath

16

his philosophic outlook there lingered ineradicably an affection for the faith of his youth and of his fathers. It was purely sentimental, but it vitiated his judgement on those rare occasions when he permitted himself at all to turn his attention to the problems that were afflicting England. Unconsciously, imperceptibly, this had created at Trevanion Chase the atmosphere in which Margaret had been reared. In addition to this, and probably in common with the majority of the gentry of her day – certainly so if we are to believe those who kept King Philip informed of the state of public opinion in England – she could not exclude from her heart sympathy with the Queen of Scots now languishing in an English prison and in peril of her life. The Lady Margaret might be imbued with some of the widespread English antipathy to Spain and resentment of its operations against men of her own English blood; she might shudder at the tales of the activities of the Holy Office; but all this was tempered in her by a disposition to regard King Philip as a Spanish Perseus intent upon the deliverance of the Scottish Andromeda.

Gervase's angrily silent departure she observed with a smile. Afterwards she grew thoughtful. Could the wound be so deep that he would not come again, she wondered. She confessed frankly to herself that she would be sorry if that were so. They had been good friends, Gervase and she; and it was far from her wish that their friendship should end like this. Apparently it was also far from Gervase's wish. He was back again in two days' time, his indignation having cooled, and when she hailed his appearance with a "Give you welcome, Master Pirate!" he had enough good sense to laugh, realizing that she no more than rallied him. He would have kissed her according to the fraternal custom which, had grown up between them, but this she denied him on the score of his beard. She could not suffer to be kissed by a hairy man; she would as soon be hugged by a bear.

As a consequence of this assertion, he appeared before her on the morrow shaved like a puritan, which sent her into such an ecstasy of mirth that he lost his temper, laid rough hands upon her and kissed her forcibly and repeatedly in pure anger and lust to show her that he was master, and man enough to take what he lacked.

At last he let her go, and was prepared to be merry in his turn. Not so the lady. She stood tense and quivering, breathing hard, her face white, save for a red spot on each cheek-bone, her red-gold hair in disorder, and flames in her vivid blue eyes. For a long moment those eyes pondered him in silent fury. This and the outraged dignity which he read in every line of her tall supple figure abashed him a little, rendered him conscious that he had behaved like an oaf.

"Faith!" she said at last with ominous composure of voice, "you must think yourself still in San Domingo."

"In San Domingo?" quoth he, labouring to discover the inference.

"Where you no doubt learnt to mishandle women in this fashion."

"I?" He was scandalized. "Margaret, I vow to God... "

She, however, cared nothing for his vows and interrupted them. "But this is Trevanion Chase, not a city conquered by pirates; and I am the Lady Margaret Trevanion, not some unfortunate Spanish victim of your raid."

He was wounded and indignant. "Margaret, how can you suppose that I...that I..." He became inarticulate. Indeed, there were no words for it that a lady could tolerate. And she, perceiving that she had found the heel of her Achilles, turned the arrow in the wound to avenge herself.

"Such ready expertness argues abundant practice, sir. I am glad to know, even at the cost of the indignity, the quality of those adventures which were left out of your brave narrative to my father. As you boasted, sir, you've learnt a deal on the Spanish Main. But in your place I shouldn't practise in England what you learnt there."

He read in her tone, as she intended that he should, a depth of conviction against which he felt that protestations and arguments would be idle. It would need evidence to dispel it, and where should he find evidence? Moreover, she was no longer there to listen to arguments. She had departed whilst he was still deep in his dumb, bewildered mortification. Useless to go after her in her present mood, he assured himself. And so he went home to Arwenack, trusting dejectedly that time would efface the bad impression he had made and modify the terrible assumptions to which he had given rise.

Time, however, was denied him. Before the month was out there came a summons from Sir Francis recalling him to Plymouth. If he was a clumsy lover, there is no doubt that he was a very promising seaman, as Drake had observed, and Drake had urgent need of all such men. War was coming. That was now beyond all doubt. A great fleet was building in the Spanish dockyards, and in Flanders the Prince of Palma was assembling a mighty army of the best troops in Europe for the invasion of England so soon as the fleet should be ready to cover his passage.

Gervase went to take his leave of Margaret and her father. Lord Garth he found as usual in his library, his gaunt spare frame wrapped in a bed gown, his head covered by a black velvet cap with ear-flaps, his mind fathoms deep in scholarly speculation. The fiddling of Nero during the burning of Rome seemed to Gervase a reasonable, pardonable trifle of conduct, compared with the Earl of Garth's absorption at such a time in the works of men who had been dead a thousand years and more. To startle him out of this unpatriotic lethargy, Master Crosby talked of the Spanish invasion as if it were already taking place. His lordship was not startled. A man who is obsessed by the platonic theory that the earth, the sun, the moon and all the visible heavenly bodies are so much sediment in the ether, with a more or less clear perception of all that this connotes, cannot be expected to concern himself deeply with the fortunes of such ephemeral things as empires.

The traditions and duties of gentility imposed it upon him to dissemble his impatience at the unwelcome interruption of his studies and to utter a courteous God-speed which should straightly put an end to it.

From his lordship, Gervase went in quest of her ladyship. It was a fine autumn day, and he found her taking the air in the garden with a company of gallants. There was that handsome fribble Lionel Tressilian who was too much at Trevanion Chase these days for Gervase's peace of mind. There was young Peter Godolphin, a kinsman of Margaret's, it is true, but not of such near kinship that he might not aspire to make it nearer. And there were a half-dozen other beribboned lute-tinklers, stiffly corseted in modish narrow-waisted doublets, their trunks puffed out with Spanish bombast. He descended upon them with his news, hoping to dismay them out of their airy complacency as he had hoped to dismay the earl.

Ignoring them, he flung his bombshell at the feet of Margaret.

"I come to take my leave. I am summoned by the admiral. The Prince of Parma is about to invade England."

It made some little stir, and might have been more but for the flippancy of young Godolphin.

"The Prince of Parma cannot have heard that Mr Crosby is with the admiral."

It raised a general laugh, in which, however, Margaret did not join. It may have been this little fact that lent Gervase the wit to answer.

"But he shall, sir. If you have messages for him, you gentlemen who stay at home, I will do my best to bear them."

He would gladly have quarrelled with any or all of them. But they would not indulge him. They were smooth and sleek, whilst Margaret's presence made him set limits on his display of the scorn they aroused in him.

When presently he departed, Margaret went with him through the house. In the cool grey hall she paused, and he stood to take his final leave of her. Her eyes were very grave and solemn as she raised them to his face.

"Is it war indeed, Gervase?"

"That is what I gather from the letters I have had and the urgency of this summons. I am to leave at once, the admiral bids me. Every man is needed."

She laid a hand upon his arm, a beautiful tapering hand it was, looking oddly white on the dark crimson velvet of his sleeve. "God keep you, Gervase, and bring you safely back," she said.

It was a commonplace enough thing to say in the circumstances. But the tone she used was a tone he had never heard in her voice before. It should have heartened him, who normally was bold enough, and upon occasion, as we have seen, almost overbold. He might have kissed her then and had no reproach for it. But he couldn't guess it, any more than he could guess that not to take the advantages a woman offers is an even worse offence than to take advantages which she does not offer. So while his heart beat fast with hope at that gentle tone and liquid gaze, it beat also with trepidation.

He gulped and stammered: "You... You'll wait, Margaret?"

"What else? Would you have me follow after you?"

"I mean... You'll wait for me; for my return?"

She smiled up at him. "I think it's very likely, sir."

"Likely? Not certain, Margaret?"

"Oh, certain enough." She had not the heart to rally him. He was going on a business from which he might never return, and the thought made her very tender, gave her almost a foretaste of the sorrow that would be hers if he should be counted among the fallen. She took pity on his halting, and generously gave him the answer he lacked the courage to demand. "It is not likely that I shall marry anyone else, Gervase."

His heart bounded. "Margaret," he cried.

And then Peter Godolphin came mincing into the hall to inquire what it was that kept her ladyship from her guests.

Gervase, wishing him in hell, was forced to cut short his leave-taking. But he was content enough. He took the slim hand that lay upon his sleeve and kissed it reverently.

"Those words, Margaret, shall be as a cuirass to me." Upon which poetical assertion, almost as if ashamed of it, he abruptly departed.

Chapter 3

In Calais Roads

War was not so immediate as Gervase had supposed. Indeed, there were good reasons why neither Spain nor England should desire irrevocably to engage in it.

King Philip, however, urged by the Pope to do his duty as the secular arm of the Faith and dethrone his excommunicated sister-in-law, was, after all, anything but a fool and not unreasonably self-seeking. He must therefore pause to ask himself what profit would accrue to himself from such an enterprise. God and Time and he – King Philip liked to contemplate that conjunction – made up a slow-moving trinity. It was not as if there were any prospect of making England a Spanish province like the Netherlands. The only temporal result would be to place Mary Stuart upon the English throne and the political consequences of this would be to strengthen the French influence which Mary Stuart represented by virtue of her French alliances. The only way to avoid this and to profit Spain would be for Philip to marry Mary and share her English throne. But Philip had no wish to do anything of the kind. He may have observed that the lady's husbands were not lucky. He did not therefore see why Spanish blood and Spanish gold should be poured out for the profit of France. From the temporal point of view, the business was much more the concern of the French king than it was Philip's. There remained the spiritual point of view: the importance of restoring the unadulterated Catholic faith to England and bringing her spiritually once more under the subjection of Rome. Now this was Rome's business, and if the Pope wanted Philip to do Rome's business for him, it was fitting that the Pope should bear the expenses of the enterprise. But when Philip laid this reasonable argument before the Pope, His Holiness – the great Sixtus V – fell into such a rage that he flung his dinner plates about the room.

That was the situation in Spain through the autumn and winter of 1586.

In England nothing could be further from the intention or wish than to declare war. Spain was, after all, the mightiest empire of the day. Her possessions were vast, her wealth fabulous, her strength colossal. The inexhaustible riches of the Indies were at her command, the finest troops in the world served under her banners. Clearly this was not an empire to be challenged. But since danger threatened from it, preparations must be made to meet that danger, if only in obedience to the old Roman maxim that who desires peace should prepare for war.

Hence those naval activities to which Gervase Crosby was summoned; the ship-building, the drilling, the storing of arms, the manufacture of gunpowder, and all the rest. The conflicting orders from Court reflected the uncertainty of the outlook. On Monday came instructions to mobilize the fleet, on Wednesday to disband it, on Saturday to mobilize it again, and so on interminably. But the adventurers, the privateers, took no heed of these ever-fluctuating orders. They went steadily ahead with their preparations. It may have been in the mind of Sir Francis that if war did not come there would still be work for his hands in plucking some more feathers from Spain's rich Indian plumage. He was, there can be no doubt of it, a pirate at heart. Let England not reproach him with it, but be thankful.

In the early part of the year, the whole aspect of the situation was changed by the execution of the Queen of Scots. It was deemed that her removal, so long advocated by farsighted statesmen, by putting an end to plots and intrigues which aimed at enthroning her, and the

Catholic religion with her, in England, must remove the menace of a war which was to be waged for this very purpose.

The effect, however, was the exact opposite. King Philip took the view that if he were now to exert himself as the secular arm of the Church, the fruits of his endeavours would no longer fall into the lap of France. There being no longer a Queen of Scots to be placed upon the throne of England, King Philip might occupy it himself, converting England into a Spanish province so soon as he should have done his duty by executing the bull of excommunication and deposition which had been launched against his heretical sister-in-law. Now that a direct profit was perceived from the affair, the arming for a crusade against heretical pravity went forward amain; the brothers of St Dominic were sent up and down the land to preach the sanctity of the cause; Catholic adventurers from every country flocked in to offer their swords. The hounds of God were straining at the leash. At last King Philip was to loose them at the throat of heretical England.

It occurred to Sir Francis Drake that common sense demanded that something should be done to mar these preparations. To sit back in patience while your avowed enemy arms himself at all points to destroy you is the attitude of the insane.

So Sir Francis went off to London and the Queen. His proposals made her nervous. She was still negotiating a treaty of peace with King Philip through the Spanish ambassador. King Philip, she was assured, wanted peace, on the strong advice of the Prince of Parma, who was finding more than enough to do in the Netherlands.

"So do we want peace, madam," the blunt Sir Francis answered. "I might do something to ensure it."

She questioned him as to his intentions. He had none. He didn't know what he should do until he got there – he did not quite know where – and saw for himself what might be possible. In any treaty of peace she would get the best terms by showing her strength, and so removing all suspicion that she treated because of weakness.

"We'll put on a brag, Your Grace," the sailor laughed.

He was a difficult man to resist when his long, steady grey eyes were upon you. A sturdy fellow of middle height, now in his fortieth year, too powerfully built for grace, but of an engaging countenance with his crisp brown hair and the pointed beard which dissembled the inflexibility of his mouth. The Queen yielded, if reluctantly.

Because he perceived the reluctance, he lost no time in fitting out, and he was away in the *Buonaventura* with a fleet of thirty sail at his heels on a fine April morning, not more than a few hours before the arrival of a courier to detain him. Perhaps he had word that these countermandings were on the way.

Six days later he was in Cadiz Roads discovering for himself what there was to be done, and seeing it clearly there before him in the shipping that crowded the harbour. Here lay the elements of that great expedition against England: the transports, the provision vessels, even some of the mighty ships of war that were now fitting.

What was to be done was as clear to him as how to do it. He went in on a flood tide. He took them unawares. Such an act as this was the last audacity Spain could have expected even from one so audacious and endemonized as El Draque. They ran the gauntlet of the hail of shot from the Spanish batteries, sank the guardship with a broadside, scattered a fleet of galleys that ventured momentarily to oppose them, and swooped down upon their prey.

Twelve days they stayed in Cadiz harbour, during which at his leisure Drake stripped the ships of all that could be useful to him, then set them on fire and so destroyed a million ducats' worth of shipping. When he sailed out again, having, in his own words, thus singed the beard of the King of Spain, he did so in the assurance that the Armada would not sail that year. Not that year would the troops of the Prince of Parma be landed on English soil.

He was correct enough in his estimate, for it was not until May of the year following that the Invincible Armada of a hundred and thirty vessels sailed out of the Tagus in the wake of the *San Martin*, the stately flagship of the Admiral, the Duke of Medina-Sidonia. The fleet sailed in a state of grace. Every man of the thirty thousand distributed through the ships had confessed himself, received absolution of his sins, and had communicated. Every ship had been especially blessed by the Primate of Spain; every mainmast-head carried a crucifix; on the great banner flown by the Admiral, the red and gold standard of Spain, the figures of the Virgin and her Son had been embroidered and the motto "Exsurge Deus et vindica causam tuam"; there was great provision for the care of the souls of those crusaders – greater than the provision for the care of their bodies; for whilst the ships carried two hundred priests they carried fewer than a hundred surgeons. Majestically this mighty fleet, as formidable in spiritual as in temporal armament, advanced on the blue water.

There were delays and difficulties; enough of them to have suggested that the Deity was none so eager to vindicate His cause at the bidding of Spain or through the arm of Spain.

But at last, at the end of July, the invincible fleet was in the Channel and the season of English waiting was at an end. It had not been wasted so far as Drake and the privateers were concerned. Most of them had been at their stations ever since the return from Cadiz, and they had found abundant work for their hands.

They slipped out of Plymouth without any kind of ostentation, and some fifty of them, low-hulled ships, gave the towering Spaniards an exhibition of close-hauled sailing which made them rub their eyes. Reaching easily to windward, their low hulls offering comparatively little target, they crossed the Spanish rear, and whilst themselves out of range of the Spanish cannon, they poured from their own more powerful guns broadside after broadside with deadly effect into those great floating castles. The Spanish ships suffered the greater mortality from being overcrowded: this because they counted upon time-honoured boarding tactics. But the English, outsailing them, and refusing to grapple or be grappled, showed them a new and disconcerting method of sea-fighting. In vain the Spaniards cursed them for cowardly dogs who would not come to hand-grips. The English answered them with broadside and slipped away through the water to go about and empty into them the guns on the other quarter.

To Medino-Sidonia this was all very exasperating in its difference from all that he had expected. The good Duke was not a sailor, nor indeed a fighting man of any kind. He had pleaded his incompetence when the King had placed this responsibility upon his shoulders. He had been abominably sea-sick when first they put to sea, and now he and the mightiest fleet the waters of the world had ever seen were being chased up the Channel like a herd of bullocks before a pack of wolves. The Andalusian flagship, with her commander Don Pedro Valdez, the ablest, as he was the most gallant admiral in that fleet, had come to grief and had been constrained to surrender; other vessels had suffered dreadfully from the damnable tactics of the endemonized heretics before the close of the first day of action, which was Sunday.

On Monday both fleets were becalmed, and the Spaniards licked their wounds. On Tuesday the wind had veered and the Spaniards had the weather gauge. Now was their chance to sail the English down and grapple them. At last, in the wind He sent them from the East, God lent a hand to the vindication of His cause. But the devil, it became clear to them, fought on the side of the English. Sunday's history was repeated, in spite of the wind from the east. English broadsides continued to crash through Spanish bulwarks from ships that were either out of range or else so low in the hull that they offered no target at all, and by vespers the noble *San Martin* was leaking like a sieve through her fractured timbers, six feet of solid oak though they were.

On Wednesday there was another pause. On Thursday a further hammering, and on Friday, at last, the Duke saw nothing for it but to endeavour to establish communications with the Prince of Parma, from whom he would require supplies and what other assistance the Prince could bring him. With this intent he brought his battered fleet to anchor on Saturday in Calais Roads, neutral waters, into which the English would not dare to follow him.

But that the English did not mean to lose sight of him he understood when he perceived them at anchor a couple of miles astern.

The Spaniards were licking their wounds again; cleaning up the ships, effecting repairs where possible, tending the wounded, putting the dead overboard.

The English, half a league away, were considering the position. In the main cabin of the *Ark Royal*, the flagship of the Lord Admiral, Howard of Effingham, his lordship sat in council with the principal officers of the fleet. They were under no delusion as to the Spaniards' reason for anchoring in Calais Roads, or the danger to themselves and to England in allowing him to remain there. The Armada after all was not yet sensibly impaired. She had lost but three ships, and could easily spare them. What she could spare less easily was the confidence which had been shaken by those first knocks exchanged, or indeed the lives that had been lost; but men could be replaced by Parma; courage and confidence could be restored by rest; damages could be repaired; the ships could be revictualled, and Parma could renew also their ammunition, which must be running low. Here was one set of reasons why the Duke of Medina-Sidonia could not be left in peace where he now lay. Another was in the fact that the English supplies were becoming exhausted, and they could not wait here indefinitely for the Spaniards to come out of neutral waters. Something must be done.

Drake was for burning them out. A strong flood tide was due that night setting towards the Spanish anchorage. This could be used to float a fleet of fireships down upon them. Seymour, Sir John Hawkins, Frobisher and the Lord Admiral himself were heartily in accord. But it would be blindfolded work unless first by daylight they took some more accurate observation of the Spanish position than was possible at their present distance. Therein lay the difficulty. Hawkins offered a suggestion. The Lord Admiral weighed it, and slowly shook his head.

"Too desperate a chance," said he. "The odds are a hundred to one, a thousand to one against his return."

"It depends upon whom you send," said Drake. "Odds of that kind are to be reduced by skill and courage."

But Howard would not yet hear of it. They discussed other means, and dismissed them one by one, returning at last to that first suggestion.

"I think it's that or nothing," Hawkins submitted. "Either that or we go to work blindfolded."

"We may have to go to work blindfolded after that," Lord Howard reminded him, "and we shall have sacrificed some gallant lives."

But Drake had an answer to this. "Every man of us makes a gamble of his life. We should not be here else, or being here we should never engage in action. I am of Sir John's opinion."

Lord Howard's fine eyes considered him. "Do you know of a man for such an enterprise?"

"I have him under my hand here. He came aboard with me, and is waiting now on deck. A strong lad of his hands, with brains to act quickly in an emergency. He hasn't yet learnt to be afraid of anything, and he can handle a boat with any man. I first proved his mettle at San Domingo. He's been with me ever since."

"Almost too good a man to lose in this affair," Lord Howard deprecated.

"Nay. He's the sort of man that won't be lost. I'll send for him if your lordship says so, and we'll put the matter to him."

And that is how Mr Crosby comes into this famous council of war and, as it were, into history. His youth, his inches and his gallant bearing when he presented himself won him the sympathy of those hard-bitten seamen. His seemed too fair a life to offer up on the ruthless altar of Bellona. But when Drake had expounded to him the task ahead, the laugh with which he took it for a jest, an escapade, won him the love of every man present, and most of all of Drake because the lad so nobly justified his captain's boast of him. Aglow with eagerness, young Crosby listened to a recapitulation of what was required and how he was to obtain it. Himself he suggested that as the afternoon was waning, no time should be lost. He had best start at once.

Lord Howard shook him by the hand at parting. The Admiral's lips smiled, but his eyes were wistful as they surveyed this smiling audacious lad whom he might never see again. He strove for a moment to say something.

"When you return," he said, and keen ears might have noted that he stressed the "when" as men do when a word is changed between thought and utterance – "When you return, sir, I shall be glad if you will seek me."

Gervase bowed to the company, flashed them a smile, and was gone, the sturdy Sir Francis labouring after him up the companion-ladder. They went back to Drake's ship the *Revenge*. The boatswain piped all hands on deck. Sir Francis told them what was needed: a dozen volunteers to go with Mr Crosby and ascertain the exact position of the Spanish ships. There was not a man would have refused to follow Gervase, for many of them had followed him before and knew him for a leader who never flinched.

That afternoon the Duke of Medina-Sidonia, moodily pacing the poop of the *San Martin* with a group of officers, beheld to his amazement a sailing pinnace detach herself from the English lines to bear down upon the Spanish anchorage. He and those with him stood at gaze. So did others on the Spanish ships, in the utter inactivity of men who can but observe the unfolding of a marvel they do not understand. Straight towards them came the little craft, rippling through the light waves, straight for the Spanish flagship.

It must be, opined the Duke, that she bore him a message from the English. Perhaps his guns had mauled them more than he suspected. Perhaps the loss of life had been such that they would be willing to make terms. Fatuous imaginings possible only to a landlubber. Politely his mistake was pointed out to him, also that this pinnace bore no flag of truce, as she must have done if she sought a parley. Whilst they were still conjecturing, she was under their counter.

Gervase Crosby stood in the stern-sheets, himself handling the tiller. With him sat a youth with a writing-tablet and a pen. In the bows a gun had been mounted and a gunner stood with lighted match beside it. The little craft sped on, circled the *San Martin* completely, and as she circled fired a shot at her. Drake would have described this as putting on a brag. The object of that piece of swagger was to deceive the Spaniards as to the real purpose of the visit. Meanwhile Gervase's eyes were measuring the distance from the shore, and taking in the position of the other ships relatively to the flagship, and his details were rapidly being written down by the improvised secretary.

It was done, and he was already leaving the Spaniards astern before one of their officers recovered from his surprise at this impudence to ask himself if something else did not lie behind it. Whether impudence or not – something was due here. He commanded it, and a gun executed the command. But, trained too hastily, its shot, which could easily have sunk the frail boat, tore harmlessly through her mainsail. Other ships roused themselves, and there was a cannonade. But it was loosed too late by at least five minutes. The pinnace was already beyond the short range of the Spanish guns.

Drake was in the waist of the *Revenge* awaiting him when Gervase climbed aboard.

"I ask myself," said Sir Francis, "what particular kind of luck protects you. By all the laws of war and of chance and of common sense you should have been sunk before ever you got within a cable's length of them. What's this?"

Gervase had proffered the sheet of notes which he had dictated.

"Lord!" he said. "You bring the methods of the counting-house with you. Come away to the Admiral."

That night eight vessels thickly coated with pitch drifted down in the dark upon the tide, controlled by long sweeps, in the wake of their leader, which was steered by Gervase Crosby. This, a trivial task from the point of view of danger, compared with his earlier one, he had almost insisted upon undertaking as being the logical corollary to his inspection of the positions. At comparatively close quarters, slow matches were lighted aboard each vessel. The crews slipped silently overboard to the waiting pinnace, and the ships were left to drift down the short remainder of the way upon the Spaniards. When as they got amongst them they suddenly broke into flame one after the other, they scattered panic through the invincible fleet. These English, it seemed, had every resource and artifice of hell at their command. It was conceived, reasonably enough, that the fire-ships were full of gunpowder – as indeed they would have been if the English had possessed powder to spare – and knowing the fearful havoc they would work upon exploding, the Spaniards, without waiting to weigh anchor, cut their cables and stood out to sea.

At dawn, Medina-Sidonia found the English bearing resolutely down upon him, and on that day was fought the most terrific action that the seas had ever known. When evening fell the power of the Armada was definitely broken. Thereafter, in the days that followed, it but remained to drive into the high latitude of the North Sea where they could do no harm, the seventy surviving ships of the hundred and thirty that had sailed so proudly from the Tagus as the instrument by which God should vindicate His cause.

Medina-Sidonia asked nothing better than to be allowed to go. He had endured all the sea-fighting to which his stomach was equal, and was glad enough to drive before the wind away from any further risk of action. Like sheepdogs herding a flock, the English ships hung on their heels until they were past the Forth; then left them to the winds and the God in whose name they had sailed forth on their crusade.

Chapter 4

Sir Gervase

On a fair August day, Mr Crosby made one of a numerous company assembled in a spacious panelled chamber of the palace of Whitehall.

It was a day of calm, and of blue skies, delusive interlude in the fury of the weather which had lately turned stormy, with frequent tempests that shook the earth and the heavens and made seamen thankful that they had turned back when they did from the pursuit of the Spaniards, and so had brought their ships in safety to the Thames before the change set in.

The sun shone radiantly through the leaded panes of the tall windows overlooking the river and the Palace steps, where the barges were now moored which had brought the Admiral and his numerous company to answer the summons of the Queen of England.

Mr Crosby, in mingled pride and awe to find himself in so considerable and distinguished an assembly, looked about him with interest. The room was hung with pictures, all of which were veiled; there was an Eastern carpet of brilliant variegated colouring on a square table by which he was standing in the room's middle; against the panelling were ranged some chairs, tall-backed and carved, each bearing upon its scarlet velvet an escutcheon whereon the leopards of England, or on gules, were quartered with the lilies of France, or on azure.

These chairs were empty, all save one, which was taller and ampler than the rest and equipped with arms ending in carved and gilded leonine heads.

In this chair, placed between two of the windows with its back to the light, sat a woman whom at first glance you might have supposed an Eastern idol, so bejewelled and bedizened was she. Her leanness was dissembled by a bulging farthingale. Her red-raddled face was lean and sharp with a thin aquiline nose and a very pointed, ill-tempered chin. The darkness of her eyebrows had been supplied by a pencil, and her lips were of a startling scarlet in which Nature had no hand. Above the brow, which was almost masculine in its loftiness and breadth, towered a monstrous head-tire of false yellow hair in which a bushel of strung pearls were interwoven. Rows upon rows of pearls covered her neck and breast as if to supply again the pearly beauty long since faded from her skin. From the summit of her gown a collar of lace of the proportions of an enormous fan spread itself upright behind her head. Pearls were slung from it; jewels blazed in it; more jewels smouldered in her gown, a cloth of gold wrought with an uncanny embroidery of green lizards. She made some play with a handkerchief that was edged with gold lace, and this served two purposes: to display a hand which as yet by time was extremely beautiful, and to conceal her teeth whose ageing darkness no art could yet dissemble for her.

Behind her and to right and left of her chair were ranged in line her ladies-in-waiting, a dozen women of the noblest and loveliest in England.

Mr Crosby had heard the Queen described more than once by Lord Garth. In painting the portrait of the lady whom his ill-fated friend had loved, Roger Trevanion yielded to one of his few remaining enthusiasms, and out of this it may be that he coloured the picture over-generously. Hence, and forgetting that forty years were sped since the Earl of Garth had last beheld her, Mr Crosby had entered the august presence in expectation of a radiant vision of feminine beauty. What he beheld dismayed him by its disparity with his mental portrait.

Her immediate supporters, too, added to the incongruity of the picture. The one upon her left was a tall lean gentleman in all black. His sharp-featured countenance ended in a long white beard which entirely failed to lend that crafty face a patriarchal air. This was Sir Francis Walsingham. In ludicrous contrast with him stood the Earl of Leicester on her right. Once reputed the handsomest man in England, he was now corpulent and ungainly of body, inflamed and blotchy of countenance. His gorgeous raiment and the arrogance with which he carried his head served only to heighten the absurdity of his aspect.

That the Queen did not find him absurd was instanced by the place he occupied, and still more by the fact that the forces of England which were to have resisted Parma's landing had been under the Earl of Leicester's supreme command. As a deviser and leader of pageants, it is probable that he had not his equal in England, if, indeed, in Europe. But it was fortunate for England, and for Leicester, that English seamen had made it unnecessary for him to exercise those talents in attempting to withstand the Prince of Parma.

With these same valiant English seamen was this assembly now concerned. Lord Howard of Effingham, the Lord Admiral, towering straight and tall before the Queen, was rendering her a first-hand account of those actions in the Channel which had delivered England from the awful menace of Spain. His lordship was brisk and succinct in his narrative. At moments too succinct to please her grace, who now and again would arrest him to crave more details of this or closer explanation of that. This occurred when the Lord Admiral spoke of the difficulty in which they found themselves when Medina-Sidonia was at anchor in French waters, and related that having made a closer survey of his position they sent in fireships to burn him out. He would have swept on with no more than that, to relate the morrow's action, but the Queen checked him in terms of his own trade.

"God's death, man! Haul down some of your sail. You drive so fast before the wind that we cannot follow. This survey at close quarters, how was it made? You have not told us that."

He supplied the details in a silence of intense attention which may have inspired him to a certain liveliness of phrase. The Queen laughed. So did others, thrilled by the narrative of personal valour.

"Faith," she told him, "you're better as a sailor than a story-teller; you leave out the choicest morsels." Then came a question that sent a quiver through Mr Crosby. "What was the name of the man who sailed that pinnace?"

Gervase heard his own name. It terrified him. It seemed to his straining ears that Lord Howard rolled it out in tones of thunder upon the silence. He blushed like a girl, shifting uncomfortably on his feet, and saw as if through a mist the faces of some of those of his acquaintance who stood about him, as they now turned their heads to give him a smile of friendly satisfaction. Then his thoughts flew to Margaret. If only she could have been there to hear him named she must have accounted herself justified of her faith in him and her promise to become his wife.

The Lord Admiral's narrative drew to a close. The Queen pronounced it, in a voice made sonorous by the depth of her emotion, as brave a tale as the world had ever heard, and alluded to her thankfulness to God for this good and prosperous success to those who had fought this battle against the enemies of His Gospel. Not Spain alone, but England too – and, from the results, with better justification – might account herself the instrument of divine justice.

Followed the presentation by the Lord Admiral of the captains of the fleet under his command and other officers who had distinguished themselves in that great battle in the Channel. To each the Queen spoke some word of commendation, whilst upon three of them she bestowed the accolade with a sword supplied by the Earl of Leicester.

After that Lord Howard's place was taken by the Vice-Admiral, Sir Francis Drake, upon whom devolved the duty of presenting the captains and some other officers of the privateers, nearly all of them West-country gentlemen of family, many of whom had fitted ships at their own charges. The sturdy seaman rolled forward on his short thick legs as if a heaving poop were under his feet. He was resplendent in a suit of white satin which gave his bulk the appearance of having been suddenly increased. His beard was newly-trimmed, his crisp brown hair sedulously combed and oiled, and there were rings of pure gold in the lobes of his close-set ears.

He bowed low, announced his purpose in a voice that was like a trumpet-call, and began his presentations.

The first was a neighbour of Mr Crosby's, Oliver Tressilian of Penarrow. He was half-brother to that Lionel Tressilian who came too much to Trevanion Chase for Mr Crosby's peace of mind. But you would have looked at the men in vain for evidence of relationship. Where Lionel was fair and mincing, elegant, soft and sleek as a woman, this Oliver, tall, resolute and swarthy, was of an almost overwhelming maleness. His mien was commanding, his bearing proud to the point of arrogance. To behold him as he made now his leisurely advance was to recognize him for one born to mastership. And although still young, his deeds already bore out the promise of his person. He had been schooled in seamanship at the hands of Frobisher; he had come to the support of Drake with a strong ship of his own, and to his audacity and resource as much as to any other cause had been due the capture of the Andalusian flagship, an event which early in the fight had put such heart into the English seamen.

The Queen's dark short-sighted eyes conned him with unmistakable admiration as he knelt at her footstool.

The sword flashed up and descended smartly upon his shoulder. "Such men as you, Sir Oliver, are to be considered as persons born for the preservation of the country." Those were the terms in which she dubbed him knight.

None grudged him the honour. He was one for whom a great future was predicted, and it was not to be foreseen that by the wickedness of men, the apparent inconstancy of his mistress and finally the operations of the Holy Office, the fame for which he was reserved was to be won under the banner of Islam. As a Moslem Corsair, Sakr-el-Bahr, the Hawk of the Sea, he was destined to become one of the scourges of Christianity. It was a destiny none could have prophesied as he rose proudly from his knees that day, honoured and commended.

After him, one by one, came the other privateers. First the captains, and then those lesser officers who had served with more than ordinary distinction. And the first of these whom Sir Francis named was Gervase Crosby.

He stood forth, tall and supple. He had dressed himself – or rather Killigrew had seen to it that he was dressed – in a brave suit of murrey velvet, with slashed cannions to his trunks and rosettes to his shoes. He wore a short cloak in the Italian fashion, and a narrow white ruff sharpened the outline of his face. Excessively young for a man of his deeds he looked in his shaven beardlessness; for never since Margaret's condemnation of beards nearly a year ago had he suffered the hair to grow upon his face.

The Queen's dark eyes seemed to soften a little as they watched his approach, and they were not the only feminine eyes that pondered him with admiration. More than one of her maids of honour considered him with interest.

He went down on his knees to kiss her hand, and she frowned almost in perplexity as she surveyed the top of his head with its rippling auburn hair worn close. Having kissed her beautiful hand, he would have got to his feet again.

"Here's haste!" said she in her gruff voice. "Kneel, child, kneel! Who bade thee rise?"

Realizing his fault he blushed to the nape of his neck and continued kneeling. She turned to Sir Francis.

"Is this he who went sailing in the pinnace among the Spanish ships in Calais Roads?"

"The same, Your Grace."

She looked at Gervase again. "God's death! Why it's a child!"

"His age is older than his looks, and his deeds are older than his age."

"They are so," she agreed. "By God, they are!"

Mr Crosby was increasingly ill-at-ease and wished from his heart that she would make an end of this. But she was not minded to make an end just yet. His young comeliness gave his exploit a special heroism in her feminine eyes, stirred a little enthusiasm in her intensely feminine soul.

"That was a brave thing you did," she told him gently, to be gruff with him the next moment. "God's death, child, look at me when I speak to you." I suspect that she desired to see the colour of his eyes. "It was as brave a thing as I've heard this day, and God knows a feast of valour has been spread before me. Don't you agree, Sir Francis?"

Sir Francis drew himself up a little from his deferentially bending attitude.

"He was schooled by me in seamanship, madam," he replied, as who would say: "What else do you expect from a pupil of that academy?"

"It deserves, I think, some special mark of favour, both to reward it and to encourage others to the like."

And then, a bolt from the blue to him who had been very far from expecting any guerdon, the flat of the sword smote him on the shoulder, and the command to arise, so long delayed to his discomfort, came in terms which made him realize that a man may be in too great haste to get up from kneeling to a sovereign.

Standing, he marvelled that he had not earlier observed her singular beauty; that upon his first glimpse of her he had wanted to laugh. What, he wondered, could have ailed him.

"God bless Your Majesty," he blurted out in his intoxication.

She smiled at him, and there was something wistful in the lines of her ageing mouth and reddened lips. She was unusually gracious that day.

"He has blessed me richly already, lad, in giving me subjects such as these."

He effaced himself after that, and went to join Oliver Tressilian, who offered to carry him back to the Fal in his ship.

Gervase was in haste to return, to carry to the lady whom he pictured waiting there, this dazzling, bewildering news of his advancement. Drake permitting it, and excusing him from the great thanksgiving service that was to be held in St Paul's, he departed on the morrow with Tressilian. Sir John Killigrew, who had been in London during the past ten days, went with them. Of the bitter feud that was later to mar the good relations between Killigrew and Tressilian there was as yet no sign. Sir John, however, was elated by the achievement of his young kinsman.

"You shall have a ship of your own, boy, if I have to sell a farm to fit it," he had promised him. "All I ask," he added, for with all his generosity there was a practical mercenary streak in him, "is a quarter share in the ventures you will undertake."

That ventures were to be undertaken was readily assumed, as also that they would be more than usually profitable now that the might of Spain upon the seas had been so signally impaired. And this was the subject of most of their talk during the voyage to the Fal on Sir Oliver's ship, the *Rose of the World*. He had named her so, it is to be supposed, in honour of Rosamund Godolphin, whom he loved, and upon the assumption – erroneous, I believe – that her name was a contraction of Rosa Mundi.

On the last day of August, the *Rose of the World* rounded Zoze Point and came to anchor in Carrick Roads.

Sir John and his kinsmen took their leave of Tressilian and went ashore at Smithwick to climb the heights to stately Arwenack, whence on a clear day the view extended to the Lizard, fifteen miles away.

No sooner did they reach it than Gervase was away again. He would not even stay to dine, although it was already passed the hour of dinner. Now that Tressilian was home, the news of events in London might reach Trevanion Chase at any moment, and this was dangerous to the satisfaction which Gervase hoped to derive from being the first to announce to Margaret those details which concerned himself. Killigrew, perceiving the reason of his haste, rallied him upon it, but let him go and sat down to dine alone.

Although the distance from door to door was less than two miles, the properties adjoining, yet such was Gervase's haste that, having called for a horse, he must ride it at the gallop.

In the avenue approaching the big red house with its tall twisted chimneys he found a groom in the blue livery of the Godolphins waiting with three horses, and learned that Peter Godolphin and his sister Rosamund, together with Lionel Tressilian, were at the Chase, having stayed there to dine. As it was already close upon three o'clock they would soon be leaving. Gervase was relieved. The sight of the waiting horses had led him almost to fear that despite the haste he had made he might have been forestalled.

He found them in the garden, even as on that day, two years ago, when he had gone to the Chase to take his leave of Margaret. Then, however, he had been an aspirant for fame. Today he returned in the effulgence of achievement. Success had crowned him, the Queen had knighted him. His name would be repeated among Englishmen; it would be inscribed upon the scroll of history. The memory of that accolade at Whitehall invested Sir Gervase with a new assurance. The dignity of knighthood had entered into his blood, was reflected in his bearing.

He sent ahead the servant who received him, to announce him.

"Sir Gervase Crosby, may it please your ladyship."

Thus did he break his news to them as he came briskly, in his brave murrey suit, his head high, in the servant's wake.

For a moment Margaret was breathless. The colour ebbed from her face to come surging back on a flood tide. Amazement smote similarly her three companions, those two gallants and the sister of one of them, the gentle, fair-haired, saintly-looking Rosamund Godolphin, still a child of not more than sixteen years, but already woman enough to have fired the heart of the masterful elder Tressilian.

Gervase and Margaret looked at each other, and for a heartbeat may have seen naught but each other. Had he found her alone, there can be no doubt he would have taken her in his arms, as he accounted his right by virtue of her last words to him at parting two years ago. The unwelcome presence of those others compelled some measure of circumspection. He must confine himself to taking her hand and, bending low, content his lips with that as an ernest of more to come anon when he should have driven out those intruders.

To this task he addressed himself from the outset.

"I landed less than an hour ago on Pendennis Point," he announced, so that Margaret might judge for herself with what eager speed he had sought her. He turned to the younger Tressilian. "Your brother brought us back from London in his ship."

Rosamund broke in with startled eagerness.

"Oliver is home?" It was the tall slim girl's turn to go pale and breathless, whereat her handsome brother frowned. Although prudence and expediency made him maintain a pretence of friendliness with the Tressilians, there was no real love lost between him and them. He found them in rivalry with him on every hand. His interests were beginning to clash with theirs in the countryside, and he viewed with anything but favour the affection which had sprung up between his sister and the elder of them. There was an unpleasant surprise in store for him from Gervase.

"The *Rose of the World*," he said, answering the lady, "is anchored in Carrick Roads, and Sir Oliver will be home by now."

"Sir Oliver!" both men echoed in a breath. And Lionel repeated the questioning exclamation: "Sir Oliver?"

Gervase smiled, almost with condescension, and hung upon his answer an account of how he had received his own honours.

"He was knighted by the Queen in the same hour as myself at Whitehall on Monday last."

Margaret stood with her arm about the waist of the willowy Rosamund. Her own eyes sparkled, whilst Rosamund's looked oddly moist. Lionel frankly laughed his pleasure at his brother's advancement. Peter Godolphin alone saw here no cause for satisfaction. This thing would make these Tressilians more insufferable than ever; it gave them an unquestionable advantage over him in local influence. He sneered. He was very ready always with his sneers.

"Faith! Honours must have fallen thick as hail."

Sir Gervase caught the sneer, but kept his temper. He met it by assuming a still loftier condescension. He looked down his nose at Mr Godolphin.

"Not quite so thickly, sir, and only where the Queen's discernment perceived them to be deserved." He might have let the matter lie upon that reminder that to sneer at honours is to sneer at who bestows them. But he pursued the matter a little further. Pride in the advancement which had come upon him so unexpectedly may have intoxicated him a little, considering his youth. "I quote, I think her majesty, or if not her majesty at least Sir Francis Walsingham. I will not swear which of them it was who said but I know that it was one of them – that England's best make up the twenty-thousand that sailed out to meet and break the might of Spain. A score of knighthoods, sir, comes to but one for every thousand. None so thick a shower when all is said. Had every man been knighted, it would still have been foolish to sneer at a measure which could but serve to distinguish them hereafter from those who stayed at home, and – sheltered themselves behind their valour."

It made an awkward silence, and a little frown of perplexed annoyance descended upon the brow of the Lady Margaret. Then Peter stiffly answered him.

"You use a deal of words, sir, to say little, and your meaning is obscured in verbiage."

"Will you have the marrow of it?" wondered Sir Gervase.

"In heaven's name, no!" It was Margaret who spoke, a determined resolute Margaret. "We'll have no more of this. My father, Gervase, will be glad to see you. You'll find him in the library."

It was a dismissal, and deeming it unjust, it made him angry. But still he veiled his annoyance. He smiled quite pleasantly. "I'll stay until you are free to take me to him."

43

Upon that, in secret resentment, and with the curtest of nods to Gervase, the men took their leave, and Godolphin carried off his sister with him.

When they had gone the Lady Margaret looked at her lover with gloom in her eyes and a wry little smile on her lips. Slowly she shook her head at him. "It was ill done, Gervase."

"Ill done? God lack!" To remind her of the cause, he mimicked Peter Godolphin with an exaggerated simper. " 'Faith! Honours must have fallen thick as hail!' Was that well done? Am I to be rallied by any popinjay for what my merits have earned me? Am I to kiss the rod of his providing and turn the other cheek? Is that how you would have your husband behave?"

"My husband!" said she, and stared at him. Then she laughed. "Remind me, pray, of when it was I married you. I vow that I've forgot."

"You'll not have forgot that you promised to marry me?"

"I remember no such promise," said she in the same light tone.

He weighed the words rather than the manner. They set him breathing hard, caused him to pale under his tan. "Will you go back on your word, Margaret?"

"And now you are unmannerly."

"I am concerned with more than pretty manners, madam." He was growing vehement, overbearing, and she ever calm and cool, disliking vehemence either in herself or others, began to be seriously annoyed. He hectored on. "There was a promise you gave me in the hall, there, as I was leaving: a promise that you would marry me."

She shook her head. "As I remember it, my promise was that I would marry no man but you."

"Why what's the difference?"

"It lies in that I may keep that promise and yet keep to my intention of following the Queen's example and continuing all my days in my maiden estate if I so choose."

He turned it over in his mind. "And do you so choose?"

"I must until I am persuaded to choose otherwise."

"How may you be persuaded?" he demanded, almost challengingly, wounded in his tenderest sensibilities and simmering with indignation at what he must account an unworthy quibble. "How may you be persuaded?"

She looked him between the eyes, standing straight and tense. "Certainly not in any way that you've yet chosen to pursue," said she, quite calm and cool and mistress of herself.

The elation in which he had come, the pride in his knightly rank so newly-attained, the swagger it had lent him, all fell from him now. He had thought to dazzle her – and, indeed, to dazzle all the world – with his honours and the echo of the deeds that had earned them. Realization was so vastly different from his exalted expectations that his heart turned to lead in his breast. The auburn head which he had carried so proudly even at Whitehall was lowered at last. He contemplated the ground. He became humble.

"I'll choose any way that you may desire for me," he said, "for I love you, Margaret. To you I owe my knighthood, for the deeds that won it me were inspired by you. In all I bore myself as if your eyes had been upon me, with no thoughts save to do that which should give you pride in me could you behold it. The reward I have won and all that may follow upon this are naught to me unless you share them with me."

He looked up, and saw that he had touched her, melted her a little from the smooth hardness of her mood. She was smiling now with a hint of tenderness. He set himself to follow up the advantage.

"I vow you use me ill," he protested, and thus introduced again contentious matters. "You give a chilly welcome to the eager haste in which I seek you."

"You choose to be quarrelsome," she reminded him.

"Was I not provoked? Was I not sneered at by that Godolphin whelp?" And he became impatient. "Is all that I do wrong, and all that he does right in your eyes? What is Mr Godolphin to you that you espouse his quarrels?"

"He is my kinsman, Gervase."

"Which gives him licence to affront me. Is that your meaning?"

"Shall we forget Mr Godolphin?" said she.

"With all my heart," he cried, whereupon she laughed and took his arm.

"Come and pay your duty to my father. You shall tell him of your fine deeds upon the sea, and I will listen. I may be so beglamoured by the tale as to forgive you everything."

It did not seem to him in justice that he had need of forgiveness. But he desired no more disputes.

"And then, Margaret?" he asked her eagerly.

She laughed again. "Lord, what a man it is for outracing time! Can you not await the future in patience without ever seeking to foretell it?"

He looked at her in doubt a moment. Then he thought he read a challenge in her eyes. He took the risk of acting upon it. He caught her in his arms, and kissed her. And since she suffered it this time without resentment it would seem that he had read aright the challenge.

They went in to disturb the studies of the earl.

Chapter 5

Flotsam

Don Pedro de Mendoza y Luna, Count of Marcos and Grandee of Spain, opened his eyes and looked up through the pallid dawn at the grey cloud masses overhead. It was some little while before his senses understood what his eyes beheld. Then he grew conscious that as he lay there supine upon the shore he was cold and stiff and sick. By this he knew that he was still alive; though how this happened, and where he might be, were matters yet to be investigated.

Painfully, upon joints that seemed almost to creak as they moved, he brought himself to a sitting posture, and gazed out across the heavy ground-swell of the opal-tinted sea into the spreading flush of the September dawn. His senses reeled under the effort, sky and sea and land all rocked about him, and he was seized with nausea. He ached from head to foot, ached as if he had been stretched upon the rack; his eyes smarted acutely; there was an unspeakably bitter briny taste in his mouth, and his mind was in such troubled confusion that it could render him no proper account of himself. He was conscious that he lived and suffered. Beyond that it is to be doubted if he was so much as conscious of his own identity.

His nausea increased, and he became violently sick, whereafter, exhausted, Nature compelled him to lie down again. But as he lay now, the oppressing cloud began to lift from his brain, clearing the outlook for his consciousness. Soon memory resumed her sway. He sat up again, more alertly this time, and at least no longer nauseated. His eyes ranged once more over the sea, more purposefully now, seeking upon the waters some sign of that towering galleon which had suffered shipwreck in the night. The reef upon which she had gone to pieces showed boldly in silhouette against the quickening sky, a black line of jagged rocks upthrusting from a white foam of thundering breakers. But of the galleon not so much as a mast or spar was to be seen. And the storm, too, had passed, its fury spent, leaving no indication of its passage save that oily ground-swell. Overhead the cloud mass was being broken up, dissolving, and patches of blue sky increasingly revealed.

Don Pedro sat forward, his elbows on his knees, his head in his hands, his fine long fingers thrust into his damp clammy hair. He remembered now that dreadful swim of his, instinctive and without orientation in the blackness of the night. The unquenchable animal instinct of self-preservation it was that had compelled it. Reason had no part in the effort. For whilst he possessed the clear assurance that land could not be far, he had no means of telling in that impenetrable darkness the direction in which it lay. Therefore, with little hope of reaching it, he supposed himself to be swimming through eternity.

He remembered how when exhaustion began at last to cramp his limbs and paralyse further effort, he had commended his soul to his Maker, to that God who had proved so extraordinarily insensible of the fact that His were the battles which Don Pedro, and so many other tall Spaniards now stiff and cold, had gone forth to fight. He remembered how in those last moments of consciousness a wave had suddenly seemed to seize him in its coils, lift him high and bear him swiftly forward upon its crest, then loose its grip of him and leave him to crash down upon the beach with a force that had driven out what little breath yet lingered in his tortured lungs. He remembered his instant deep thankfulness, quenched the next moment in the realization that he was being sucked back by the undertow.

The horror of it was upon him again. He shuddered now as he thought of the frenzy with which he had clawed that foreign shore, driving his fingers deep into the sand, to grip and save himself from the maw of hungry ocean before the strength to battle should be spent with consciousness. That was the last thing he remembered. Between that point and this there was a blank which his reason now set itself to bridge.

The tide was on the ebb when they had struck the reef. This had permitted his last effort to be availing. Thus had the retreating sea been foiled of her prey. But, in faith, that monster had been fed to a surfeit as it was. The galleon was gone and with her some three hundred fine tall sons of Spain. Don Pedro checked the surge of thankfulness for his own almost miraculous preservation. Was he, after all, more fortunate than those who had perished? He had been dead, and he was alive again. It amounted scarcely to less. The dark dread portals had been crossed when consciousness was extinguished. For what had he been thrust back into the world of life? His respite in this barbarous, heretic, excommunicate land could be no more than temporary. Escape must be impossible. Upon discovery it would be demanded of him that he suffer death again, and suffer it probably with indignity and amid torment infinitely worse than those which last night he had undergone. Far indeed from returning thanks for his preservation, let him give rein to his envy of those compatriots of his who would wake no more.

Drearily he looked about him, surveying the rocky little cove of that nook-shotten isle on which the sea had spewed him up. The swiftly-growing light showed him a desolate deserted space, walled in by cliffs like some vast prison. No dwelling was visible here or anywhere on the heights above. All about him rose these sheer red cliffs fringed on their summit by the long grass that was waving in the freshening breeze.

He knew that he was somewhere upon the coast of Cornwall. This from what the navigator of the galleon had told him last night just before they were dashed upon the rocks by the fury of that infernal tempest which had swept them leagues out of their course; a tempest which had come down upon them just when they appeared to have weathered all their perils, to have conquered adversity, and to confront a clear run home to Spain. Never again would he behold the white walls of Vigo or Santander upon which two days ago he had so confidently been expecting soon to look.

In imagination a picture of them rose before him, all bathed in sunshine, the vines laden now with their ripe purple clusters among which the brown-skinned, dark-eyed Galician or Asturian peasants would be moving with their vintage baskets on their shoulders, to pile from these the grapes into the ponderous wooden bullock-carts identical in every detail with those which the Romans had brought into Iberia nearly two thousand years ago. He could hear them singing at their labours, the wistful heart-wringing songs of Spain, subtle compounds of joy and melancholy that quicken a man's blood. So confidently two days ago had he been anticipating the sight of all this to heal the wounds which body and soul had taken in this ill-starred adventure. From the white church on the summit there above Santander the Angelus of dawn would even now be ringing. As if he heard it with the ears of his flesh, the home-sick, storm-battered Don Pedro disengaged his legs from a tangle of seaweed, struggled to his knees, crossed himself and recited the salutation to the Mother of God.

After that he sat down again dejectedly to consider anew his position.

Suddenly he laughed aloud, a laugh of deep and bitter irony. He laughed at the contrast which he discovered between the manner of his coming ashore in England and that which had so confidently been planned. He had shared the assurance of his master, King Philip, in a triumphal progress which no human power could withstand. He had looked upon England as already beneath the heel of Spain, its bastard and excommunicate Queen driven forth in ignominy, and this Augean stable of heresy cleansed and purified and restored to the True Faith.

What else was to have been expected? Spain had launched upon the seas an armament that was invincible by temporal forces, fortified by spiritual weapons which must render it invulnerable to the Powers of Hell, offering herself as an arm through which God should vindicate His cause. It was incomprehensible, incredible, that from the outset the elements should appear to have stood in league with the heretics. He reviewed the whole adventure from the first issuing of the fleet from the Tagus, when at the very outset adverse winds had created confusion, losses and delays. In the Channel the wind had almost constantly favoured the lighter craft of the endemonized heretical dogs who had harried them. And even when all hope of effecting a landing in England had been abandoned, and the surviving ships of the Armada, driven to circumnavigate this barbarous island, asked no more of Heaven than that they should be permitted to reach home again, the elements had persisted in their incomprehensible hostility.

As far as the Orkneys they had hung together. There in a fog ten of the galleons had gone astray. Sixty ships, including the *Conception*, commanded by Don Pedro de Mendoza y Luna, had clung to the *San Martin*; and with her had ventured farther north, running short of food, the water fouling in their casks and disease breaking out amongst their crews. Their pressing needs drove them to seek the coast of Ireland where half of them were wrecked. In a gale off the Irish coast the *Conception* was separated from the remnant of the fleet at a time when her crew were by thirst and famine rendered too exhausted to handle her. By a miracle they made Killiberg, and here Don Pedro obtained fresh provisions and fresh water. Thus he had been able to revive his fainting seamen, preserving them only so that they might be drowned upon the coast of Cornwall, from which he had been again preserved to end perhaps yet more miserably. Was there a curse upon them that the gift of life at the hands of Heaven should be the gift to be most feared?

Of the fate of the other consorts of Medina-Sidonia's flagship Don Pedro had no knowledge. But judging their case by his own when he had parted from them, he had little cause to suppose that any of them would ever reach Spain again, or if they reached it that they would bear anything but skeletons into Spanish harbours.

In his dejection at this final ruin so far as he himself was concerned, Don Pedro reflected that the ways of the Deity were altogether beyond understanding. One explanation, it was true, existed. The launching of the Armada might be regarded as an ordeal by battle in the old sense: an appeal to God to deliver His judgement between the old-established faith and the reformed religion; between the Pope and Luther, Calvin and the rest of the heresiarchs. Was it in answer to this that God had spoken thus through the winds and the waves which He controlled?

Don Pedro shuddered at the thought, which, as he himself perceived, went perilously near to heresy. He dismissed it, and from the past turned his attention more closely to the present and the future.

The sun was breaking through and quickening the dispersal from the heavens of the cloudy remnants of last night's tempest. Don Pedro rose painfully to his feet and wrung what he could of the sea water from his doublet. He was a tall gracefully-shaped man of scarcely more than thirty, and not even the sodden state of his garments could extinguish their elegance. His dress alone would have proclaimed his nationality. He was all in black, as became a noble of Spain and a lay tertiary of St Dominic. His velvet doublet, peaked and tapering to an almost womanish waist, was faintly wrought with golden arabesques. In its present wet state it had almost the appearance of a damascened cuirass. From a girdle of black leather embossed with gold a heavy dagger hung upon his right hip above his ballooning trunks; his hose, a little rumpled now, was of black silk; the canons of his boots, of fine Cordovan leather, had slipped down, one to the level of his knee, the other to his very ankle. He sat down again to pull them off, first one and then the other, emptied out the water by which they were logged and drew them on again. He removed from his neck the handsome collar of Dutch point, which hung like a dishclout now that the sea had washed all the starch from it. He wrung it out, considered it a moment, then cast it from him in disgust.

Giving now in the full daylight a closer attention to his surroundings, he was startled to perceive the real nature of certain dark objects which dotted the little strip of beach. These, carelessly observed when he had first looked about him whilst the light was dim, he had assumed to be rocks or clumps of seaweed.

He made his way towards the nearest of them with dragging feet. He paused to bend over it, recognizing it for the body of Hurtado, one of the officers of the ill-fated galleon, a gallant stout-hearted fellow who had laughed at perils and discomforts. Hurtado would laugh no more. Don Pedro fetched a sigh that was in itself a requiem and passed on. A little farther he came upon a man still bestriding in death the spar upon which he had ridden ashore. Seven other bodies lay, some sprawled, some huddled, upon the sands where the sea had cast them up. These, some timbers, a chest and few odd furnishings represented all that was left above water of the splendid *Conception*.

Don Pedro considered his late comrades with that solemnity which the dead must ever command. He breathed a prayer for them even. But upon his finely-chiselled face – of the colour of ivory, its warm pallor stressed perhaps by the small black moustache and stiletto beard – there was no shade of regret for their fate. Don Pedro was equipped with a finely-balanced cold intelligence which could suppress emotion in the weighing of realities. These men were more fortunate than himself in that they had died but once, whereas he was destined, he supposed, to endure another and infinitely more cruel death in this hostile land.

It was a reasoned assumption, and by no means merely the apprehension of illogical panic. He was acquainted with the fierce hatred of Spain and Spaniards that was alive in England. He had seen flashes of it during his sojourn at Elizabeth's Court, where he had spent two years in the train of his cousin, the Ambassador Mendoza – he who had been compelled to leave England when Throgmorton betrayed his complicity with the adherents of the Queen of Scots in a plot against the life of Elizabeth. If that hatred had been so lively then, what must it be today, after years of alarms culminating in the dread into which the coming of the Armada had flung this God-abandoned country? He knew his own feelings for a heretic; he knew how he would deal with one at home; how, indeed, he had dealt with some. Was he not a lay tertiary of St Dominic? These feelings supplied him with a standard by which to measure the disposition of heretics towards himself, and the fate that must inevitably await him at the hands of the heretics.

He paced back slowly to Hurtado's body. He remembered to have observed that there was a rapier girt to it, and Don Pedro coveted the weapon. This covetousness was entirely of instinct. Reason supervening as he stooped to unbuckle the belt, he paused.

His sombre eyes looked out over the heaving waters as if to question the infinite of which the ocean must ever seem the symbol. What use to him a sword?

Don Pedro was a cultured and learned gentleman who had studied at the University of St James of Compostella, and afterwards applied his learning in the world and the courts he had frequented. Hence he had developed a habit of philosophic reflection. He had learnt that to strive against the ultimate inevitable is a puerile effort, unworthy of an intelligent mind. Where an evil is unavoidable, the wise man goes to meet it and so makes a speedy end. Let him abide, then, here in this deserted spot until he perished of hunger and of thirst; or, if he went forward, let him cover his face like a roman and receive death from the first hand raised against him.

Thus philosophy. But Don Pedro was still young; the blood flowed strongly in his veins, and the love of life was quick within him. Philosophy, after all, is an arid business, concerned with speculations upon the why and wherefore of things, with theories upon past and future, upon origin and destination outside of absolute human ken. Life, on the other hand, as apprehended by the senses is concerned with the moment; it is not vague, but definite, real and self-assertive. Where life flows strongly, the reality of what is must ever conquer speculations of what may be, and life will seize every chance, however slender, of preserving itself.

He stooped again and, completing this time his task without further hesitation, buckled the dead man's sword to his own loins. Nor was this the end of the fortification he craved against the immediate future. His men had all received their pay before the fleet sailed from the Tagus, and there had been, alas, no chance of spending any of it. The last precaution of each had been to strap his bag of ducats to his waist. Don Pedro loathed the task, but went about it at the dictates of common sense, and in the end stuffed a heavy purse into his sodden doublet.

By now the sun was already well above the horizon, and the last of the storm-clouds was dissolving in the blue. The sunshine and some exertion which it had been necessary to employ had partly restored Don Pedro's circulation, had at least delivered him from the earlier ague in which he had shivered. He became conscious that he was hungry and thirsty and that his mouth was bitter as a brine-pan.

He stood looking out to sea again, considering. Over the sunlit waters a flock of gulls wheeled and circled ever nearer to the shore, screaming shrilly. Whither should he direct his steps? Was it possible that in this desolate land of England there might be folk so charitable as to take pity on a fallen enemy in extremes? He doubted it. But unless he went to ascertain, the few pains he had already taken to provide for emergencies would be utterly wasted and a certain and painfully slow death would await him here. After all, that was the worst that could await him elsewhere, and it was not quite certain. A chance undoubtedly existed. Thus you perceive how the instinct of life had come already to effect a change in his outlook, and to irradiate it with a slight measure of hope.

He moved along that strip of Cornish beach, looking for some break in the wall of cliff, for some path that should lead up to those green heights on the level of which no doubt there would be men and dwellings. He climbed a shallow wall of black and jagged rocks which, springing from the cliff, ran athwart the sands to bury themselves in the water and no doubt continue under it, just such a treacherous reef as that upon which the *Conception* had gone to pieces. In the tiny cove beyond he spied quite suddenly the debouching of a dingle adown which a little brook came hurrying turbulently seaward. The sight of it was blessed in his eyes, the voice of it sang a song of salvation in his ears.

He reached the edge of it above the shore, flung himself prone upon the sparse wet grass where the soil was still sandy and gratefully lowered his head to drink as drinks the animal. No Andalusian wine, no muscadine, had ever tasted one half so sweet to him as this long draught from that sparkling Cornish brook. He drank avidly to quench his burning thirst. and cleanse his mouth of that bitter briny flavour. Then he washed the salt from his eyes and beard and from the undulating black hair that grew to a peak in the middle of his fine brow.

Refreshed, his spirits rose, and the reaction from the pessimism of his awakening was complete. He was alive, and he was in the full glory of his youth and strength. He had been wrong – impious and insensible to God's grace – to envy his poor dead comrades. Contritely he fell now upon his knees, and did what it would have become a pious gentleman of Spain to have done earlier: returned thanks to Heaven for his miraculous preservation.

His orisons ended, he turned his back upon the sea and began the ascent of the gently rising ground. The dingle was densely wooded, but a beaten track where the way had been cleared ran along the brook with its little cascades and deep pools, where here and there he beheld the flash of the golden flank of a trout which his shadow startled. Tall blackberry bushes tore at him as he advanced and thereby drew his attention to their fruit. He was thankful for the discovery of this manna, and proceeded to break his fast. It was very jejune fare; the berries were small, none too ripe and their pulp was scanty. But Don Pedro was not fastidious that morning. Misfortune schools us in the appreciation of small gifts. He ate with relish until a crackling sound in the undergrowth across the stream disturbed him. He stood as still as the trees that sheltered him, lest any movement on his part should betray his presence. His ears were strained to listen and identify the sounds.

Someone was moving yonder. He was not at all alarmed. It was not easy to alarm Don Pedro. But he was alert and watchful, since whoever came must of necessity be an enemy.

Quite suddenly this enemy was revealed, and not quite the enemy that Don Pedro had looked for. Through the alders beyond the stream crashed a great liver-coloured hound, snarling and growling as it came. It stood poised a moment on the farther bank, now barking furiously at this black intruder whom it had sighted. Then with short yelps it ran hither and thither seeking a passage, and at last heaved itself across in a terrific leap.

Don Pedro leaped at the same moment. Nimbly he sprang upon an opportune rock, and out flashed Hurtado's rapier. This infernal dog should receive a cold sharp welcome.

But even as the hound bounded forward to the assault, a clear imperious voice detained it.

"Down, Brutus! Down! Hither to me! Hither at once!" The dog checked, hesitating between indulgence and obedience. Then as the command was repeated, and the mistress who uttered it appeared between the trees, it turned, and with a final yelp, perhaps of disappointed anger, went bounding back across the brook.

Chapter 6

Surrender

Sword in hand, statuesquely from his rocky plinth, Don Pedro bowed until his trunk was at right angles with his shapely legs. He hoped that he was not ridiculous.

The lady across the brook whom he thus saluted belonged to a type which to a son of Spain must ever seem the most delectable by virtue of that natural law which renders opposites inter-attractive.

Her cheeks were delicate as apple-blossoms; her hair was of the ruddy golden of ripe corn, and tied with great simplicity, without any of those monstrous affectations which Elizabeth had rendered fashionable in England. Her eyes were deeply blue, and the surprise now staring out of them gave them a look of startled innocence. She was tall, he observed with approval, and of those most sweet proportions which ripening womanhood alone can display. Her dress marked her in his eyes for a person of quality. Her peaked stomacher and ridiculous farthingale – though less ridiculous by much than mode described – proclaimed to him clearly that here was no rustic Diana for his Endymion. And not only her dress but her bearing and the self-assured manner in which she now confronted this noble-looking and – in his rumpled, sodden garments – rather fantastic stranger, went further to announce her quality.

"Sir, would you have killed my dog?"

Now it was not for nothing that Don Pedro de Mendoza y Luna had spent three years in London in the Ambassador's train and gone about the Court. He spoke English better than many Englishmen, and beyond a slight exaggeration of the vowel sounds there was little in his speech to betray the foreigner.

"Madam," he answered her smoothly, "I trust you will not count it a lack of gallantry in me that I am reluctant to be eaten by a lady's dog."

His accent and the light humour of his answer set her staring harder.

"Now, God a' mercy!" she ejaculated. "You'll not have sprouted here, like a mushroom, in the night. Whence are you, sir?"

"Ah! Whence!" He shrugged. A melancholy smile invested his fine sombre eyes. "That is not to be answered in a word."

He came down from his rock and in three active strides, from boulder to boulder, was across the brook. The crouching hound half-rose and growled at his approach, whereupon the lady bade him down again, and cut him across the body with a hazel switch to quicken his obedience.

Don Pedro stood before her to explain himself. "I am no better than a piece of wreckage; some of the flotsam from a Spanish galleon that foundered on the rocks down there in last night's storm. I am all that has come ashore alive."

He saw the sudden darkening of that fair face, the recoil before him in which if there was fear there was more repugnance. "A Spaniard!" she exclaimed in the tone we use when we mention evil and detested things.

He sank his head between his shoulders; spread his hands in deprecation. "A very sorry one," said he, and on that sighed plaintively.

Almost at once he saw racial prejudice cast aside for womanly pity. She observed more closely his condition, his sodden garments and dishevelled head, and saw that it bore out his tale. She pictured to herself the thing he told her, and was stricken at the thought of that sunken galleon and the loss of life.

Upon her face he read the reflection of this uprush of compassion, for he was very skilled in the deciphering of human documents; and being too a very subtle gentleman, he perceived his course, and promptly took it.

"My name," he said, and said it with a certain conscious pride that was not to be mistaken, "is Don Pedro de Mendoza y Luna. I am Count of Marcos, a Grandee of Spain, and your prisoner." On that he went down upon his knees, and proffered her the hilt of the sword which he still held naked in his hands.

She fell back a pace or two in sheer surprise. "My prisoner?" Her brows were knit in bewilderment. "Nay now; nay now."

"And it please you," he insisted. "It has never been imputed to me, and I hope it never may be, that I want for courage. Yet finding myself shipwrecked, alone in a hostile land, I am in no case to offer resistance to my capture. I am like a garrison that is forced to capitulation and merely asks that it may capitulate without hurt to honour. On the beach down there I had a choice of alternatives. One was to walk back into the sea which has rejected me, and drown. But I am young, as you observe, and suicide is the certain gateway to damnation. I preferred, then, the other alternative, which was to make my way to the haunts of men, and upon finding one who was of a quality to receive my sword, to make surrender. Here at your feet, lady, my quest is ended almost as soon as it began." And again he proffered her the blade, held now across his two hands.

"But I am not a man, sir." She was obviously nonplussed.

"Let all men thank God with me for that," he cried. Then more solemnly continued: "In all ages it has been deemed proper that valour should yield to beauty. For my valour I will beg you to accept my word until such time as it may be tested, when the test, I trust, will be in your own service. For the rest your mirror and the eyes of every man will vouch. And as for your quality, I were blind or a clown did I not perceive it."

That the situation piqued and pleased her from the very outset is as certain as that the astute Don Pedro judged confidently it must.

It was so tinctured with romance that its appeal to a lady of any heart and imagination must prove beyond resistance. Only the extraordinary nature of the adventure made her hesitate, aroused a doubt on the score of the practical fulfilment of this Spanish gentleman's proposal.

"But I have never heard the like. How can I take you prisoner?"

"By accepting my sword, madam."

"But how can I hold you?"

"How?" he smiled. "It is easy to hold the captive who desires captivity. Who would desire liberty that might be your prisoner?"

His eyes grew so ardent as to leave no vagueness in his meaning. She flushed under that regard of his, as well she might, for Don Pedro went very fast indeed. "I surrender me," he said. "Yourself shall fix my ransom and make it what you will. Until it comes from Spain I am your prisoner."

He saw that her hesitation was still far from conquered. Perhaps, indeed, his momentary ardour by its prematureness had increased it. Therefore he had recourse to utter frankness, confident that by revealing the full extent of his peril and thus arousing her compassion, he would prevail upon her. He showed her that it was upon her mercy that he counted; that it was his faith in her gentleness and her pity for his plight that impelled him to take this course which she accounted extraordinary and which was certainly unusual.

"Consider," he begged her. "In the hands of another it might go very ill with me. I intend no insult to your countrymen's sense of what is in honour due to an unfortunate and helpless enemy; of what is prescribed by all the usages of chivalry. But men are the creatures of their passions, of their feelings; and the feelings today of Englishmen for Spaniards..." He broke off, and shrugged. "You know them. It may well be that the feelings of the first Englishman I met will conquer his notions of what is becoming. He may summon others to help him cut me down."

"Would so much be needed?" she flashed at him, touched by his sly imputation that no one Englishman would suffice to take a Spaniard.

But he knew women, and he answered without hesitation, though in accents that sounded humble and self-deprecatory. "I think so, lady. And if you deny me now I must resolve your doubts by making proof of it."

He knew that she would not, and knew that the half-challenge of his answer struck the right note, and preserved him a figure of dignity in misfortune, a man who would condescend only within certain definite honourable limits to accept shelter from his peril. If he made it plain that he sought compassion from her, he also made it plain that he sought no more than he might accept without loss of self-respect.

She perceived dearly enough that if she assented to his odd proposal, if she accepted him for her prisoner, it would be hers to shield him. She would be doing a worthy thing; for Spaniard though he might be, he was human and a gentleman. That she had the power to carry this thing through and claim him for her own against any aggressor, reflection made her gradually confident. He had rightly gauged her mettle and her quality. In all that Cornish countryside there was probably none strong enough to stand against her imperious will once she determined to exert it.

The combined appeal to her womanliness and her sense of the romantic carried the day with her. She accepted his surrender, and this in terms of a generosity for which she was sure that there was abundant chivalrous precedent.

"Be it as you will then, sir," she said at last. "You shall be my prisoner. Give me your parole of honour that you will attempt no escape, and you may retain your weapons, holding them in trust for me."

Still on his knees, the sword still proffered, he bowed his head, and solemnly gave the oath required.

"Before God and Our Lady, by my honour and my faith, I swear to hold myself your captive, and that I shall not leave you until yourself you restore me the liberty which I here surrender."

Upon that he rose, and sheathed his rapier. "Is it a presumption, madam, to ask my captor's name?"

She smiled, for all that there still abode in her a shade of uneasiness at the eccentricity of this transaction.

"I am the Lady Margaret Trevanion," she replied.

"Trevanion?" He manifested a faint quickening of interest. "Are you by chance of the family of the Earl of Garth?"

She was justifiably surprised that a Spaniard should be so well-informed upon English family matters.

"He is my father, sir." And she expressed her astonishment in her question: "What do you know of the Earl of Garth?"

"I? Nothing, alas. Though that is a deficiency in me which the fortune of war should now repair. But I have heard my father speak of him and the near escape he had of losing his head in the service of your present Queen when Mary Tudor reigned in England. My father was here in the train of King Philip in those days when he was the Queen of England's husband, and I think he knew your father well. It is an odd link between us, if you please."

The link was none so odd as Don Pedro assumed or would have it appear. His father had been one of a cloud of Spanish noblemen who had come and gone about the Court of Queen Mary at a time when the Lord Admiral Seymour and his friends were prominent in the public eye and particularly in the eye of King Philip and his following, whose position in England was menaced by their activities.

"From the memory of his own misfortunes and the perils in which he all but lost his life, my Lord Garth may not be without sympathy for the misfortunes of another." Then, lest he should appear to plead too much, he essayed to diminish it by humour. "The first of these misfortunes, my lady, and the peril of life most pressing upon me at the moment comes from hunger."

She smiled. "Come, sir. I will see what may be done to mend it and the rest of your condition."

"The rest of my condition? *Valga me Dios!* There's naught amiss with the rest of my condition."

"Come," she commanded, and led the way, the hound bounding forward ahead.

Don Pedro, obediently, as became a prisoner, followed closely, and began at last to be truly thankful for his miraculous preservation.

Chapter 7

Margaret's Prisoner

They made their way upwards through a dell by a winding path that was all dappled with the sunlight beating through a ramage still dripping from last night's storm. The lady and her hound went ahead. Don Pedro followed, partly because to follow became his condition, partly because the pathway was scarcely wide enough to admit of their going abreast.

As they neared the summit, where there was open ground, a lusty male voice carolled suddenly above them. The actual words of his song have been lost, and they do not greatly matter. The burden of it was that life on the rolling sea was a jovial life, a roving life, and a rolling life. It fetched a laugh from Don Pedro, whose sea-memories at the moment were anything but jovial.

At the sound the girl looked over her shoulder at him, hanging a moment in her stride, and there was the ghost of a smile on her lips. It might have been supposed by one whose shrewdness was less satanic than the Spaniard's that she smiled in sympathy with his laugh, perceiving the wry humour of it. Don Pedro, however, caught in that smile something different, something mystifying to which he did not hold the clue. He was to hold it presently, when the singer disclosed himself, which was after they had brushed past the last of those wet branches and stood upon the open moorland all gold and purple in the morning sunshine.

Don Pedro beheld a tall young gentleman, tawny of head and care-free of countenance, who hailed her ladyship's emergence into the open with a glad cry and a light of gladness in his laughing eyes. He advanced upon long legs that were cased in thigh-boots of untanned leather; he rolled a little in his gait – a roll which it is to be feared he exaggerated, so that all might know him at sight for the terrible seaman he accounted himself. He was bareheaded, and his wind-tossed hair, bleached in patches by the same sun which had burnt his skin to its pleasant tan, increased the fresh young comeliness of his appearance. He carried a fowling-piece on his shoulder.

Her ladyship's dog bounded joyously forward to greet him, and for a moment hampered his own eager advance upon her ladyship, who meanwhile expressed surprise at his being abroad so early. He explained himself briefly. There was a fair at Truro, and a company of mummers who, it was said, had once played before Her Majesty in London. He had ridden over betimes to offer to escort her thither if it should be her pleasure to attend the play which was to be given after dinner in the yard of the Trevanion Arms. Hearing that she had gone walking, he had followed on foot; and to improve the occasion he had borrowed Matthew's fowling-piece hoping to take back a hare or a grouse for his lordship's supper. From all this, rapidly delivered, he broke off abruptly to inquire, in Heaven's name, who might be her companion.

There were several ways in which her ladyship might have presented her prisoner. Of these she mischievously chose the least explanatory and at the same time the most startling.

"This, Gervase, is Don Pedro de Mendoza y Luna, Count of Marcos."

The young seaman's eyes grew round; his brows came together. "A Spaniard!" quoth he, very much as he might have said: "A devil!" And almost instinctively he swung the fowling-piece from his shoulder to the crook of his arm, in readiness for action. He repeated his ejaculation on a higher note: "A Spaniard!"

Don Pedro smiled. He commanded upon occasion a smile of melancholy weariness, and this he now employed. "A very wet one, sir," he said in his precise and careful English.

But Sir Gervase scarcely looked at him. His eyes, question laden, were chiefly upon her ladyship.

"How comes a Spaniard here, in God's name?"

It was Don Pedro who answered him. "The sea, in rejecting me, was so benign as to cast me at the feet of her ladyship."

Quite apart from his being a Spaniard, Gervase disliked him on the spot. It is possible that Don Pedro intended that he should, for such was the dissimilarity, mental and physical, between these two that in whatever circumstances they might have met no love is conceivable between them. There was no man more skilled than Don Pedro in the art of subtle injury, that injury of tone and glance which is the more to be resented because allied with civil words which give no ground whatever for complaint.

"You mean that you have been shipwrecked?" Gervase questioned with a blunt aggressiveness.

Don Pedro's fine features were illumined by his faint weary smile. "I expressed it more gallantly, I hope. That is the only difference between your words and mine."

The young man came nearer. "Well, well," said he, with the least suspicion of swagger. "It is fortunate I met you."

Don Pedro bowed. "Sir, your courtesy places me in your debt."

"Courtesy?" quoth Sir Gervase. He uttered a short laugh. "You take me amiss, I think." And to avoid any possible further misunderstanding, added curtly: "I trust no Spaniard."

Don Pedro looked at him. "What Spaniard asks your trust?" he wondered.

This Sir Gervase disregarded. He came to business. "We will begin," he informed her ladyship, "by depriving him of his weapons. Come, Sir Spaniard. Hand them over."

But here at length her ladyship interposed. "You'll go your ways, Gervase," she informed him lightly, "and meddle in matters that concern you. This is not one of them."

Momentarily he was rebuffed. "What's that?" Then he shrugged and laughed. "This does concern me. It is a man's business. Come, sir, your weapons."

But Don Pedro merely smiled, in that easy weary way of his. "You are too late, sir, by half an hour. These weapons are surrendered already. I hold them merely on parole and in trust for my captor. I am the Lady Margaret Trevanion's prisoner."

Sir Gervase first grew solemn in astonishment, then loosed his laughter. In this there was an indiscreet note of contempt which angered her ladyship and summoned a flush to her cheeks by which the young man should have taken warning.

"Midsummer frenzy!" he crowed. "Who ever heard of a man being a woman's prisoner?"

"You have just heard it, sir," Don Pedro reminded him.

Her ladyship became disdainful. "You are young, Gervase, and the world lies before you for your instruction. Let us on, Don Pedro."

"Young!" was all that his indignation would permit him to ejaculate.

"Young, ay!" she answered him. "And beset by all the faults that are the marks of callowness. You detain me, I think?"

"It is my intent, by Heaven!" He stood squarely and angrily in their way.

Don Pedro might have offered to remove him. But Don Pedro used his wits. He perceived here, both in her ladyship and in Sir Gervase, certain symptoms which he thought he recognized. His own situation bristled with danger; he was very delicately poised; and he must be careful to do nothing that would disturb his precarious balance. So he remained aloof from the contention of which he was the subject.

Sir Gervase meanwhile made haste to put aside his wrath before the anger in Margaret's eyes. He perceived betimes his error, though he did not perceive that her indignation sprang chiefly from the very fact that he bore himself ill.

"Margaret, this is a thing best…"

She broke in upon his pleading tone. "I have said that you detain me." She was very haughty and peremptory. There was perhaps in her humour a touch of that perversity inherited from her perverse mother.

"Margaret!" His voice quivered with dismay and incredulity; his honest eyes, so blue against the tan of his face, were troubled. "I desire only to serve you; to… "

"No service is here required; certainly no service such as you importunately offer." And for the third time: "Come, Don Pedro," she commanded.

Sir Gervase fell back now, too deeply offended to offer another word. She moved on, Don Pedro following obediently, and it was upon him that Sir Gervase vented in his fierce scowl some of his seething anger. The Spaniard met the scowl with a bow than which nothing could have been more courteous and deferential.

To Sir Gervase, as he stood there following them with his brooding eyes, the glory had departed out of that September morning, and the joy in which he had come seeking Margaret was all withered in his heart. He accounted himself monstrously ill-used by her, and this not entirely without reason.

For a week now he had spent the greater part of each day in her company, either at the Chase itself or else walking or riding with her, and the relations between them had been so close and warm that he was assured his period of probation was at an end, and that soon she would consent to become openly betrothed to him.

There was no coxcombry in the lad. If on the one hand he had begun confidently to assure himself that she loved him, on the other her love for him must remain an abiding miracle for which in his own person and endowments he could find no sufficient cause. It was, like the unearned gifts which sometimes fall from Fortune's lap, something to be accepted in wondering gratitude and without question.

But this morning's events had destroyed all this again. Clearly he did not love him. She found in his company beguilement of her leisures. Time may have hung heavily upon her hands at Trevanion

Chase with that dull, bookish father, and she was glad to have him ride with her, hawk with her, escort her upon occasion to Penrhyn or Truro, take her sailing or fishing in the estuary. But love, real love for him, clearly there could be none in her heart, else she would not use him as she did, would never have humbled him in this fashion, and denied him what clearly lay within his rights where this shipwrecked Spaniard was concerned. It was all incredible and exasperating. He was, he found it necessary to assure himself, a man of some account. The Queen had knighted him for his, part in the action with the Armada, he held Her Majesty's commission, which imposed upon him certain duties here in Cornwall. The apprehension of this Spaniard washed ashore from one of the galleons that had escaped the action in the Channel was clearly within these duties, and, Margaret or no Margaret, he would accomplish it and refuse to be put off by an absurd romantic surrender to herself which this Spaniard might have made. And not so absurd, after all, that surrender, reflected Sir Gervase. Far from it. It was an instance of Spanish craft and Spanish cunning to play upon the romanticism of a woman for his own ends and the preservation of his own skin.

Thus after long and careful deliberation Sir Gervase took his resolve. He would follow them to the Chase, and relieve Lord Garth and his daughter of this undesirable guest, whatever the subsequent consequence to himself. That done, he would go seek Sir Francis Drake, or any other leader about to put forth in quest of fresh adventure, and bring to the enterprise that fine ship of his own which Sir John Killigrew was fitting for him.

Thus you behold him come striding into the hall at Trevanion Chase, and not to be detained there by old Martin, who was the master of his lordship's comparatively meagre household. He thrust the fowling-piece into the servant's hands, brushed him and his remonstrances aside, and stalked into the library, where Margaret and her prisoner were closeted with the earl.

Sufficiently vexed and perturbed was his lordship already. Here was no mere question of one of those momentary interruptions which never failed to irritate him, but a matter likely to be fruitful of all manner of disturbances and likely to keep the peace he desired for his household in hourly danger of being shattered. The dim remaining perceptions of the obligations of his station, however, had been stimulated by the link which at the very outset Don Pedro had sought to establish through his father's acquaintance with the earl in the distant days of Queen Mary's reign. This had lent his lordship grace to dissemble at least some part of his dismay at the intrusion and, all the inconveniences which it adumbrated.

The spare, grey-faced old recluse had looked up from under his shaggy brows with almost friendly eyes, and a faint smile moved under the narrow, square-cut beard, once auburn but now almost white.

"Oh yes. I remember Don Esteban de Mendoza. I remember him very well. He was your father, eh?" The smile broadened a little. "I had reason to esteem him."

He fell into abstraction, pondering events that were abruptly dragged from the tomb of oblivion. He recalled that of all the Spaniards at the court of Queen Mary, Don Esteban de Mendoza was probably the only one who had not thirsted for the blood of the Princess Elizabeth. When danger to her was most threatening from the activities of Renaud, it was Don Esteban who had warned the Lord Admiral, and this warning was so timely as to have been perhaps the means of preserving Her Grace's life.

It was his recollection of this that prompted his next words. "The son of Don Esteban de Mendoza stands in no great peril in, England. There must be a score of gentlemen ready to serve you for your father's sake. The Queen herself, once reminded of the past, should stand your friend, as your father once stood hers."

"It is possible," said Don Pedro, "that they may prefer to remember that I commanded a galleon of the Armada. Recent events must ever be more present than remote ones. And, in any case, between me and those gentlemen who might befriend me lies almost the whole of England, where it is not humanly possible today that a Spaniard should be loved."

It was at this point that Sir Gervase broke unbidden upon the conference in that musty library, bringing with him into it some of the vigorous freshness of the moorlands and the sea. He was a little excited and extremely vehement, both of which were conditions which his lordship detested. By virtue of the Queen's commission which he held, he proposed to relieve Lord Garth at once of this unwelcome intruder. He announced the intention rather than offered a service, which again was not the happiest way to deal with his lordship.

His lordship administered a reproof. "This commission which you hold from Her Grace gives you no right to break in upon me when I am private. I excuse it because I perceive the zeal by which you are moved. But this zeal, Gervase, is misplaced and unnecessary. Don Pedro has already surrendered himself a prisoner."

"To Margaret! To a woman!" cried Sir Gervase, and accounted it superfluous to do more than state the fact. Its absurdity was self-revealing. "Let him surrender himself to the justices of Truro, until order can be taken about him. By your leave, my lord, I will, myself, escort him thither now."

"And risk having him torn in pieces in the streets," said her ladyship. "That would be chivalrous."

"There would be no danger of it if he went with me. You could trust to my escort."

"I should prefer to trust to these walls," he was answered.

They made Sir Gervase more and more impatient.

"But it is fantastic," he insisted. "Who ever heard of a woman holding a prisoner? And how is she to hold him?"

It was Don Pedro who answered, smoothly urbane. "It is honour, sir, that holds a prisoner who has given his parole. I am bound more securely by that than by all the chains with which your Truro jail could load me."

This, of course, was not easily answered without using an offensiveness difficult to justify. Gervase was still seeking grounds upon which to dispute with them, when Margaret swept all argument aside with the reminder that her bedraggled prisoner was weak and faint, wet, cold and hungry, and that whatever might ultimately be resolved about him, commonest humanity dictated that their immediate care should be to feed and clothe and rest him.

His lordship, who perceived thus the possibility of an early return to the study of the Phoedo and the Socratic arguments upon the immortality of the soul, seized the opportunity of putting an end to all discussion and delivering his library from its invaders.

Chapter 8

Don Pedro's Letter

Don Pedro was treated at Trevanion Chase with all the consideration due to an honoured guest, and this in a house famed for its hospitality, despite the apparently inhospitable character of its master.

Lord Garth's revenues were by far the greatest of any nobleman in the West of England; his personal expenditure was insignificant; and he gave little thought or care to the manner in which his considerable wealth was laid out by his stewards, Francis Trevanion – an impoverished cousin upon whom he had bestowed the office – and Howard Martin, the chamberlain grown old in his service. He trusted these men implicitly, not so much because they were trustworthy or because his own nature was trustful as because by trusting them he was relieved of those economic cares and minor domestic details which he regarded as the troublesome, necessary futilities of life. His wealth was more than abundant for all that his station might require of him in his household; and whilst of an intense personal frugality, he had no desire that any economy should be practised, regarding such practices, indeed, as an irritating waste of things infinitely more valuable than money.

What the Lady Margaret required for herself or considered should be provided for another, she had merely to signify either to Francis Trevanion or to Martin, according to the nature of the requirement. She was invariably obeyed without question.

By her orders now a servant was appointed to minister to the personal wants of Don Pedro; their guest was provided with fresh linen and what else he lacked for his bodily comfort, and he was afforded a spacious chamber in the southwest wing of the mansion, whence he had a fine view of the downs and the sea, that accursed sea which had played the traitor to him and his fellow-countrymen.

To this chamber Don Pedro was confined for a week by a fever which attacked him on the very evening of his arrival, as a very natural result of all that lately he had undergone. This fever raged so furiously in the course of the next two days that a doctor was fetched from Truro to attend him.

Thus the fact of his presence at Trevanion Chase became bruited abroad and afforded presently matter for sensational discussion in every hamlet between Truro and Smithwick. Soon there were rumours – false rumours – of other Spaniards who had come ashore alive from that galleon, whose wreckage had supplied active and in some instances profitable occupation to the locality, and extravagant stories went up and down the countryside.

The constable came from Truro to pay Lord Garth a visit. He accounted it his duty to inquire into this affair and to suggest to his lordship that it behoved him to lay the matter before the justices.

His lordship was contemptuous of the justices, and arrogantly unable to perceive how anything that happened at Trevanion Chase could be the concern of any but himself. In some respects his outlook was almost feudal. Certainly nothing could have been more remote from his intentions than to seek the justices in this or any other matter.

He expressed himself in some such terms. He adopted a judicial tone. He admitted the presence at Trevanion Chase of a Spanish gentleman who had come ashore from the wreck. But as this coming ashore could not be regarded in the light of an invasion or as a hostile act against the peace of the realm, he was not aware of any statutory enactments under which the justices might take proceedings against Don Pedro. In any case, however, Don Pedro had formally surrendered himself to the Lady Margaret; he was virtually a prisoner at Trevanion

Chase, and his lordship accepted whatever responsibility this might entail, and denied the right of anyone to demand of him an account of his actions in this or any other matter.

He was by no means certain that the right did not exist; but he thought that the surest way of saving himself trouble was to deny its existence. To clinch his arguments he presented the constable with a crown and sent him to the kitchen to get drunk.

No sooner was he rid of the constable than he was plagued by Sir John Killigrew, who came to express the unsolicited opinion that this Spanish gentleman should be sent to the Tower to join there his distinguished compatriot Don Pedro Valdez.

His lordship began to experience exasperation. If he refrained from heat, it was because manifestations of heat were foreign to his nature. But he did not mince matters in pointing out to Sir John that he considered the subject of the visit an unwarrantable intrusion, and that he was well able to take order about Don Pedro without advice or assistance from his neighbours. He condescended, however, to explain that Don Pedro's case was rather exceptional; he deserved some consideration out of regard for his father's attitude towards the Queen in the old days. In this, his lordship asserted confidently, there was at least a score of gentlemen still in England who would support him. Sir John withdrew defeated, to face his kinsman Gervase, who had inspired the visit, and to explain to him its failure.

"After all, it is his own affair. The responsibility lies with him," said Killigrew with an airy tolerance very different from the patriotic indignation in which he had set out. "One Spaniard more or less is no great matter when all is said, and there's no mischief for the fellow's hands here in Cornwall."

Sir Gervase did not at all agree with him. He denounced the whole thing as outrageous. At best it was an untidy business, and the young seaman liked things ship-shape and in their proper places. The proper place for Don Pedro de Mendoza y Luna, in his opinion, was the Tower. His hostility to the Spaniard was increased, if not indeed entirely begotten by the attitude towards himself which her ladyship had taken up concerning the fellow. He failed entirely to perceive that it was his own rather boyish self-sufficiency and almost arrogant assumption of authority which had piqued her into this attitude.

Considering himself affronted by her disregard, he allowed the days to pass without attempting to approach her. But he had news of her – of her and her prisoner – which did not at all lessen his indignation.

The neighbouring gentry accepted the fact of the Spaniard's presence at Trevanion Chase with an equanimity that appalled him. From the Godolphins, the Tregarths and the younger Tressilian he actually heard the man's graces, wit and accomplishments extolled. This when Don Pedro's fever had abated and he was once more abroad, and being treated – as the reports showed – as an honoured guest. What Sir Gervase overlooked in permitting himself to be fretted by these reports was the fact that the aim of those fribbles was deliberately to stab him by them, and so avenge the hurt to their mean selves proceeding from the honours which had given him an ascendancy over them.

So Gervase sulked at Arwenack and gave his mind ostensibly to matters concerned with the fitting of his ship as if no Lady Margaret existed, until one morning, some twelve days after Don Pedro's coming, a groom rode over from the Chase with a note from her ladyship in which she inquired the reason of Sir Gervase's protracted absence and required him to come in person that very day and explain it to her. That he had registered the irrevocable resolve of sailing for the Indies without seeing her again did not prevent him from instantly obeying the summons of that note, little suspecting that it was in the interest of Don Pedro that his presence and services were required.

The fact was that with the recovery of his strength Don Pedro's mind turned naturally enough to the recovery of his liberty and to his repatriation. He approached the matter skilfully and delicately, as he did all things.

"There is," he informed her ladyship, "a matter of some urgency to be discussed between us, which only my condition has suffered me to postpone until now."

They had lingered at the breakfast-table when the meal was over and after his lordship and Francis Trevanion had withdrawn. The latticed windows stood open, for the weather was still warm. Don Pedro, facing them, could look out from his seat at the table upon the long stretch of smooth green lawn, brilliant as enamel in the morning sunshine, to the cluster of larches which cast a black shadow along its farther edge.

The Lady Margaret looked up quickly, her attention arrested by the unusual gravity of his tone. He answered the question of that glance.

"It becomes necessary that as my captor your ladyship should settle the ransom that is due."

"The ransom?" she frowned a little in surprise and perplexity. Then she laughed. "I don't perceive the necessity."

"It exists, my lady, none the less, and it is for you to state the sum. And let me add that to state a light one were to pay me a poor compliment."

Her perplexity increased. Her thoughtful eyes seemed to be pondering the table of dark oak with its strip of white napery and the crystal and silver glistening upon it. This, she thought, was to push the comedy a little far. At last she said: "Though I accepted your surrender when you made it, because...because, forsooth, it seemed a pretty thing to do, yet in reality you are to account yourself no more than our guest."

A smile flickered over the narrow handsome face. "Ah, no!" he cried. "Do not commit the error of assuming that I am no more than that nor the imprudence of announcing it. You must bethink you that if I am your guest, you are guilty of harbouring me, of affording me shelter. You are surely aware that there are heavy penalties already for harbouring Catholics, and no doubt there will be added ones for harbouring Spaniards who have been in arms against England. For your own sake as much as for mine, then, let it be quite clear that I am your prisoner, and that it is as your prisoner that I abide here. You will remember, too, that you are committed to it by what you told Sir Gervase on the morning of my surrender to you. Without that assurance from you and from his lordship, Sir Gervase would have taken me, and I do not care to think how it might have fared with me. I know that sooner than be dragged into some public place I must have withstood arrest by him; and since he was armed on that occasion with a fowling-piece, it is more than likely he would have shot me. You will see, then, when all this is considered, that honour will not permit me to owe my life and safety to a subterfuge."

It was, of course, a piece of sophistry; for none was more aware than himself that the very nature of his arrest was in itself a subterfuge. The argument, however, sufficed to deceive her, and she confessed to herself that it was unassailably sound.

"I understand," she said. "All this being so, and since you insist, yourself you shall name your ransom." He smiled mysteriously, thoughtfully fingering the long pearl-drop in his right ear.

"Be it so," he said at length. "Depend upon it, my lady, that I shall do myself the fullest justice. It remains now for you to lend me your aid so that I may procure this ransom."

"Ah, yes?" She laughed now, thinking that here surely he must find himself completely baffled.

But he was to reveal the unfailing quality of his resource which already had found a way. He leaned forward across the board. "I will write a letter, and it will be for you to see that it is carried."

"For me?"

He explained himself. "From the estuary below, from Smithwick and elsewhere, fishing yawls and other such craft are daily putting out to sea. It is amongst these that we must find a messenger to bear my letter. It is in this that of necessity I must depend upon your ladyship."

"You think I could prevail upon an English seaman to make a Spanish port at such a time as this?"

"That were, of course, a ludicrous suggestion, and I am not being ludicrous. I am earnest. All is well between England and France and my letter shall be addressed to one who is known to me in the port of Nantes. The rest we may leave to him. He will forward it to its ultimate destination."

"You have it all thought out!" she said, eyeing him almost mistrustfully.

He rose, slim and very elegant in his Spanish clothes, which the care of the efficient Martin had restored to their pristine quiet splendour. "Could I suffer myself to remain indefinitely a burden upon your noble hospitality?" he protested, his attitude one of dismay at a thought that did him wrong. But his eyes very watchful of her.

She laughed quite freely at that, and rose in her turn. On the gravel outside she had caught the approaching crunch of hooves, and knew the sound to herald the approach of groom and falconer. They were to ride that morning on the open moorland, and Don Pedro was to see for himself how hawks are trained in England.

"A courtly dissimulation of your haste to leave us," she rallied him.

"Ah, not that!" he exclaimed with a sudden fervour. "It is not charitable to think so of me, who am so little master of my destinies."

She turned her shoulder to him, and looked out of the window. "Here is Ned with the horses, Don Pedro."

A slow smile lifted a little his black moustachios as he considered the back of her neat head. He thought he detected annoyance in her when she discovered how maturely he had considered his plans for removing himself. Her manner had turned frosty, and her subsequent laughing indifference had been so much feminine dissimulation to cover her self-betrayal. Thus reasoned Don Pedro and took satisfaction in this reasoning. It received a check when, as they rode that morning, she told him that if he would write his letter, she thought she knew of a channel by which it could be set upon its journey. After her flash of resentment at his intentions he had hardly expected such ready acquiescence in measures which were to lead to his ultimate departure.

Thus it fell out that on the morrow when he had written his letter – couched in Latin so that it might baffle any vulgar person who might be tempted to investigate its contents – she dispatched her little note to Sir Gervase.

He came at once, arriving at eleven, just as they were sitting down to dine, for they kept country hours at Trevanion Chase. At table he had leisure to observe for himself the courtly grace, the urbane charm and ready easy wit which had been reported to him of Don Pedro. And as if perceiving the tactical error of his earlier downrightness where the Spaniard was concerned and seeking to make amends, he employed towards him a studied courtesy which Don Pedro returned with interest.

When dinner was done, and the earl had withdrawn in strict accordance with his inveterate habit, her ladyship desired Sir Gervase to come and admire with her the last of the year's roses. Sir Gervase, asking nothing better, departed with her, leaving Don Pedro and Francis Trevanion alone at table.

There were certain harsh truths she was to hear from Sir Gervase by way of chastisement upon which forgiveness would follow the more sweetly. But as they paced her rose garden, enclosed within tall and trimly-cut hedges of yew to shelter the blooms from the sea gales, she adopted towards him, so distracting and unusual an air of shyness that the remnants of his ill-humour were dissipated unuttered, and all the ill things he had rehearsed to tell her were forgotten.

"Where have you tarried all these days, Gervase?" she asked him presently, and by this question, for which once he had hoped so that he might return one of the dozen scathing answers he had prepared, flung him into some slight confusion.

"I have had affairs," he excused himself. "The fitting of my ship has engaged me closely with Sir John. And then... I did not think that you would be needing me."

"Do you come only when you think you are needed?"

"Only when I think I am welcome, which is much the same thing."

She gasped. "The unkind imputation!" she cried. "You are welcome, then, only when you are needed? Fie!"

His confusion increased. As usual she was putting him in the wrong where he knew that he was right.

"There was your Spaniard here to beguile your leisures," he said gruffly, angling for a contradiction.

"A courtly person, is he not, Gervase?"

"Oh, courtly enough!" he growled impatiently.

"I find him vastly diverting. There is a man who has seen the world."

"Why, so have I. Was I not with Drake when he sailed… ?"

"Yes, yes. But the world I mean, the world of his knowledge, is different from yours, Gervase."

"The world is the world," said Gervase sententiously. "And if it comes to that, I've seen a deal more of it than ever has he."

"Of the savage world, yes, Gervase. His knowledge is of the civilized, cultural world, as his person shows. He has been to all the courts of Europe and is learned in their ways and in many other ways. He speaks all the languages of the world, and plays the lute like an angel, and sings… Should'st hear him sing, Gervase! And he… "

But Gervase had heard enough, and interrupted her. "How long does he abide here, this marvel of the ages?"

"Only a little while longer, I fear."

"You fear?" Disgust ineffable rang in his voice.

"What have I said?" she wondered. "Have I angered you, Gervase?"

He snorted impatiently and strode on, planting his feet with ferocity. For all that he had sailed with Drake, seen much of the world and learnt many things, there had been few opportunities upon that voyage to study the tortuous ways of woman.

"What are you going to do with him?" he asked. "Has your father reached a resolve?"

"It is no concern of my father's. Don Pedro is my prisoner. I am holding him to ransom, and he shall go home so soon as the ransom comes."

This first took him by surprise, then afforded him some slight matter for mirth.

"If you are waiting for that, there's no ground for your fears that he'll soon be leaving you."

"You make too sure. He has writ a letter to a man in Nantes, who will proceed to Spain to obtain the ransom."

Sir Gervase was utterly discourteous. "Bah!" he sneered. "It would become you better to send to Truro for the constable and deliver Don Pedro to the law of the land."

"And is that all you've learnt of the usages of chivalry in your sailings with Sir Francis Drake? I think you had better sail again and travel farther."

"Chivalry!" said he. "Moonshine!" Then from futile contempt he turned again to more practical considerations. "He has writ a letter, you say. And who's to carry the letter?"

"That is a difficulty, of course. He perceives it himself."

"Oh, he does, does he? He must indeed be a man of perceptions. He can actually see an object when it stands before him. There's discernment!" And Sir Gervase laughed, well pleased to have found this weakness in the Spaniard's equipment.

He was less pleased when Margaret pointed out the consequence. They had come to the end of the enclosed garden, to a semi-circular stone seat that was half recessed into the thick yew hedge. With a sigh of resignation, she seated herself.

"He bides here for ever, then, it seems!" She sighed again. "A pity! I am sorry for him, poor gentleman. To be a prisoner in a foreign land can be no enviable fate. It is like being a thrush in a cage. But there! We will ease his condition all we can, for myself I am well content that he should remain. I like his company."

"Oh, you like his company? You confess to that?"

"What woman would not? He is a man whom most women would find adorable. I was lonely until he came, with my father always at his books, and no one to bear me company but such foolish fellows as Lionel Tressilian, Peter Godolphin or Ned Tregarth. And if you are going a-sailing again, as you say you are, I shall soon be lonely once more."

"Margaret!" He was leaning over her, in his eyes all the ardour aroused by that unusual confession.

She looked up at him, and smiled with some tenderness. "There! I've said it! I didn't mean to say so much."

He slipped into the seat beside her and put his arm about her shoulders.

"You understand, Gervase, don't you, that I should desire to keep so welcome a companion as Don Pedro by me?" His arm fell away as if it had been water. "I mean when you are gone, Gervase. You wouldn't have me lonely. Not if you love me."

"That is to consider," said he.

"What is to consider?"

He sat forward now, his elbows on his knees. "This letter that he has written: what exactly did he hope from it?"

"Why, his ransom and the means to return to Spain."

"And he had no thought of how it might be got to Nantes?"

"Oh yes. He thought the skipper of some yawl or fishing boat might carry it. His difficulty lay in inducing such a skipper to do him this service. But no doubt Don Pedro's wits will find a way. He's very shrewd and resourceful, Gervase, and he..."

"Yes, yes," said Gervase. "Perhaps I can save him trouble."

"You, Gervase? What trouble can you save him?"

He got to his feet abruptly. "Where is this letter?"

She considered him round-eyed. "Why, what now? What is the letter to you, Gervase?"

"I'll find a skipper to carry it to Nantes. It shall be there within a week at most. Another week or two to get his ransom here, and he may go his ways again to Spain or to the devil."

"Would you really do so much for him, Gervase?" said her innocent ladyship.

Gervase smiled grimly. "Get me the letter. I know of a boat that sails with the tide tonight, and if the price will warrant it her skipper will even run to the Loire."

She rose. "Oh, the price will warrant it. Fifty ducats for the bearer, to be delivered to him against the letter by the person to whom it is addressed."

"Fifty ducats! 'Sdeath! He's a wealthy man, this Spaniard!"

"Wealthy? His wealth is incalculable. He is a Grandee of Spain. The half of the Asturias are his property and he has vast vineyards in Andalusia. He is a nephew of the Cardinal-Archbishop of Toledo, he possesses the close friendship of the King of Spain, and… "

"To be sure, to be sure," said Gervase. "Get me this letter, and leave the rest to me."

He could be depended upon to act zealously in the matter, for by now no one could have been more completely persuaded than Sir Gervase Crosby of the propriety of speeding so illustrious, wealthy, accomplished, highly connected and attractive a gentleman from Trevanion Chase.

Chapter 9

The Assault-at-Arms

The letter was duly despatched, and in consideration of this fact Sir Gervase might well have practised patience for the little while that Don Pedro was likely to continue at Trevanion Chase. But young men in love are notoriously impatient, and matters were not eased for Gervase when he found the Lady Margaret rendered all but inaccessible to him by the claims upon her of her prisoner.

Whenever Gervase sought her now, there was no chance of being private with her for more than a moment. If she were not away, riding or hawking with the courtly Spaniard, there were ever visitors at the Chase, and the Spaniard was invariably the centre of interest. Either he entertained the company with amusing narratives out of his wide experience, or else he charmed them with plaintive, passionate Andalusian songs, and he was so skilled a performer on the lute that he could ring from it an unsuspected power of melody.

That the Lady Margaret should remain indifferent to his undeniable fascination was incredible, particularly to Sir Gervase. When the witty, versatile, accomplished Don Pedro exerted himself to please, there is no doubt he could be dangerous. And it was obvious to all that he was exerting himself now. Those Cornish gallants who had paid an assiduous court to the Lady Margaret until Sir Gervase had elbowed them out of his way looked on and smiled to see him thrust aside in his turn by another. In Don Pedro they beheld their own avenger, which in itself went far to dispose them in Don Pedro's favour.

Lionel Tressilian made a simpering jest of it to his grim half-brother Sir Oliver. But Sir Oliver did not laugh with him.

"God's light!" he cried. "It's a shameful thing that a pestilential Spaniard who shelters himself behind a woman's petticoat should be fawned upon by a pack of unlicked English whelps. He should have been handed over to the justices. Since my Lord Garth is too indolent to oppose his daughter, if I were in Gervase Crosby's place, I'd make short work of this Don Pedro."

Chancing on the morrow to meet Gervase in Smithwick, the elder Tressilian spoke his mind freely and bluntly as was his habit. He blamed Gervase's weakness for accepting this comedy of Don Pedro's surrendering his sword to a lady and for suffering himself to be thrust out of his proper place by such a man. The youth of the place were making a jest of it; and it was high time Gervase showed them that it was not only upon the seas that he could deal with Spaniards.

This supplied the drooping spirits of Gervase with the necessary spur, and coming that afternoon to Trevanion Chase he decided to take action, though not necessarily of the violent kind at which the downright uncompromising Sir Oliver had hinted. That were neither just where the Spaniard was concerned, nor prudent towards Margaret. But it was necessary that his own position should be properly defined. Being informed by Martin that her Ladyship was in the arbour with Don Pedro, he decided to make a beginning with the earl.

The earl, who had shifted from philosophy to history, its proper correlative, was poring over a colossal volume of Herodotus when Sir Gervase invaded his privacy.

"My lord," the young man announced. "I am come to talk to you of Margaret."

His lordship looked up peevishly. "Is it really necessary?" he wondered. "I suppose you are come to tell me once again that you want to marry her. I don't oppose it if she doesn't. Marry her if she will have you. Go and ask her."

If this was a subterfuge to be rid of his intruder, it failed.

"She will not listen to reason these days," Sir Gervase complained.

"Reason? Whoever made love in terms of reason with any hope of success? I begin to understand your failure, sir."

"My failure is due to this damned Don Pedro." He smacked a speck of dust from a tome that lay under his hand upon the table. "Until this Spaniard was washed up here out of Hell I had every hope to be married before Christmas."

His lordship frowned. "What has Don Pedro to do with this?"

"With submission, my lord, I say you spend too much time with books."

"I am glad you say it with submission. But it hardly answers my questions."

"It were well that you spared some leisure from your studies to keep an eye upon your daughter, sir. She and this Spaniard are too much alone together; much more than is befitting a lady of her station."

The earl smiled sourly. "You are endeavouring to tell me that Margaret is a fool. My answer is that you're a fool to think so."

But Gervase would not be put off. "I say that all women are fools."

His lordship sniffed. "I nothing doubt that your misogyny has its roots in a wide experience." Seeing the blank look in the young man's eyes he explained himself. "I mean that you'll have known many women."

"As many as I need to," quoth Gervase, non-committal.

"Then it is high time you got yourself married. A God's name what do you stay for?"

"I have already told your lordship. This infernal Spaniard stops the way. At this very moment he sits at her feet in the arbour, thrumming his pestilent lute and languishing his Malaga love-songs."

At last his lordship appeared really scandalized. "And you tarry here while this is doing? Away with you at once, and send her hither to me. I'll make an end of this. If I have any authority over her she shall many you within a month. Thus at last I may have peace. Away with you."

Sir Gervase departed on that agreeable errand, whilst his lordship returned to investigate the fortunes of Cyrus and Cambyses.

The tinkling of the lute, the rich melodious voice of the Spanish Grandee guided Sir Gervase to the arbour. Unceremoniously he interrupted the song with his message.

"Margaret, his lordship asks for you. He is in haste."

She departed after some questions to which he returned equivocal replies.

The two men were left together. Don Pedro, having bowed to the departing lady, sat down again, and crossed his shapely legs that were cased in shimmering black silk, a quality of hose almost unknown in England, the very pair in which he had swum ashore. With the lute lying idly in his lap, he made some attempts at polite conversation. These were impolitely discouraged by the other's monosyllabic answers. At last Don Pedro ignored his companion, and once more gave his attention entirely to the instrument, a pretty thing out of Italy of ebony inlaid with ivory. His fingers swept the chords. Very softly he began to play a quick Sevillian dance measure.

Sir Gervase, in that state of irritation which distorts all things and magnifies the distortion, chose to perceive in this a deliberate affront, a subtle form of mockery. Perhaps the rippling character of the measure added colour to the assumption. Anger surged up in him, and acting upon it, suddenly he dashed the lute from the thrummer's hands.

The Spaniard's dark eyes looked at him in black astonishment from out of that handsome, ivory-coloured face. Then, observing his aggressor's fiery countenance, he smiled a slow faint smile inscrutable of meaning.

"You do not like music, eh, Sir Gervase?" he inquired with quiet, derisive courtesy.

"Neither music nor musicians," said Gervase.

The Spaniard continued unruffled, regarding him now with a faintly quickened interest.

"I have heard that there are men like that," said he, implying that he now looked for the first time upon a member of that species. "The sentiment, or the lack of it, I can understand if I cannot admire it. But the expression of it which you have chosen I do not understand at all."

Already Sir Gervase realized that he had done a stupid, boorish thing. His anger with himself was increased by the utter failure of his action to provoke Don Pedro out of his lightly scornful urbanity. Almost he could admire the Spaniard's weary impassivity, and he was certainly made the more sensitive of his own loutishness by contrast. This merely served to fan his rage.

"I should have thought it plain enough," he answered.

"Of course if this onslaught upon the Lady Margaret's unoffending lute was merely an instance of rustic want of manners, let me assure you that it was entirely unnecessary."

"You talk too much," said Gervase. "I meant no harm to the lute."

The Spaniard uncrossed at last his graceful legs, and rose with a sigh. His face wore now a look of weary melancholy.

"Not to the lute? To me then, eh? The harm was for me? You desire to offer me an affront? Am I to assume this?"

"If it will not strain your capacity for assumption." Committed to it now, Gervase could not draw back.

"But it does. I assure you that it does. Being unconscious of having given offence, or of ever having lacked for courtesy towards you…"

Sir Gervase broke in. "You are, yourself, the offence. I do not like your face. That jewel in your ear savours the fop, and offends my sense of niceness. And then your beard is odious, and in short, you are a Spaniard, and I hate all Spaniards."

Don Pedro sighed even as he smiled. "At last I understand. Indeed, sir, you appear to have a very solid grievance. I am ashamed of myself for having afforded it. Tell me, sir, what I may do to please you?"

"You might die," said Gervase.

Don Pedro fingered his beard, ever suave and cool before the hot anger of the other, which his every word, with its undercurrent of contempt and mockery, was deliberately calculated to increase.

"That is a deal to ask. Would it amuse you," he wondered almost plaintively, "to attempt to kill me?"

"Damnably," said Gervase.

Don Pedro bowed. "In that case, I must do what I can to oblige you. If you will stay for me until I get my weapons, I will afford you the gratifying opportunity."

With a nod and a smile, he departed briskly, leaving Gervase in a fury the half of which was directed against himself. He had behaved with an outrageous clumsiness before that impeccable master of deportment. He was ashamed of the boorish manner in which he had achieved his object with one whose bearing throughout had been an education in the manner in which these matters should be handled by men of birth. Deeds alone could now make amends for the shortcomings of his words.

He said so in a minatory tone to the Don, as presently they made their way together to a strip of lawn behind a quickset hedge where they would be entirely screened and private.

"If you ply your sword as keenly as your tongue, Don Pedro, you should do fine things," he sneered.

"Do not be alarmed," was the smooth answer.

"I am not," snapped Sir Gervase.

"There is not the need," Don Pedro assured him. "I shall not hurt you."

They had rounded the hedge by now, and Sir Gervase, in the act of untrussing his points, fell roundly to swearing in answer to that kindly promise.

"You entirely misapprehend me," said Don Pedro. "Indeed, I think there is a good deal in this that you do not apprehend. Have you considered, for instance, that if you kill me, there will be none to question your right to do so; but if I were to kill you, it is odds that these barbarous compatriots of yours would hang me in spite of my rank?"

Gervase paused in the act of peeling off his doublet. Dismay overspread his honest young face. "As God's my life I had not thought of that. Look you, Don Pedro, I have no desire to place you at such a disadvantage. This thing cannot go on."

"It cannot go back. It might be supposed that I pointed out the delicacy of the situation so as to avoid the issue. And that my honour will not suffer. But, I repeat, sir, you have no cause for alarm."

The taunting confidence angered Sir Gervase anew. "You're mighty sure of yourself!" said he.

"Of course," the Don agreed. "Could I consent to meet you else? There is so much that you overlook in your hot haste. Consider that, being as I am a prisoner on parole, to permit myself to be killed would be lacking in honour, since to die by an act in which I have a part were tantamount to breaking prison. It follows that I must be very sure of myself or I would not consent to engage."

This was more than Gervase could endure. The Spaniard's dignified imperturbability he had admired. But this cold bombast disgusted him. He flung aside his doublet in a rage and sat down to pull off his boots.

"Is so much necessary?" quoth Don Pedro. "Myself I abhor damp feet."

"Each to his taste," he was curtly answered. "You may die dry-shod if you prefer it."

The Spaniard said no more. He unbuckled his sword belt, and cast it from him with the scabbard, retaining the naked rapier in his hand. He had brought sword and dagger, the usual combination of duelling weapons; but discovering that Sir Gervase, who had come unprepared for this, was armed with rapier only, Don Pedro accommodated himself to his opponent.

Lithe, graceful and entirely composed he waited now, bending. the long supple steel like a whip in his two hands, whilst his opponent completed his elaborate preparations.

At length they faced each other, and engaged.

Sir Gervase, as he had already proved upon more than one occasion, was endowed with the courage of a mastiff; but his swordplay was, like his nature, downright, straightforward and without subtleties. By sheer strength of brawn he had earned himself among seamen something of a reputation as a slashing swordsman, and he had come to conceive that he was a match for most men with the weapon. This resulted not from self-sufficiency, but from ignorance. His education was far from complete, as Margaret frequently and unkindly reminded him. Something was to be added to it this afternoon.

The true art of fence was in its infancy. Lately born in that fair land of Italy, which has mothered all the arts, it had as yet made comparatively little progress in the rest of Europe. True there was a skilled Italian, a Messer Saviolo, in London, who gave instructions to a few choice pupils, and similarly there were masters sprouting up in France and Spain and Holland. But in the main your gallant, and your soldier in particular, depended upon his strength to bear down an opponent's blade and hack a way to his heart. To this he added sometimes certain questionable tricks of fighting, which were of less than no avail should he chance – as Sir Gervase chanced today – to be opposed to one of those few swordsmen who had made a study of this new art and mastered its principles.

You conceive the disconcerting astonishment of Sir Gervase when he found the slashing cuts which he aimed at the lithe Don Pedro, with all the weight of his brawn behind them, spending themselves upon the empty air, rendered harmless and powerless as they were met by a closely played deflecting blade. It was like witchcraft to the uninitiated, as if the Spaniard's sword were a magic rod, which at contact robbed his own, and his arm with it, of all strength. Then he grew angry, and his play became wilder. Don Pedro might have killed him twenty times without exertion. It was indeed this lack of exertion on the Spaniard's part that infuriated the sturdy young seaman. Don Pedro scarcely stirred. He kept his arm shortened and used his forearm sparingly, depending chiefly upon the quick play of his wrist to be everywhere at once with the very greatest economy of time and action. Thus in a manner that to Gervase seemed increasingly uncanny, the forte of that blade was ever presented to the foible of his own, sending every cut and every thrust irresistibly yet effortlessly awry.

Gervase, already breathing heavily and beginning to perspire, broke ground so as to attack in another quarter. But he had his labour for nothing. The Spaniard merely pivoted to face him, and to re-engage as before. Once Gervase made as if to hurl himself forward, so as to come to grips with his opponent; but he was checked by the Spaniard's point, flicked upwards to the line of his throat. If he advanced he must impale himself upon it.

Baffled and winded, Sir Gervase fell back to breathe. The Spaniard made no attempt to follow and attack. He merely lowered his point, to ease his arm, whilst waiting for the other to resume.

"You become heated, I fear," he said. He showed no sign of heat himself and was breathing easily. "That is because you use the edge too much, and therefore labour with your arm. You should learn to depend more upon the point; keep the elbow closer to the body, and let your wrist do the work."

"'Sdeath!" roared Gervase, in fury. "Do you give me lessons?"

"But do you not begin to perceive that you need them?" quoth the affable Don Pedro.

Sir Gervase leapt at him, and then things happened quickly. Quite how they happened he never understood. The Spaniard's sword deflected his fierce lunge, but less widely than hitherto, and now blade ran on blade until the hilts crashed together. Then quite suddenly Don Pedro's left hand shot out and closed upon Sir Gervase's sword wrist. The rest was done with the speed of thought. The Spaniard dropped his sword. His now empty right seized Gervase's rapier by the quillions and wrenched it from his grasp before the design was so much as suspected.

Thus Sir Gervase found himself disarmed by seizure, his weapon now in his opponent's hand. Enraged, hot and perspiring he stood, whilst the Spaniard, smiling quietly, bowed to him as if to signify that he had done his part and the affair was at an end.

And then, as if this measure of humiliation were not in itself sufficient, he suddenly became aware of Margaret's presence. She was standing by the corner of the quickset hedge, wide-eyed, white-faced, her lips parted, her left hand pressed to her breast.

How long she had been there he did not know; but in any case long enough to have witnessed his discomfiture. In that bitter moment Sir Gervase accounted it no mercy that Don Pedro had not run him through the heart.

Sick and foolish, oddly pale now under his tan, despite the heat in which the combat had put him, he watched her swift, angry approach.

"What is this?" she demanded, turning first to one and then to the other and withering each with her glance.

It was, of course, Don Pedro who, never for a moment losing his composure, afforded her an answer. "Why, nothing. A little sword-play for the instruction of Sir Gervase. I was demonstrating for him the art of the new Italian school of fence."

He proffered the sword to Sir Gervase, hilt foremost. "Enough for today," he said with his courteous smile. "Tomorrow, perhaps, I shall show you how the estramaçon is to be met and turned aside."

By his infernal subtlety the man invested what he said with an air which conveyed quite plainly the very thing he pretended to conceal: how generously he had spared his opponent.

Her ladyship considered him a moment in haughty dignity. "Pray give me leave apart with Sir Gervase," she commanded frostily.

The Spaniard bowed, took up his rapier from the ground and then his sword belt, and obediently departed.

"Gervase," she said peremptorily, "the truth! What passed between you?"

He gave her truthfully enough the details by which he knew himself to be shamed.

She listened patiently, her face white, her lip at moments trembling. When he had done and stood hang-dog before her, it was some moments before she spoke, as if she were at pains to choose her words.

"You were bent, it seems, upon saving me the trouble of disobeying my father's wishes?" she said at last between question and assertion.

He was in no doubt of her meaning. But the heart was all gone out of him. He continued to contemplate the trampled turf. He perceived how fitting it was that she should refuse to marry such an oaf as himself, clumsy in all things. He had no courage left to defend himself or plead his cause.

"Well?" she demanded. "Why don't you answer me? Or have you talked yourself dumb with Don Pedro?"

"Perhaps I have," he answered miserably.

"Perhaps you have!" she mocked him. "Good lack! Would it have helped you to have got yourself killed?"

In reply he set her a question which he might well have set himself, ay, and found the answer to it in her present angry agitation.

"Since you would not have cared, why all this heat and bother?"

Excitement betrayed her. "Who says I would not?" she snapped, and almost bit out her tongue when the words were sped.

They had a transfiguring effect upon the man before her. He stared at her, and fell to trembling. "Margaret!" he cried in a voice that rang out. "Would'st have cared, Margaret?"

She took refuge in feminine dissimulation. She shrugged. "Is it not plain? Do we want the justices here to know how you met your death, and a scandal about our heads that may send an echo as far as London?"

He gulped and lapsed back into his dejection. "Was that all you meant? Was that all?"

"What else could you suppose I meant? Get you dressed, man. My father is asking for you." She began to turn away. "Where did you say you left my lute? If you've broken it I'll not forgive you easily."

"Margaret!" he called to her as she was departing.

By the quickset hedge she paused, and looked at him over her shoulder.

"I've been an oaf," he pleaded miserably.

"Upon that particular at least we can agree. Aught else?"

"If you'll forgive me... " He broke off, and moved towards her. "It was all for you, Margaret. I was maddened to see this Spaniard ever in your company. I can't endure it. We were so happy until he came... "

"Myself I've not been unhappy since."

He swore beneath his teeth. "It's that! It's that!"

"It's what?"

"My cursed jealousy. I love you, Margaret. I'd give my life for love of you, Margaret dear."

"Faith, I believe you," she taunted him, "since I found you engaged in the attempt." She moved away a pace or two, then paused again. "Get you dressed," she repeated, "and in Heaven's name get sense," she added, and was gone. But as he was gloomily trussing his points, she was back again.

"Gervase," she said, very grave and demure now. "If my forgiveness matters, you'll promise me that we shall have no more of this."

"Ay," he answered bitterly, "I promise."

"You swear it," she insisted, and for all that he swore it readily enough he had not the wit, it seems, to fathom the reason of her concern. A little coxcombry would have helped him here. But there was no coxcombry in Sir Gervase Crosby's composition.

Chapter 10

The Ransom

Sir Gervase departed that day from Trevanion Chase in the deepest humiliation he had ever known. In another this humiliation might have turned to gall, urging him to a mean vengeance in one of the forms which the circumstances placed so readily at hand. In Sir Gervase, however, it inspired only self-reproach. He had behaved abominably. He had borne himself like an ill-mannered schoolboy, and Don Pedro had dealt with him precisely as his case and condition required, administering, with a magnanimity that was in itself a cruelty, a corrective birching to his soul.

That Margaret must now utterly despise him seemed inevitable; that she should be justified of her contempt was intolerable. Thus in his almost excessive humility had he interpreted her indignation. Blinded by it – for humility can be as blinding as conceit – he had never seen the fierce concern behind it.

His opponent's case was little better than his own. It was in vain that Don Pedro defended himself by specious arguments, or paraded the magnanimity and restraint to which Sir Gervase owed it that he had come off the field without physical hurt. The Lady Margaret did not desire that Sir Gervase should owe anything to the magnanimity of any man. It was detestable to her that he should be placed in such a position, and this detestation she divided impartially between himself and the man who had placed him there. Towards Don Pedro her manner was now aloof and frosty. She allowed him to perceive that she had formed her opinion of his conduct and desired to hear no explanations since no explanations could modify the view she took.

After supper that evening, however, he made a vigorous attempt to put himself right in her eyes. She was withdrawing with her cousin Francis in the wake of her father, when he begged her to stay a moment. In yielding it is possible that her intent was to render him yet more fully aware of her indignation.

"I vow," he said, "that you use me cruelly in being angry with me for a matter which it was not in my power to avoid."

"It is not my desire to hear more of it."

"And now you are unjust. There is no deeper injustice than to condemn a man unheard."

"I do not need to hear you, sir, to know that you abused your position here, that you abused the trust I placed in you when I allowed you to retain your weapons. The facts themselves are all I need to know; and the facts, Don Pedro, have lowered you immeasurably in my esteem."

She saw the spasm of pain ripple across that narrow, clear-cut face, and look at her out of those great liquid and undeniably beautiful dark eyes. This it may have been that, softening her a little, suffered her now to listen without interruption to his answer.

"Than that," said he, "you could inflict upon me no crueller punishment, and it is an irony that it should fall upon me for actions in which from end to end I was guided only by the desire to retain an esteem which I prize above all else. I abused your trust, you say. Will you not hear my answer?"

He was so humble, the pleading note in his voice so musical, that she gave her consent with a reluctance that was only apparent. He offered, then, his explanation. Sir Gervase had come to him with the clear intention of provoking a quarrel. He had dashed the lute from Don Pedro's hands, he had alluded in the grossest terms to Don Pedro's physical attributes.

These affronts he could have forgiven, but to forgive them would have justified Sir Gervase in accounting him a coward, and that he could not have forgiven because it would have hurt his honour. Therefore, to avoid the unforgivable, he had consented to meet Sir Gervase Crosby, but this only because no doubt of the issue existed in his mind and he could depend upon his resolve to use his weapons only for a defensive purpose, so as to render negative the combat. He had displayed his mastery of those weapons, not in any braggart spirit, but merely so as to place his courage above reproach when he should come to decline any further quarrels that it might be sought to put upon him.

It made up a strong case, and his manner of presenting it was impeccable in its modesty. But her ladyship was not disposed, it seemed, to clemency; for whilst she confessed herself, as perforce she must, satisfied with his arguments, the tone in which she confessed it was frosty and distant; and frosty and distant her manner continued in the days that immediately followed. She no longer showed any concern for the entertainment of her prisoner. She left him to his own devices, to seek exercise in lonely brooding walks, or to employ his wits in agricultural and forestry discussions with Francis Trevanion, while she rode abroad with Peter and Rosamund Godolphin, or entertained these and other visitors, to the Spaniard's exclusion, in her own bower.

Thus for Don Pedro three dismal days passed sluggishly. She observed his dejected countenance when they met at table and was satisfied that he should suffer, the more so because as a consequence of the events Sir Gervase had not been seen at Trevanion Chase since he had departed in defeat. If she could have guessed the full extent of Don Pedro's suffering, things might have been different. In regarding the melancholy reflected on his pale face and in his liquid eyes as a histrionic adaptation to what he conceived the requirements of the case, she did him less than justice.

Don Pedro suffered in all sincerity, and the wistfulness which she detected in his eyes when they observed her arose from his very soul.

It was inevitable, by the attraction of opposites, that this dark-complexioned typical son of the South, thrown into such close and constant association with that tall, golden girl whose cheeks were as delicately tinted as the apple blossoms, whose eyes were so unfathomably calm, so blue and so frankly level in their glances, should have lost his heart to her. She was so different not only from the languishing, sheltered, ill-informed women of his native Spain, but from any woman that he had ever met in any other part of Europe. The liberty which she enjoyed so naturally, having known naught else from childhood, gave her at once a frankness and a strength which afforded her maidenhood a stronger bulwark than ever was supplied by a barred casement or a vigilant duenna. She was innocent without ignorance, frank without boldness, modest without simpering, and maddeningly attractive without deliberate allure. In all his life and all his travels, Don Pedro had never met a lady half as desirable nor one whose permanent conquest could be a source of deeper pride. And all had been going so well and promisingly between them until that unfortunate matter with Sir Gervase Crosby, whom, from despising, Don Pedro now began to hate.

Thus for three days he pined in the chill exclusion to which she doomed him. On the evening of the fourth something happened to restore him to the centre of the canvas, his proper place in any picture of which he was a part.

They were at table when a servant brought word that a gentleman – a foreign gentleman – was asking for Don Pedro. The Spaniard, having craved and been granted leave, withdrew to the hall where this visitor waited.

The worldly consequence of Don Pedro de Mendoza y Luna was to be inferred from the amazing celerity put forth to serve him by those who were the recipients of that letter dispatched to Nantes. Their speed was so little short of miraculous that within some eighteen days of the sailing of the yawl that had borne the letter the bearer of the answer presented himself at Trevanion Chase.

Don Pedro, coming with swift eager steps into the spacious grey hail, checked abruptly at sight of the man who awaited him, a squarely built fellow, in brown homespun and long sea-boots, black-bearded, and tanned like a sailor. Under his arm he bore a bulky package wrapped in sailcloth. He bowed to the Spaniard, and announced himself in French.

"At your service, monseigneur, I am Antoine Duclerc, out of Nantes."

Don Pedro frowned and stiffened. His manner became haughty.

"How is this? I had thought that Don Diego would have come in person. Am I, then, become of so little account?"

"Don Diego has come, monseigneur. But it would hardly be prudent for him to land."

"He becomes prudent, eh?" Don Pedro sneered. "Well, well! And who are you?"

"I am the master of the brig that went to fetch him out of Santander. She is lying-to a couple of miles from shore with Don Diego aboard, awaiting your excellency. It is arranged we take you off tonight. I have a boat in the cove under the cliff there and a half-dozen stout Asturians to man it."

"Asturians?" Don Pedro seemed surprised and not displeased.

"We shipped a Spanish crew at Santander by Don Diego's orders."

"Ah!" Don Pedro came nearer. "And the ransom?"

The Frenchman proffered the package from under his arm. "It is here, monseigneur."

Don Pedro took it and sauntered across to the window. He broke the heavy seals and with his dagger ripped away the envelope of sailcloth, laying bare an oblong ebony box. He raised the lid. Nestling on a cushion of purple velvet lay a string of flawless, shimmering pearls, every bead of which was nigh as large as a sparrow's egg. He took it in his hands, setting the empty box upon the window-seat.

"Don Diego has done well," he said at last. "Tell him so from me."

The seaman looked his surprise. "But will your excellency not tell him so yourself? The boat is waiting…"

Don Pedro interrupted him. "Not tonight. It leaves me no time to make my little preparations. You shall come again at dusk tomorrow, when I will be ready."

"As your excellency pleases." Duclerc was uneasy. "But delays are dangerous, monseigneur."

Don Pedro slowly turned, and slowly smiled. "All life is dangerous, my friend. And so at dusk tomorrow in the little cove where the brook joins the sea. God accompany you."

Duclerc bowed and departed. Alone, Don Pedro stood bemused a moment, holding that priceless string in the cup of his two hands, admiring the lustre of the pearls so chastely iridescent in the waning sunshine of that autumn evening. He smiled faintly, musingly, as he considered precisely how he should present them. At last he lightly tied together the two silken ends and returned to the dining-room.

He found that his lordship and Francis had departed, and that Margaret was now alone, occupying the window-seat and gazing out over the parterres, from which the glory of the flowers had almost entirely passed. She glanced over her shoulder as he entered; but his hands were now behind him, and she caught no glimpse of the thing he carried.

"Is all well?" she asked him.

"All is very well, my lady," answered he, whereupon she resumed her contemplation of the sunset.

"Your visitor is from…overseas?" she asked.

"From overseas," he replied.

He sauntered across to her, his feet rustling in the fresh rushes with which the dining-room floor was daily spread. He stood close behind her at the window, whilst she, waiting so much as he might choose to tell her, continued to gaze outward. Very quietly he raised his hands, poised that splendid necklace for a moment, and then let it slip over her golden head.

She felt the light touch upon her hair and then, quite cold, upon her bare neck, and she leapt instantly to her feet, her cheeks aflame.

She had conceived that what she felt was the touch of his fingers. And for all that he smiled as he stood now bending slightly forward, he was stabbed by the swift resentment of what he saw she had imagined.

Perceiving her error and seeing the necklace hanging there upon her white skin, she laughed a little, between awkwardness and relief.

"Sir, I vow you startled me." She took the pearls in her fingers to examine them, and then realizing the magnificence of what she beheld, she fell breathless and some of the colour slowly faded from her cheeks.

"What is this?"

"The ransom that I have had fetched from Spain," he answered simply.

"But…" she was aghast. She knew something of the value of jewels enough to discern that here upon her bosom lay a fortune. "But this, sir, is beyond all reason. It is of enormous price."

"I told you that if you left it to me I should set a high value upon myself."

"It is a prince's ransom," she continued.

"I am almost a prince," he deprecated.

She would have said more on the same score, but that he brushed the matter aside as trivial and of insufficient moment to engage their notice further.

"Shall we waste words upon so slight a thing in an hour when every word of yours to me is become more precious than all the foolish pearls upon that string?"

Here was a new bold note upon which he had never yet dared to touch, a lover's note. She stared at him blankly, taken by surprise. He swept on, explaining any ambiguities in the words he had used already. "The ransom is delivered, and the hour of my departure is approaching – too swiftly, alas! So that I have your leave, your consent, my release from the parole which binds me, I sail tomorrow night for Spain."

"So soon?" said she.

It seemed to him, no doubt deluded by his hopes, that she spoke wistfully; the shadow which crossed her face he assumed to be of regret. These things were spurs to his desire. He was a little breathless, a little stirred out of his habitual calm composure.

" 'So soon?' you say! I thank you for those words. They hold the very seed of hope. They lend me audacity to dare that in which I must otherwise have faltered."

The ring of his voice was not to be mistaken, nor the gleam of his dark eyes, nor yet the flush that came to warm the ivory pallor of his cheeks. All her femininity vibrated to it; vibrated in alarm.

He leaned over her. "Margaret!" It was the first time he had uttered her name, and he uttered it in a caressing murmur that lingered fondly over each vowel. "Margaret, must I go as I came? Must I go alone?"

She saw that she must deliberately misunderstand him so as to leave him a clear line of retreat from an advance in which it was not desired that he should continue. "You'll have friends on board, I make no doubt," she answered with simulated lightness, seeking to steady the fluttering of her heart.

"Friends?" He was scornful. "It is not friends I lack, or power, or wealth. These are mine in abundance. My need is of someone to share all this, to share all that I can bestow, and I can bestow so much." He went headlong on before she could check him. "Will you waste your lovely life in this barbarous corner of a barbarous land, when I can open all the world to you, render you rich and powerful, honoured, envied, the jewel of a court, a queen of queens? Margaret!"

She shrank together a little. It was impossible to be angry unless it were with herself for a lack of circumspection which justified the presumption of his speech. And yet in the manner of it there was nothing presumptuous. It was respectful, pleading, humble. He had said no word of love. Yet every word he had uttered spoke of it with a convincing eloquence; his accents of entreaty, his very attitude of supplication were all instinct with it.

The prospect he held out was not without allurement, and it may even be that for a second the temptation to possess all that lay within his gift may have assailed her. To be powerful, rich, honoured, envied. To move in the great world: to handle destinies perhaps. That was to drink the full rich wine of life, to exchange for the intoxicating cup of it the insipid waters of this Cornish home.

If the temptation assailed her, it can have done so only for a moment, during that little pause of a half-dozen heartbeats. When she spoke she was calm and sane again and true to herself. She answered him quite gently.

"Don Pedro, I will not pretend to misunderstand you. Indeed that were impossible. I thank you for the honour you have done me. I esteem it that, my friend, believe me. But… " She lingered a moment on the word, and raised her shoulders in a little shrug. "It may not be."

"Why not? Why not?" His right arm was flung out as if to encircle her. "What power is there to hinder?"

"It is the power to compel that is wanting." She rose, and her eyes, candid, pure and true, almost on a level with his own, looked him squarely in the face, whilst she dealt his hopes the blow that should completely shatter them. "I do not love you, Don Pedro."

She saw him wince as if she had struck him. He fell back before her a little, and half turned away; then, with a swift recovery, he came back to the assault.

"Love will come, my Margaret. How should it not? I shall know how to awaken it. I could not fail in that, for love begets love; and to such love as I pour upon you your own love must respond." He was white to the lips, so that his beard seemed to take on a deeper shade of black. His vivid eyes glowed with passion and entreaty. "Ah, trust me, child! Trust me! I know, I know. I am wise… "

She interrupted him very gently. "Not wise enough to see that this importunity must give me pain." Then she smiled, that frank clear smile of hers, and held out her hand to him, as a man might have done. "Let us be good friends, Don Pedro, as we have been since the day I took you prisoner."

Slowly, compelled to it, he took her hand. Meanwhile the fingers of her left were touching the pearls upon her bosom. "These I shall treasure less for their worth than for the memory of a pleasant friendship. Do nothing now to spoil it."

He sighed as he bowed low over the fingers he grasped. Reverently he bore them to his lips.

Before the irrevocable note of her voice, before that friendly frankness, which in itself made a stouter barrier between them than mere coldness could have done, he confessed himself defeated. He made no boast when he said that he was wise. He was skilled beyond the common in deciphering human documents, and his skill did not permit him here to persist in error.

Chapter 11

The Departure

If Don Pedro's skill in the deciphering of human documents was great, as I have said, great, too, were his longings. And longings blunt the senses to all things outside of their own aim. So that, by the following morning, Don Pedro had come to doubt the accuracy of his reading of Margaret and the irrevocable quality of the decision she had made. This hope renewed and fortified the longings from which it sprang.

Desire was something which this spoilt child of fortune had never been schooled to repress. With him it had ever been but the sweet preface to possession. He had never known the meaning of denial. He knew it now, and the torment of it. All night that knowledge and that torment abode in him, until he swore at dawn that he would not submit, could not endure it to continue.

Outwardly, however, on that last day of his at Trevanion Chase he showed nothing of his inward suffering. Sharp searching eyes might have detected the imprint of it on his countenance, but in his manner no hint of it was betrayed. He had been well schooled in the art of self-possession; it had been one of his maxims that who would prevail must never allow his purpose to he read.

And so, whilst pain searched his soul, whilst the hunger for Margaret, sharpened by her denial of him, gnawed at his heart, he smiled as affably as ever and preserved unchanged his cool, urbane, impassive air.

So completely did this deceive her that she came to conclude that his heart was not so seriously involved as his words had seemed to imply. He had been swept away, she thought, by a momentary yielding to emotional impulses. She was glad and relieved to discover it. She liked him more than any man she had ever met save one; and she must have suffered had she remained under the conviction that she had sent him forth in pain.

She had shown the pearls to her father, who had curtly pronounced them fripperies, whereupon, in protest and so as to compel his attention, she had ventured a hint of their value. It had not impressed him.

"I can well believe it," he had said. "There's naught in the world so costly as vanity, as you may come to learn in time."

Then she told him what the gift implied; that Don Pedro's ransom being paid he now claimed the liberty to depart, and would be leaving them that evening.

"Very well," said the earl, indifferently.

It chilled her. So that he was left alone in this musty library to pursue, over quagmires of human speculation, the will-'o-the-wisp of knowledge, whoever chose might come and go at Trevanion Chase. She might depart, herself, and not be missed. Indeed, he might regard her presence as no more than a source of interruptions, and would perhaps welcome, as putting a definite end to these, her departure overseas to Spain. But another there was, who would not be so indifferent. The thought of him warmed her again, and she found in his protracted absence a deserved reproach to herself for her harshness with him. She would send him a note to tell him that Don Pedro was leaving that evening, and to bid him come and receive his forgiveness at her hands. It was jealousy of Don Pedro that had driven him, and she now perceived how right had been the instincts in him which had prompted it. There had been more occasion for it than ever she had suspected.

With Don Pedro that day she was kind and courteous, and he made this possible by the masterly circumspection I have mentioned. He had no packages to make. What odds and ends he had caused to be procured for him whilst there, to eke out his temporary wardrobe, he now bestowed upon the servant who had ministered to him, together with a rich gift of money.

Old Martin, too, was handsomely rewarded for his attentions to the Spanish prisoner, who had known how to command his regard.

After an early supper, going as he came, with no more than the clothes in which he stood, Don Pedro was ready to depart. To his lordship, still at table, he addressed a very formal graceful speech of thanks for the generous entertainment he had received at Trevanion Chase, of which his heart would ever hold and cherish the most pleasant memories. To Heaven also he expressed his deep gratitude for having vouchsafed him the good fortune of falling into such noble, kindly, generous hands as those of the Earl of Garth and his daughter.

The earl, having heard him out, gave him answer in phrases springing from his innate courtliness, the courtliness which had been his before the events had driven him to become a hermit. He concluded all by wishing Don Pedro a felicitous voyage to his own land and all happiness in his abiding there. Thereupon he effaced himself, leaving his daughter to speed the departing voyager.

Martin fetched Don Pedro his weapons, a hat and a cloak. When he had assumed them, Margaret went with him to the hall, and then down the steps, and on through the garden with scarcely a word passing between them. Their farewells might quite properly have been spoken at the door. But it was as if he drew her on with him by the very force of his will.

On the edge of the spinney she halted, determined to go no farther, and put forth her hand. "We part here, Don Pedro."

Having halted with her, he now faced her, and she saw the pain that flickered in his melancholy eyes. "Ah, not yet!" It was a prayer. He became almost lyrical. "Do not deprive my soul of those few moments I had hoped to savour before darkness closes over it. See,

I have been a miracle of reticence, a model of circumspection. Since you said what you said to me yesterday, by no single word or glance have I importuned you. Nor would I now. Yet I ask of you one little thing; little to you but meaning so much – dear God, how much! – to me. Walk with me but a little way farther: to that blessed spot in the dell, where first my eyes were gladdened by the lovely sight of you. There, where I looked my first upon you, let me look my last, and thus departing count all a dream that happened in between. Of your sweet charity, accord me this, Margaret!"

She was not stone to resist this perfervidly poetical heart-broken supplication. After all, as he said, it was such a little thing to ask. She consented. Yet on the way through the gloom that was gathering in the dingle no word was spoken.

Thus in silence they came to their first meeting-place.

"It was here," she said, "Yonder you stood on that white rock, when Brutus leapt at you."

He paused, considered her, and fetched a heavy sigh. "Your greatest cruelty was when you stayed him." He paused again, still considering her, as if he would print each feature forever on his brain. And then: "How grudgingly," pursued that very subtle gentleman, "you accord me the exact alms I begged of your charity. ' 'Twas here!' you say, and on the very spot, careful to an inch of ground, you halt. Well! Well!"

"Ah, no," she answered him, her generous heart responding to the touch of that skilful player. "I'll bear you company yet a little farther."

He breathed his thanks, and they continued the descent, following the course of the brook, which was the merest trickle now. And as they went, there came from the beach below the grating of a keel upon the shingle.

Forth from the shadows of the trees they stepped on to the edge of the sands, now shimmering faintly in the evening light. By the water's edge there was a boat, and about it, dim and shadowy, a dark group.

At sight of this Don Pedro raised his voice, and called some words in Spanish. Two men instantly detached themselves and came speeding up the beach.

Margaret put forth her hand for the third time, and her tone was brisk and resolute.

"And now, farewell! God send you a favourable wind to Spain and bring you safely home."

"Home?" said he sadly. "An empty word henceforth. Ah, stay! Stay yet a moment!" His grip upon her hand detained her. "There is something yet I wish to say. Something I must say before I go."

"Then say it quickly, sir. Your men are almost here."

"It is no matter for them. They are my own. Margaret!" He seemed to choke.

She noticed that his face shone oddly white In the deepening twilight, that he was actually trembling. A vague fear possessed her. She wrenched her hand free. "Farewell!" she cried, and abruptly turned to go.

But he sprang after her. He was upon her. His arms went round her, holding her close and powerless as in a snare of steel. "Ah, no, no," he almost sobbed. "Forgive, my Margaret! You shall forgive! You must; you will, I know. I cannot bear to let you go. Be God my witness, it would kill me."

"Don Pedro!" There was only anger in her voice. She sought to break from him; but he held her firmly. Such an indignity as this had never touched her pure young life, nor had she ever dreamt of such a possibility. "Let me go!" she commanded, her eyes scorching him with their fury. "As you are a gentleman, Don Pedro, this is unworthy. It is knavish! Vile!"

"A gentleman!" he echoed, and laughed in furious scorn of all such shams as in this moment he accounted them. "Here is no gentleman. We are just man and woman, and I love you."

At last she understood the full villainy of his purpose, sensed the utter remorselessness of his passion, and a scream sped upwards through the dingle. Came a roar from above to answer her. Almost inarticulate though it was she recognized the voice and thrilled at the sound of it as never yet she had thrilled. Twice she called his name in ringing accents of fearful urgency.

"Gervase! Gervase!"

Momentarily she was released, and then, almost before she could realize it and attempt to move, a cloak was flung over her head to muffle her. She was lifted from her feet by strong pinioning arms, and hurried swiftly away. After her bearers came Don Pedro at speed.

"Handle her gently on your lives, dogs," he thundered in Spanish to his men. "Make haste! Away! Away!"

They gained the boat as Gervase came through the trees on to the open beach. One of the Spaniards levelled a musketoon across the bows to make an end of that single pursuer. Don Pedro kicked the weapon into the sea.

"Fool! Who bade you take so much upon yourself? Push off! And now give way! Give way!"

They floated clear as Gervase came bounding to the water's-edge. Nor did the water check him. On he came, splashing through it.

"Don Pedro, you Spanish dog!" he cried in mingled rage and anguish.

The boat drew off under the stroke of his six long oars and swiftly gathered way.

Yet Gervase in his mad agony went after it to his armpits. There he checked, raving, with the wash of the boat about his neck. He raised an impotent fist and shook it in the air.

"Don Pedro!" he called across the water. "Don Pedro de Mendoza! You may go now. But I come after you. I shall follow you, though it be to Hell!"

Don Pedro in the sternsheets, catching the note of agony in those accents, looked through the gloom at the man who had wielded the musketoon.

"I was wrong," he said. "It would have been a mercy to have shot him."

Chapter 12

The Secretary of State

My Lord Garth sat peacefully over his books, lighted by four tapers which Martin had lately placed upon his table. He was labouring over the Phaedrus, and by an odd coincidence relishing the simple explanation afforded by Socrates of the tale of the abduction of Oreithyia by Boreas from the banks of the Ilissus. To his lordship thus engrossed came a wild, dishevelled figure, squelching water from his boots at every stride.

This was Sir Gervase Crosby. But such a Gervase Crosby as his lordship had never yet seen or heard.

"Afoot, my lord!" came the thundered exhortation. "Afoot and be doing! Enough of books, by God!" With a blow of his brawny fist he swept the tome from under his lordship's eyes and sent it crashing to the ground.

My lord considered him, blinking in his supreme amazement.

" 'Od's light!" said he. "Hath Brutus got the rabies and bitten thee? Art clean mad?"

The answer came on a sob. "Mad! Ay!" And he flung out his news. "Your daughter's gone; carried off by that Spanish traitor out of Hell." Scarcely coherent in his headlong passion, he delivered the full tale of it.

His lordship sat benumbed: a crumpled, shrunken figure of dismay and horror and despair. But Sir Gervase knew no mercy, and admonition followed instantly upon narrative.

"When a man has a daughter, it is his duty to her, to himself and to his God – if so be he have one – to care for her and keep watch over her. But you sit here with no thought for anything but dust and books and dead men's tales, and never trouble your mind of what be doing among the living, of what villainies may be wrought under your very nose and against your only child. And now she's gone. Gone, I say! Borne off by that villain. A dove in the talons of a hawk!"

Sir Gervase, having cast for once, under the overmastering spur of his grief, all that diffidence in which usually he approached the earl, was terrific, and irresistible. Had he but done his wooing in such a spirit the horror which now afflicted him might never have fallen across his life and Margaret's.

My lord set his elbows on the table, took his head in his hands and groaned impotently in his overwhelming misery. He seemed a man suddenly aged. The spectacle of him was pitiful. But it awoke no pity in the tortured soul of Gervase Crosby.

"Ay, groan!" he sneered at him, "Huddle yourself together there and groan in your helplessness to amend that which you had not the care to hinder." Then, abruptly, scornfully: "Give you good night!" he cried, and swung about to depart, tempestuous as he had come.

"Gervase!"

The heart-broken cry arrested him. Belatedly it pierced his distracted reason that, after all, my lord and he were fellow-sufferers. The earl had risen. He stood now, commanding himself, a gaunt figure, tall despite the scholar's stoop which almost humped his shoulders. From their momentary numbness under the shock of the news, his wits were recovering, and his will was compelling their recovery. It is for fools and weaklings to lie prostrate under grief. Lord Garth was neither. This blow was to be met, and if possible to be countered. He would gird up his loins for whatever contest might lie ahead. Under the touch of grim necessity the man of thought was transmuted into the man of action.

"Where are you going?" he asked.

"After her," the boy answered wildly. "To Spain."

"To Spain? Wait, boy! Wait! Let thought precede all action ever. Naught was ever accomplished without plan. Spoil nothing now by haste." He moved away from the table, wrapping his russet gown about him. His chin sank to his breast and on his slippered feet he slip-slopped slowly to the window. He stood there, looking out upon the park and the black bulk of the elms over which the moon was rising, whilst Gervase, impressed by the sudden energy of his tone, waited as he was bidden.

"To Spain, eh?" His lordship sighed. "You are no Perseus, and Margaret's is hardly the case of Andromeda." He swung about on a sudden inspiration. "First to the Queen," he cried. "It may be that Her Grace will still remember me, and that the memory will count for something. Moreover, she's a woman – a very woman – and she should aid a man to befriend a woman in sore need. I'll come with you, Gervase. Call Martin. Tell him to bid them prepare horses and order a couple of grooms to ride with us. Bid Francis supply us with what moneys he has at hand. We'll start so soon as it's daylight."

But Gervase shook his head as he answered impatiently: "My lord, my lord, I cannot wait for daylight. Every hour is precious now. I start for London so soon as I have changed my clothes and taken what gear I need. It was already in my mind to invoke the Queen's assistance. I was for seeking Drake or Hawkins that they might procure me audience. If you will come, my lord, you must follow. It would but delay me," he ended bluntly, "to have you with me."

A flush of indignation overspread the pallid haggard face of the student. Then he saw reason, and fetched a sigh. "Ay, I am old," he agreed. "Too old and feeble to do more than cumber you. But my name may count for something still; it may count for more with the Queen than that of either Drake or Hawkins. You shall have letters from me. I'll write to Her Grace. She'll not deny the bearer; and that will be your opportunity."

He moved briskly back to his table, cleared a space in that litter of books and papers, and sat down to write.

Sir Gervase waited with such patience as he could command whilst his lordship slowly laboured with the pen. For this was no letter that could be indited swiftly. It required thought, and in his distraction the earl's thoughts went haltingly. At last, however, it was done. My lord sealed it with his arms, engraved on a massive ring he wore. He rose to proffer it to Gervase, and almost at once sat down again, weak and shaken. The mental strain had temporarily sapped his physical vigour and made him realize to the full how unfitted he was to take an active part in the enterprise ahead of the young man.

"Indeed, indeed, I should but cumber you," he confessed. "Yet to sit here waiting... O God! Mine is the harder part, Gervase."

At last Sir Gervase was touched. He had done the earl a wrong. There was red blood in his veins, after all, and he had a heart for other things than books. He set a hand upon his shoulder.

"If you trust me, it will help you, my lord. Be assured that what man can do shall be done; that you could not yourself do more if you were in your fullest vigour. You shall hear from me from London."

He was gone like the whirlwind, and a moment later the earl, seated again at his table, his head in his hands, heard outside the receding clatter of flying hooves.

At the peril of his neck Sir Gervase rode through Smithwick; then more slowly, yet with a speed cruel to his horse, up to the winding road to Arwenack. Sir John was away from home, a circumstance which Gervase considered almost fortunate, since thus there would be no time lost in explanations. Time was to be lost, however, he discovered; a loss that was to end in a gain; for at Arwenack he found the elder Tressilian awaiting him.

They had become fast friends these two, who were brothers-in-arms and who had received the accolade on the same day and in reward of similar achievements. There had been some talk between them that so soon as Gervase's ship was ready, he and Sir Oliver should unite their forces and go forth in a joint venture. It was this very subject which Sir Oliver had come to discuss with him tonight. Instead he was to listen to Sir Gervase's furious tale, whilst Sir Gervase was ridding himself of his sodden garments.

The vigorous, black-browed Sir Oliver took fire at the narrative. He swore roundly and fully, for he was ever a rough-tongued man, at Spain and Spaniards.

"As God's my life I'll bear this thing in mind whenever and wherever I meet a Spaniard," he promised fiercely. Then he became practical. "But why ride to London? Why spend a week upon the road at a time when every day must count? The *Rose of the World* will bring you there in half the time."

"The *Rose of the World*?" Sir Gervase checked in the very act of trussing the points of his hose to stare up at his tall friend. "My God, Oliver! Is she ready for sea?"

"She's been ready this last week. I could put out at dawn."

"Could you put out tonight?" Sir Gervase's eyes were feverish with excitement.

Sir Oliver looked at him. "Give chase, do you mean?"

"What else?"

But Sir Oliver shook his head, considered a moment, then shook it again. He had a vigorous, practical mind and a mental eye that saw straight and clearly to the core of things. "We've missed the tide, or must miss it before ever we could get aboard; and then the crew's ashore and to be assembled. We could drop down the river on the first of the ebb, just after daybreak; but by then it would be too late to hope to overtake your Spaniard. And to follow him into Spain we'll need some stouter equipment than our swords." Again he shook his head. He sighed. "It would have been a rare adventure. But fortune puts it beyond our reach. So it's London first, my lad. And it'll prove the shorter road in the end. I'll away, to beat up the crew and get what I need for myself. When you've got your gear together come aboard." He set one of his great powerful hands on his friend's shoulder. "Keep up your heart, lad," he enjoined, and upon that valediction departed without waiting for any word of thanks for the readiness with which he proffered so very generous a measure of assistance.

The *Rose of the World* dropped down from her moorings at the mouth of the Penryn Creek on the first of the ebb, just as day was breaking. She unfurled her sails to the breezes of dawn, and slipped away through the water on the first stage of the adventure. It was Sunday morning. So well did the wind serve them, and so ably was the tall ship handled, that by Tuesday's dawn she came to anchor abreast of Greenwich Palace. Landing they went at Sir Oliver's instigation in quest of Sir John Hawkins, whose influence at Court should open to them its jealously-guarded doors, and that same evening, having ridden hard from Greenwich, they were conducted by Sir John into the closet of Sir Francis Walsingham at Whitehall.

In Sir Francis, Gervase beheld the tall, spare man in black with the long narrow white beard who had stood near the Queen on the day Her Majesty had given audience to the seamen. He was seated at a table that was strewn with documents, nor troubled to rise when our two gentlemen were ushered in by Sir John Hawkins, who had gone ahead to obtain the Secretary of State's consent to receive them. On his narrow grey head he wore a flat black cap with flaps which entirely covered his ears, a cap which had been fashionable in the late King's time but was rarely to be seen nowadays unless it were upon some City merchant. But, for that matter, there was nothing fashionable in all Sir Francis' attire. The young secretary industriously engaged at a writing-pulpit in one of the window-embrasures was of an infinitely more modish appearance, though similarly clad in black.

Sir John withdrew, leaving the two Cornishmen with Sir Francis.

"This, sirs," he greeted them, "is a distressing tale that Sir John tells me." But there was no distress in his formal, level voice, nor in the chill glance of those pale, calculating eyes with which he conned them. He invited them to sit, waving a bony hand to indicate the chairs that stood before his table.

Sir Oliver inclined his head in acknowledgment, and sat down, stretching his long, booted legs before him. Sir Gervase, however, remained standing. He was restless and haggard. His tone when he now spoke was almost fretful. He did not find the Secretary of State prepossessing; saw little promise of assistance in the man's chill exterior. To Sir Gervase, who expected all to share something of his frenzy, it seemed that the man had ink in his veins, not blood.

"It is my hope, sir, that I may be vouchsafed occasion to place the facts before the Queen's grace."

Sir Francis combed his beard. Behind it Sir Gervase fancied that the lips had parted in a faint smile of weary scorn. "Her Majesty shall be apprised, of course."

But this was far indeed from fulfilling the hopes of Sir Gervase. "You will procure me an audience, sir?" he said between question and intercession.

The cold eyes looked at him inscrutably. "To what purpose, sir, when all is said?"

"To what purpose?" Sir Gervase was beginning hotly, when the lean hand upheld checked the burst of indignation that was about to follow.

"If the Queen, sir, were to grant audience to every man who asks it, no single second of her day would be left for any of her other manifold and important occupations. Hence the functions of Her Majesty's ministers." He was a pedant instructing a schoolboy in the elements of worldly conduct. "Such action as may be taken in this regrettable affair the Queen would invite me to take if she were informed of it. Therefore we may without any loss show ourselves dutiful to Her Grace by sparing her this unnecessary audience."

Sir Oliver shifted in his chair, and his deep voice rang loud and harsh by contrast with the sleek level accents of the secretary.

"It is not the view of Sir Gervase that Her Majesty should be spared, or that she will thank any man for sparing her in this matter."

Sir Francis was neither startled by Tressilian's vehemence nor intimidated by the fierceness of his glance.

"You misunderstand, I think." He spoke quietly ever, with that chill disdain of his. "It is Her Majesty's person alone that I am – that we all must be – concerned to spare. Her powers, her authority, shall be exerted to the full. It is my duty to exert them."

"In plain terms, Sir Francis, what does that mean?" Gervase demanded.

Sir Francis sat back in his tall chair, leaning his capped head against the summit. His elbows resting on its carved arms, he brought his fingertips together and over them considered with interest these two furious men of action who imagined that a Secretary of State was a person to be bullied or browbeaten. "It means," he said after a deliberate pause, "that I shall make the strongest representations to the French Envoy in the morning."

"The French Envoy? What has the French Envoy to do with this?"

This time Sir Francis' smile was no longer covert. "Our own relations with Spain being at this present suspended, the intervention of the Envoy of France becomes necessary. It can be relied upon."

Sir Gervase's patience was rapidly running out.

"God's light!" he roared. "And what is to happen to the Lady Margaret Trevanion while you represent the matter to the Envoy of France and he sends messages to King Philip?"

Sir Francis parted his hands and spread them a little in a deprecatory gesture. "Let us be practicable. According to your tale this lady has already been three days upon the seas in her abductor's company. The matter can no longer be of such urgency that we should distress ourselves over an unavoidable delay in reaching her."

"My God!" cried Gervase in pain.

"That," rasped Sir Oliver, "is where the Queen, being a woman, must take a different view; a less cold-blooded view than yours, Sir Francis."

"You do me wrong, sir, as I perceive. No heat of passion will help any of us here."

"I am not sure," Sir Oliver answered him. He heaved himself to his feet. "And, anyway, the matter is one for human beings, not for statesmen. Here we stand, two men who have brought our lives and our gear to the service of the Queen's grace, and all we ask now in return is that we be brought to audience with Her Majesty."

"Nay, nay. That is not all you ask. You ask that so that you may ask something else."

"It is our right," Sir Oliver roared.

"And we demand it," Sir Gervase added. "The Queen, sir, would not deny us."

Sir Francis looked at them both with the same unrufflable composure with which he had first received them. The secretary in the window-embrasure had suspended his labours to lend an ear to this browbeating of his formidable master. At any moment he expected to hear Sir Francis declare the audience at an end. But to his surprise Sir Francis now rose.

"If I deny you," said he quietly, without the least shade of resentment, "as I account it my duty to Her Majesty, you are of those who will be stirring up interest until in the end you have your way. But I warn you that it can serve no good purpose, and is but a waste of time; your own and the Queen's. Her Majesty can but entrust the business to me, to take what steps are in the circumstance possible. However, if you really insist… "

He paused, and looked at them.

"I do," said Gervase emphatically.

He nodded. "In that case I will take you to the Queen at once. Her Majesty is expecting me before she sups, and it is time I went. If the audience proves little to your taste, if it is fruitless, as it must be, of more than could have been achieved without it, I trust you will remember to place the reproach where it is deserved."

Tall and gaunt in his black gown that was edged with brown fur, he moved to the door, and threw it open. "Pray follow me," he bade them coldly over his shoulder.

Chapter 13

The Queen

Along a gallery, with windows on their right through the blurred glass of which they caught the green sheen of the foliage in the privy garden, Walsingham led them to a closed door, kept by two stalwart young Yeomen of the Guard in scarlet with the Tudor rose embroidered in gold upon their backs. At the approach of Sir Francis they ordered their tasselled halberds, whose polished blades shone like mirrors. At a nod from him one of them threw open the door and held it wide. In silence he crossed the threshold, his companions following. The door closed after them, and they proceeded some little way along the farther gallery into which they had now stepped, until Sir Francis brought up at a door on his left, which again was guarded by two yeomen.

Sir Gervase observed that, like the others, these, too, were tall, athletic, young and handsome. The tongue of rumour certainly appeared justified when it said that the Queen liked to have splendid-looking men about her. It was asserted that the loss of a front tooth by one of these magnificent guards entailed his removal from about the Queen's person.

They went through the doorway instantly opened to Sir Francis, and found themselves in a lofty ante-chamber, very richly furnished, the golden rose everywhere conspicuous upon scarlet fabrics. Half a dozen resplendent gentlemen lounged here. A chamberlain with a wand advanced to meet Sir Francis, and at a word from him, bowing profoundly, withdrew through a small door which again was guarded by a pair of yeomen who might have been cast in the same mould as the others. He returned a moment later to announce that Her Majesty would at once receive Sir Francis and his companions.

Through the open doorway came the tinkling sound of a virginal. Her Majesty's occupations of state, thought Sir Gervase, might be manifold and important, as Sir Francis had stated; but it was clear that they were not engaging her at the moment, which may, indeed, have accounted for the promptitude of their admission to her gracious presence.

They entered. Sir Francis went down on one knee, and with his left hand covertly signalled to the others to imitate his genuflexion.

They found themselves in a small room, three of whose walls from ceiling to floor were hung with rich tapestries, illustrating scenes which Sir Gervase would not have identified even if he had had leisure to examine them. A tall mullioned window overlooked the river and the Palace steps, where the great gilded royal barge was moored amid a flock of lesser craft.

This in a glance he saw as he entered. Thereafter his eyes were upon the Queen, to whom he knelt now for the second time. She was in rose-pink today. That at least was the background of the shimmering brocade she wore, which was all embroidered with eyes, so that you might have conceived that Her Majesty looked at you from every point of her person at once. For the rest she was as richly, as monstrously bejewelled as on the last occasion when Sir Gervase had beheld her, and the great erect collar of lace, spreading like a fan behind her head, reached almost to the summit of her pearl-entwined wig.

For a moment after the gentlemen entered, she continued, engrossed in the virginals, bringing her musical phrase to a conclusion. It was one of her many vanities to be accounted a fine performer, and she deemed no audience too trivial.

A tall, fair lady stood immediately behind her. Two others, one fair, the other dark, and the dark one of a singular loveliness, were seated near the window.

The Queen's beautiful hands came to rest upon the keys, then one of them, aflash with gems, was extended to take a delicate gold-edged kerchief from the polished top of the instrument. Her dark eyes peered at them short-sightedly, deepening the web of wrinkles about her pencilled brows. She may have noticed that Walsingham's companions were fine fellows both, such as she loved to look upon. Both above the common height, if Sir Oliver were by a little the taller and more athletic, the other had the greater beauty of countenance. It is possible that the coldly-calculating Sir Francis may have weighed this circumstance in introducing them thus without preliminaries into her presence. He may have been persuaded that Her Majesty could of herself do nothing to assist them beyond entrusting their grievance to him for redress; but at least their persons would ensure him from any royal resentment at having brought them to her so that they might convince themselves of what he told them.

"What's this, Frank?" she rasped in her mannish voice. "What do you bring me, and why?" And then, without waiting for the answer, she abruptly addressed Gervase.

Sir Oliver slightly behind him, copying Walsingham, had risen already from the genuflexion. Sir Gervase, not observing this, remained humbly upon one knee.

" 'Od's eyes!" she exclaimed. "Get up, man. D'ye take me for a Popish image that ye'll kneel to me all day?"

He rose, tongue-tied and a little embarrassed, with no thought of any such fond speech as that for which her exclamation had given him an opening and such as were dear to her overweening vanity. But his looks made amends in her eyes for his lack of adulatory glibness.

"Why have you brought them, Frank?"

Briefly Walsingham recalled them to her memory as two of the knights she had lately created in token of her favour, for their achievements in the fight with the Armada.

125

"As some slight recompense for the service that already they have rendered England and as some earnest for what may yet be to come for future service, they have a boon to crave."

"A boon?" Alarm flickered in her eyes. She looked up at the tall lady beside her, wrinkling her high, pinched nose. "I might have guessed it, Dacres. God's wounds, man! If it be money, or aught that's costly, I prithee save thy breath. We are beggared by the Spanish war already."

"It is not money, Your Grace," said Sir Gervase, speaking boldly now.

Her relief was manifest. She reached for a basket of silver filigree that stood upon the virginal, and gave her care to the selection of a Portingal. It was this love of sweetmeats which may have been responsible for the dark ruin of her teeth. "What is it, then? Speak out, man. Art not shy, belike?"

That, if shy, he had by now conquered his shyness, his answer proved: "It is no boon, as Sir Francis says, Your Grace. I am come for simple justice."

She looked at him with sudden, sharp suspicion, the selected Portingal suspended delicately between finger and thumb. "Ay, I know the phrase well. *Cordieu!* 'Tis on the lips of every place-seeker. Well, well! Out with this tale of it, a God's name, and let us ha' done." The sweetmeat disappeared between her thin, raddled lips.

"First, madam," said Sir Gervase, "I am the bearer of a letter." He advanced, instinctively went down on his knee again, and proffered it. "Will Your Highness be graciously pleased to receive it."

Walsingham frowned and stirred forward a pace or two. "What's this of a letter?" said he. "You said naught to me of any letter."

"No matter for that," she told him curtly. She was examining the seal. "Whose arms are these?" She was frowning. "Whence is your letter, sir?"

"From my Lord Garth, so please Your Grace."

"Garth? Garth?" She spoke as one fumbling on her memory. Suddenly her expression quickened. "Why, that will be Roger

Trevanion. Roger… " She caught her breath, and looked at him again, searchingly. "What is Roger Trevanion to thee, child?"

"My friend, I hope, madam. I know myself his. I love his daughter."

"Ha! His daughter! So? He has a daughter? If she favours him you're fortunate in your choice. He was a comely fellow in his youth. And he married, eh? I never heard of it." Her voice grew wistful. "But, indeed, I've never heard aught of him for years. Roger Trevanion!" She sighed, and fell thoughtful a moment, the expression of her face incredibly softened. Then, as if recollecting herself, she abruptly broke the seal, and spread the sheet. She read it with difficulty.

"Why, here's a vile scrawl, by God!"

"It was writ in deep agitation and sorrow, madam."

"Was it so? Ay, so it was; so it must have been. Yet it does little more than announce the fact, commend you to me and implore my favour for you and for him, who are one in the aims of which you are to tell me. So Roger is in trouble, eh? And in trouble he remembers me at last! That is the common way. But hardly Roger's." She was musing now. "*Cordieu!* He might have remembered me before, remembered the debt I have owed him these many years. How many years, dear God!" She sighed, and fell into thought. There was no hardness now in that pinched, lined face. The dark eyes seemed to Sir Gervase to have grown moist and wistful. Her thoughts may well have been with the past, the gallant Lord Admiral who had loved her and who had paid with his head for the temerity of that love, and the man who had loved him and because of that love had risked his own head freely to serve him and to serve her. Then she roused herself to command the waiting gentlemen before her. "What is this tale you have to tell me? Out with it, child. I am listening."

Sir Gervase told it, briefly, eloquently, passionately. Once only was he interrupted and then by Walsingham when he mentioned the Spaniard's surrender and its acceptance which made of him nominally a prisoner, actually a guest, at Trevanion Chase.

"Now that was ill-done," Sir Francis had cried. "We should take steps to… "

"Take steps to hold your tongue, man," the Queen silenced him.

There were no further interruptions. Sir Gervase proceeded to the end with ever-increasing anger in the tale he was relating, so that he imparted some of his own heat to his audience – to the Queen, her ladies and even the cold Walsingham. When, at last, he had done, she smote her hands upon the arms of her chair, and heaved herself to her feet.

"Now, by God's death!" she cried in a fury that had turned her livid under her paint. "Does the audacity of these Spaniards dare so much? Is there to be no end to their insolences? Shall we suffer these things, Walsingham? One of them comes shipwrecked into this realm of mine and commits this outrage! By Heaven's light, they shall yet learn the length of a maid's arm to shield a maid; they shall feel the weight of a woman's hand to avenge a woman. They shall so, by God! Walsingham, summon me… No, no. Wait!"

She moved across the room, brushing past the two ladies near the window, who had risen. From somewhere she drew a little silver bodkin. Fragments of the Portuguese comfit were inconveniencing her. Having used the instrument, she fell to tapping with it one of the little panes.

The narrative had moved her more deeply than Gervase could have hoped. However much this may have been due to the outrage itself, there can be no doubt that a contributory factor lay in the circumstance that Roger Trevanion's daughter was the victim. The tale may have gathered poignancy and impressiveness, too, because it fell upon a mood of softness and tenderness invoked by the memory of that dear friend of her girlhood and of her girlhood's lover, and further, even, because the narrator was a stalwart, handsome fellow and a lover.

At length she swung from the window, her manner almost harsh with impatience, but an impatience of which clearly he whom she addressed was not the object.

"Come hither, child!"

He was prompt to approach her, and stood respectfully before her, apart from those others who looked on with interest and one of them with uneasiness. This was Walsingham. Knowing her as he did, he perceived that the lioness in her was aroused, and foresaw trouble for himself from such a mood. He felt a little aggrieved with Sir Gervase Crosby for having taken an advantage of him in the matter of that letter. But this at the moment was a light thing compared with the anxieties which the Queen's humour awakened in him.

"Tell me, child; tell me," she was urging the long-limbed Gervase. "What, precisely, do you seek of me? What is in your mind that I should do? Exactly what justice do you desire?"

She asked for guidance; asked it from this West-country youngster, converted, no doubt, into a firebrand by his anguish on behalf of his mistress. Here, thought Walsingham, was madness. He groaned inwardly; indeed, almost aloud. His countenance was lugubriously startled.

The answer did nothing to allay his fears. The lad's words proved him indeed a firebrand, of a rashness almost beyond the Secretary of State's belief, and the Secretary of State had great experience of human rashness.

"It is my intent, Your Grace, to cross at once to Spain. To go after Don Pedro de Mendoza."

She interrupted him. "By God! The intent is a bold one! If you are to take matters thus into your own hands, what is there for me to do?" There was in her tone the suspicion of a sneer, as well there might be at the avowal of such stark madness.

"It has been my hope, madam, that Your Grace – I scarce know how – would provide means to shield me on this journey, and to ensure my safe return. It is not that I go in fear of myself... "

"You were wiser and you did," she interrupted him again. "But to shield you? I?" She made a wry face. "My arm is long enough for much. But to protect you within the dominions of King Philip at this present time... " She broke off, and because she could not see the way to do as he desired of her, and felt herself humiliated by her impotence, she fell to cursing like a roaring captain.

When at length she paused, Sir Francis Walsingham sleekly interposed. "I have already told Sir Gervase that Your Grace will command me to pursue the proper course, and to send letters to King Philip by the channel offered by the French Envoy."

"Ha! And what doth Sir Gervase answer?"

"In all humility, Your Grace, the thing is of an urgency... "

"Why so it is, child. Sir Francis needs to learn things by experience. If he had a daughter in Spanish hands he would be less cool and simpering. The devil damn such paltry counsel."

The Secretary of State was not discomposed. "The poor wits with which I serve Your Grace are waiting to discern a more effective way of availing this unfortunate lady."

"Are they so?" She glared at him. His coolness had upon her an effect quite contrary from that which he hoped. She turned her shoulders to him, and fell to tapping the window again with her bodkin. "There should surely be some way. Come, child, ply your wits. I care not how rash your proposal. We may strike sense from it if we but hear it."

There fell a pause, Sir Gervase having no settled plan of action, or thought of how that which he sought from Her Majesty might be obtained. To break the silence came the big rough voice of Sir Oliver Tressilian.

"Have I Your Grace's leave?" He advanced a step or two as he spoke, and drew all eyes upon his dark resolute countenance.

"A God's name!" she barked at him. "Speak out if you've aught in mind that will help."

"Your Highness asks for rashness, else I should scarce dare."

"Dare and be damned, man," quoth the lioness. "What's in your mind?"

"Your Highness may not remember that the honour of knighthood which I received at Your Grace's hands was for my part in the capture of the flagship of the Andalusian squadron, the only Spanish vessel seized. We took prisoner her commander, Don Pedro Valdez, who is the greatest and deservedly the most valued of all Spain's captains upon the seas. With him we took among others seven gentlemen of the first houses in Spain. These gentlemen at this present moment all lie under Your Grace's hand. They are lodged here in the Tower."

He said no more than that. But his tone was grim and full of suggestion. It expressed, like the thing he hinted, the ruthlessness of his nature and the lawlessness that were to make him what he was destined to become. It performed the miracle of startling Walsingham at last out of his imperturbability.

"In the name of Heaven, man! What is't ye're implying?"

But it was the Queen who answered him, with a short laugh and a grimness akin to Sir Oliver's own, which sent a shiver down the spine of the secretary. "God's light! Is't not plain?" Her tone said as clearly as any words could have done that the suggestion was eminently to her taste and mood. "Dacres, set my chair to the table yonder. The King of Spain shall learn the length of my arm."

The tall lady-in-waiting pushed forward the padded, crimson chair. The Queen swept to it and sat down. "Give me a pen. So! Walsingham recite me the names of the seven gentlemen who are with Valdez in the Tower."

"Your Grace intends...?" Walsingham was white; his long beard was observed to quiver.

"Shalt know my intentions soon enough; you and that other knock-kneed fellow, Philip of Spain. Their names, I say!"

Her peremptoriness was almost savage. Walsingham quailed and surrendered the names. She set them down in that big angular writing of hers in which later ages have discovered beauty. The list completed, she sat back conning it with narrowed eyes and thoughtfully gnawing the feathered end of her quill.

Her Secretary of State leaned over her, with fearful urgent mutterings. But she blighted him with a glance and an oath. So that he fell back again. A patient man and an opportunist, he resolved to wait until her royal rage should have cooled sufficiently to render her amenable to reason. Of the unreasonable thing, the outrageous thing which upon the suggestion of that outrageous black-browed Oliver Tressilian she was about to perform Sir Francis had no slightest doubt.

She bent to her task, which was to indite a letter to the brother-in-law who at one time had so ardently aspired to become her husband, and may since have had many an occasion to thank God that he had not numbered Elizabeth among his several successive wives. She wrote rapidly, scarcely pausing to consider the shaping of a phrase, and there was something of savage determination in the way her pen bit the parchment, so that her sprawling characters were engraved upon it rather than written. It was soon done.

She signed the document with a vicious flourish that was in itself like a piece of sword-play, and called for wax and a taper that she might seal it. Her ladies moved to obey. Sir Francis endeavoured once again to remonstrate.

"If in that letter, madam, the comity of nations… "

Harshly she cropped his speech. "The comity of nations!" She laughed fiercely in the grave long face and snowy beard of him. "I have said a word about the comity of nations in this letter. It counts for naught in this affair. I've warned his Spanish majesty of that."

" 'Tis what I feared, madam… "

"Lord! Walsingham, when will you cease to be a woman?" She sank her seal into the wax.

Walsingham, now terror-stricken, murmured of the Privy Council. At that she rose in fury, the letter in her hand, to inform him that she was no ward of the Privy Council; that the Privy Council existed but to interpret her sovereign will. The outrage committed by a Spanish noble upon the person of an English maid was an insult to England. She herself was England's incarnation, she informed the Secretary, and it was for her to answer that insult. It was answered in the letter, and Sir Gervase should deliver it.

Walsingham fell back appalled but daring nothing further. The circumstances were all unfortunate and against him. He was himself to blame for his rashness in having introduced that young hothead and his worse companion to audience with Her Majesty. The harm was done. Let him provide as best he could for the consequences, whatever they might be. Further intervention here might but curtail his power of doing even so much when the time came.

The Queen proffered the letter to Gervase. "There is your weapon, sir. Get you to Spain with all speed. This shall be sword and buckler to you. Yet should it chance to fail you, depend upon me to avenge you right nobly. And so God speed thee on this knightly errand. Away with him, Sir Francis. Let me know anon how he hath fared. I charge you not to fail me, on your life."

Gervase went down on his knees to receive the package. She held out her hand to him. He kissed it respectfully and in some awe, whereupon her other hand lightly touched his rippling auburn locks.

"Art a bonnie lad and a loving heart," said she in a softened voice, and lightly sighed. "God bring thy mistress scatheless home and thee with her."

He stumbled out of her presence with Sir Oliver and Sir Francis. All three of them had more than guessed what she had written.

Sir Francis sourly took his leave of them. He would have interfered had he dared. But he was on the horns of a dilemma and was constrained to the prudence of inaction. So he suffered them to depart bearing a package that might set the world on fire.

Chapter 14

Frey Luis

Fear was an emotion which had never touched the Lady Margaret Trevanion, because in her twenty-five years of life she had never been exposed to any source of it. From the first dawn of memory in her there had been those to obey, some few to guide, but none to command her. At Trevanion Chase and along that Cornish countryside, where she was regarded as the Lady Paramount, her will had prevailed whenever and wherever it had been exerted. None had ever sought to thwart or oppose her. None had ever been lacking in respect. This partly because of the station into which she had been born, but more because she possessed a generous share of that quality of reserve and self-seclusion which is usually the result of breeding. That any should offend her in even the slightest measure was utterly inconceivable. In this assurance, and in the dignity born of it, a dignity not merely superficial but going to the very core of her being, lay her immunity from all presumptions and even from the impertinences of fatuously audacious gallantry, to which the unusual freedom of her life and ways might otherwise have exposed her.

So deep-rooted was her self-assurance, so firmly established by all past experience, that it did not forsake her even now when she found herself physically constrained, rudely handled, her head muffled in a cloak. Astonishment and resentment were her predominant emotions. Fear did not touch her, because it was incredible to her that she should have anything to fear. Unthinkable that this violence should not be kept within very definite limits. She refrained from struggling, as much because she realized the futility of a trial of strength with the arms that held her as because it was utterly beneath her dignity to have recourse to physical measures of self-defence.

Quiescent, then, she lay in the sternsheets where she had been placed, seeking to control the seething indignation which might hamper the free exercise of her wits. She was not more than half-conscious of the heave of the boat, of the creak of the rowlocks and thwarts as the men strained at the oars, and of an occasional inarticulate sound from one or the other of her rowers. Beside and immediately above her sat one whom she sensed to be Don Pedro. His arm was about her shoulders, either as a measure of repression or protection. It did not trouble her as at another time it must have done. She did not shrink in pudicity from that male contact which in another place must have awakened her resentment. There was a graver violence here to engage her indignation.

At the end of perhaps a half-hour that arm was withdrawn from her shoulders. Hands were busy with the cord which had been employed to secure the cloak about her waist. It was unfastened, the muffling garment was pulled away, and suddenly her head was free to the night air, her eyes free to take stock of her surroundings: the water about her, the stars overhead, the dark forms of the sailors heaving rhythmically on the thwarts, and the man who bent over her, his face a grey-blue in the encompassing gloom. He spoke in the voice of Don Pedro.

"You will forgive this rude audacity, Margaret?" It was a question softly uttered on a note of pleading.

She found her voice and was almost surprised at its steadiness and hardness. "We will speak of that when you set me ashore again in the cove below Trevanion Chase."

She guessed his smile rather than perceived it; that smile of subtle, mocking self-sufficiency which she knew so well, which she had rather admired but now found entirely abominable. "If I did not hope for forgiveness before then, I must kill myself with despair.

There is no return, Margaret. You are committed with me to this adventure."

She attempted to struggle up from the floor of the boat upon which she was sitting. His arm returned to encircle her shoulders and so repress her movement.

"Calm, my dear," he urged her. "You need fear no indignity, no undue constraint. You go to the high destiny I have reserved for you."

"It is for yourself that you are reserving a high destiny," she answered boldly. "Gallows-high," she explained.

He said no more. With a half sigh he sank back and was silent. He judged it better to wait until this mood of indignation should have passed, as pass he thought it must when she realized more fully how utterly now she was in his power. That realization should bend her stubbornness more effectively than any words of his. She was not yet afraid. Hers was a high spirit, and this manifestation of it but rendered her the more desirable in his eyes. She was indeed a woman worth the winning, and to win her was worth all the patience he could command. That he would win her in the end, no doubt was possible to him. Like her own, his will, too, had been ever paramount.

The boat ploughed on. She looked up at the stars overhead, and at another yellower star low down on the horizon, a star which seemed to grow as they advanced. Once she looked back; but her glance failed to pierce the gloom which now blotted out completely the coastline and all sign of land. All that it revealed to her was that Don Pedro was not alone in the sternsheets. Another sat there beside him, grasping the tiller. One more protest she made, one more imperious demand, backed by a threat, to this helmsman, to put about and convey her back to shore. The man, however, did not understand. He said something in Spanish to Don Pedro and was answered shortly and sharply in the same tongue.

Thereafter she wrapped herself once more in her angry dignity and was silent. The yellow star ahead increased in size. It was reflected in a quivering spear of light across the water. Ultimately it resolved itself into the poop lantern of a towering ship, and soon they were bumping and scraping along the black sides of a great vessel, towards the entrance ladder, at the summit of which another lantern was being held by a human figure silhouetted in black against the light from the vessel's waist.

They brought up at the ladder, and her ladyship was invited by Don Pedro to ascend. She refused. She experienced in that moment her first wave of panic, and yielded to it. She struggled, resisted, commanded, and threatened. A ropes slid down the ship's side by the ladder. A sailor caught the end and made in at a running noose. This was slipped over her head, and allowed to slide down her body as far as her knees. Then her arms were raised, and the noose came up again about her until it reached her armpits and gently tightened there. Another moment and Don Pedro had caught her up and hoisted her to his shoulder. Thus burdened, supporting her with his left arm, he grasped the ladder with his right and raised his right foot to the lowest rung. He began the ascent. She realized that if she struggled or attempted to fling herself from him, she would be suspended by the rope. Of the alternative indignities, the less was to be borne thus upon his shoulder.

In the ship's waist, where a ring of lanterns made a path of almost brilliant illumination, he set her down. The rope, which had been drawn up hand over hand in a measure as she was borne aloft, lay like a snake along the deck at her feet. Don Pedro loosed and widened the noose until it fell away from her.

At the head of the entrance ladder stood Duclerc, the master, lantern in hand. By the hatch-coamings two others waited: one of them stockily-built, and dressed as a gentleman, the other tall and gaunt, in the white habit and black scapulary and mantle of a Dominican friar, his face lost in the shadows of the pointed cowl which covered his head.

The first of these advanced briskly now, and bowing low before Don Pedro, murmured softly. This was Don Diego, the intendant or steward of the Count of Marcos, he who had fitted the ship for the voyage to England so soon as word had been brought him of his master's waiting there.

The friar remained where he was, immovable as a statue, his hands folded within the capacious sleeves of his gown. Don Pedro's glance seeming to question his presence, the alert Don Diego explained it readily. No ship in the service of Catholic Spain could sail without a spiritual guide. He invited the friar forward and presented him as Frey Luis Salcedo. Priest and noble bowed to each other with all outward resemblance of mutual deference. As the friar came upright again, his hands still folded in his sleeves, the gleam of a lantern momentarily dispelled the shadows cast about his face by the cowl. Her ladyship had a glimpse of an ascetic countenance, narrow, lean and pallid, in which glowed two sombre eyes whose glance struck through her stout soul the chill of a fear such as nothing in this adventure had yet occasioned her. In that single glance, so swiftly eclipsed, she caught something of sinister menace, of active malevolence, before which her soul shuddered as it might have shuddered in the presence of a supernatural manifestation.

Then Don Pedro was informing her that the ship's main cabin was at her service, and inviting her to follow Don Diego, who would lead the way. She stood an instant hesitating, her head high, her chin thrust forward, her glance proud to the point of defiance. At last she turned and followed the stocky figure of the intendant, being followed in her turn by Don Pedro. Until resistance could be of some avail, she must suffer them to have their way with her. This she perceived, and perceiving it, submitted, upheld ever by her dignity and assisted by the persisting incredulity that any real harm could possibly touch her.

At the entrance to the gangway under the break of the poop Don Pedro was arrested by a hand upon his arm.

He turned to find the friar at his elbow. The man had followed him. If his sandalled feet had made any sound upon the deck, this had been lost in the noise of general activity aboard as the ship broached to. There had been a creaking of blocks and halliards, a pattering of steps, and now as the helm was put up, the slatting sails filled and bellied with a succession of thuds like muffled cannon-shots. Listing slightly to larboard under the burden of the breeze, the *Demoiselle* out of Nantes with her crew of Spanish sailors slipped away through the night.

Don Pedro frowned interrogatively into the ascetic face upon which the light of a lantern swinging just within the gangway was beating fully.

The friar's thin lips moved. "This woman whom your lordship brings aboard?" he questioned.

Don Pedro was conscious of a spasm of anger. The impertinence of the question was aggravated by its contemptuous terseness. But he tempered the reply which another would have had from him to the quality of his questioner.

"This lady," he said with a slow emphasis, "is the future Countess of Marcos. I am glad to have this opportunity of announcing it to you, so that you may speak of her henceforth with a proper deference."

He turned on his heel whilst the friar was impassively bowing, and went on towards the great cabin, damning in his heart Don Diego for having taken aboard for spiritual guide a brother of the order of St Dominic. These Dominicans were all alike in their insolence, swollen with pride of power in the authority they derived from their inquisitorial functions. From the Inquisitor-General to the meanest brother they knew no respect of rank, however lofty.

A comprehensive glance at the interior of the cabin dispelled some of Don Pedro's irritation. It had been furnished in a manner worthy of its intended tenants. On the snowy napery of the table crystal and silver sparkled under the light of the swinging lanterns; cushions of crimson velvet laced with gold embellished the chairs and dissembled the rudeness of the long sea-chest ranged under the stern windows of the coach. A long mirror stood between the doors of the two cabins opening on this main one on the starboard side and another beside the door of the single cabin to larboard. A soft eastern rug of brilliant reds and blues was spread underfoot and there were tapestries to mask the bulkheads.

Beside the table, slight and sleek, stood Pablillos, one of Don Pedro's own household, fetched from his Asturian home to be now his body-servant.

Don Diego, in the circumstances, and considering the haste, had done more than well, and deserved the two words of commendation which his master uttered. Then, dismissing him, Don Pedro waved the lady to a place at table from which Pablillos now withdrew and held the chair.

She looked at him steadily. Her face was white under a cloud of red-gold, now slightly dishevelled, hair. There was also some disarray in her dull red bodice, and there was a rent in the lace collar under which her bosom rose and fell to betray the emotion she desired above all to dissemble.

"I have no choice," she said coldly, contemptuously, in protest. "Since you will waste your time to my hurt in constraining me, I must submit. But it is the act of a coward, Don Pedro, and of an ingrate. You return me evil for good. I should have left you to the fate which you prove to me that every Spaniard deserves at the hands of honest men."

With that she moved slowly forward in frosty dignity and took her place at table.

Don Pedro stood deathly pale, pain in his eyes and dark shadows under them. Against the whiteness of his face, his little pointed beard and upward-flung moustaches looked startlingly black. He betrayed no anger under the lash of her words: only melancholy. He inclined his head a little.

"The rebuke is merited, I know. But even if you deem my action base, do not blame all Spaniards for the faults of one. And even for these faults, in judging them, consider the source from which they spring." He sat down opposite to her. "It is not by his actual deeds that a man is to be judged, but by the motive which inspires them. A thousand men of honour might have crossed your path in life and retained your esteem as men of honour because moved to no action that could diminish them. I am, I trust, a man of honour...'

She uttered a short, interrupting laugh. He caught his breath, and flushed a little; but repeated himself and continued: "I am, I trust, a man of honour, as in the past you rightly judged me. I might have departed, leaving you in that persuasion, had not an overmastering, an overwhelming temptation shattered all preconceptions for me. Knowing you, Margaret, I came to love you, passionately, desperately, blindly."

"Must you continue?"

"I must. For I desire you to understand before you judge. This love of mine, growing to worship, filling me with a sense of adoration, rendered you so necessary to me that I could not face life without you." He passed a hand wearily across his pallid brow. "These things are not of our own devising. We are the slaves of Nature, pawns of Destiny, who uses us to her purpose, lashing us into obedience of her peremptory will. I did not ask to love you. I did not ever desire it of my own volition. The desire was planted in me. It came I know not whence, a behest which there was no disobeying, compelling, utterly overmastering. In what opinion you held me before tonight I scarcely know. But I think that you esteemed me. And a woman such as I unerringly judge you to be could not esteem a man whom she supposed addicted to banal gallantries, to the pursuit of trivial amours, making sacrilegiously of love a pastime and a vileness. I am no such man. This I swear to you by my faith and my honour in the sight of God and His Holy Mother."

"Why trouble to swear or to forswear? All this is naught to me."

"Ah, wait! It must be something, surely. It must have weight with you that what I have done has been done in no levity possible to some such man as I say that I am not. I have abducted you. It is an ugly word."

"A proper word to describe an ugly fact, a crime for which you shall most certainly be brought to answer."

"A crime, as you say. But it is opportunity that makes the criminal. There has never been in human man – save one, and He was more than human – so much inherent virtue that there is no point at which temptation cannot break it." He sighed. "Believe me at least

141

that I should never have done what I have done if, in addition to the temptation provided by my need, my irresistible need of you, the circumstances themselves had not conspired to force me. Time would not stand still for me. This ship could not be kept indefinitely in English waters. Every hour exposed her to the risk of seizure. So I must make haste. I spoke to you last night of love – timidly, tentatively. I was rebuffed. It was to have been feared. The disclosure came too abruptly. It startled you, disturbed you, ruffled you. In other circumstances I should have paused. I should have brought an infinite patience to my wooing, sustaining that patience by the conviction that just as in our first meeting something of you had gone out to me to mark me for your own as long as I have life, so something from me must have gone out to you with the same message, although you might not yet be aware of it. It is impossible that the emotions which stirred in me should be other than reciprocal. They were as the spark that is born of the meeting of flint and steel, to the creation of which both elements are necessary. You were not yet aware of it; that was all. But in time, in a little time, I must have awakened you to this awareness. Time, however, was not at my command. It was impossible that I could protract my stay in England." He flung out an arm in a gesture of passion, and leaned forward a little across the table. "What choice, then, had I but to resort to this villainy, as you deem it, as the only alternative to the impossibility of renouncing you?" He waited for no answer, but swept on. "I have brought you away by force that I may woo you, Margaret, that I may place at your feet all that I have and all that I am, and crown you with all the honours won already and all those yet to be won under your dear inspiration. It is known by now on this ship that I am taking you to Spain to make you Countess of Marcus, and from this moment you will be entreated by all with the deference and homage due to that rank."

He paused, his melancholy, love-lorn glance upon her in humble supplication. But neither the glance nor his words had produced any visible impression. The eyes with which she returned his glance were hard, and there was only scorn in the little smile that tightened her red lips.

"I have thought you, whilst you spoke, sometimes a knave, sometimes a fool. I perceive you now to be a sorry mixture of both."

He shrugged and even smiled, an infinite weariness in his eyes. "That is not argument."

"Argument? Does it need argument to prick the empty bubble you have laboured so to blow? By the same arguments there is no vileness in the world that cannot be justified. The facts are here, Don Pedro; you have returned evil for good; you have used me with violence and indignity, hoping to constrain me to your will; you have left anxiety and sorrow behind, in a house which sheltered you in time of stress. These facts no arguments in the world can ever dispel. The attempt upon me I tell you now is idle. I'll be no man's countess against my will, and I have no will to be yours and never shall have. If you would earn a forgiveness you may yet come to need, I ask you again to give orders to go about and restore me to my home."

He lowered his eyes and sighed. "Let us eat," he said, and spoke rapidly in Spanish to the waiting and wondering Pablillos, who at once grew busy with the dishes prepared upon a buffet.

In a spirit of admirable philosophic detachment, Don Pedro found himself admiring the courage which permitted her to answer him so firmly, to sit before him so uprightly, and to meet his eye so steadily. How differently would any other woman he had ever known have borne herself in this situation! What tears and outcries would not have deafened and nauseated him! But Margaret was tempered finely as steel. Not in all the world could he find such another mother for his sons. What men would she not bear to add lustre and honour to the house of Mendoza y Luna?

Of her ultimate surrender he was confident. The arguments he had used were sincere enough; they expressed his utter faith; and in that faith he could practise patience, a virtue impossible only where there is doubt.

She ate sparingly; but that she could eat at all was a further proof of her spirit. She drank, too, a little wine; but was careful to drink only from the same jug as that which supplied Don Pedro. Observing this caution he rated her wit as highly as her spirit. Thus her very defiances and mistrusts but served to magnify her in his adoring eyes.

The single cabin on the starboard side had been prepared for Don Pedro, and prepared luxuriously. Informed of it by Pablillos he yielded it to her ladyship, and she withdrew to it with the cold resignation which had marked her every surrender to the force of circumstances.

Alone there, her demeanour may have altered. In secret she may have yielded to fear and grief and indignation. Certain it is that when early on the following morning she sought the deck, where she might conceive herself less prisoned than in the coach, there was a haggardness which her countenance had never worn before and a redness about her eyes which may have been the result of weeping or of sleeplessness, both new experiences in the life of the Lady Margaret Trevanion. Apart from those, however, she flew no signals of distress. She had dressed herself with pains, repairing the disorder which her garments had suffered, and she had tied her hair with care. Her step was as firm as the canting deck permitted, her manner one of chill dignity and assurance.

Thus she emerged from the gangway to the waist, which, beheld now in the morning sunlight, seemed less spacious than yesternight. Her glance strayed from the square main hatch with its shot rack to the boats on the booms amidships and lingered a moment on a sturdy lad, who, engaged in polishing the brass hoops of a scuttlebutt, eyed her with furtive interest. The wind had freshened with the sunrise, and there were men aloft taking in sail. Save for the youth at the scuttlebutt she seemed singularly alone. But as she moved forward along the weather quarter away from the break of the poop she saw that there were men on the quarter-deck above. Duclerc, the sturdy, bearded French master, leaned on the carved rail, observing her. As she turned he doffed his bonnet in salutation.

Behind him two sailors were gazing up into the shrouds, following the operations there of those aloft.

She crossed the canted deck to the quarter on which she supposed that land – her England – would last have been. There was no land now in sight. She had a sense almost that the ship was in the centre of a vast aqueous globe, for the pellucid morning sky seemed one with the ocean. A nausea of dismay swept over her, and she steadied herself against the bulwarks, to become suddenly aware that she was less alone than she had believed. Against one of the forecastle bulkheads leaned a tall figure as immovable as if it had been a caryatid carved to bear the burden of that forward deck.

It was the friar. His cowl was now thrown back from his tonsured head, and his face thus fully revealed in the light of day announced him younger that she had supposed him, a man in the middle thirties. Despite its hungry, almost wolfish look, it was not an unhandsome face, and one that must anywhere arrest attention. The nose was prominent, almost Semitic, the cheek-bones thrust forward boldly, seeming to drag the sallow skin with them and leave the gaunt hollows in the cheeks. His mouth was wide, but thin of lips and firm, whilst under a jutting brow two great, dark eyes glowed sombrely.

He stood within but a few yards of where she had come to lean, his fingers closed upon his breviary, a string of beads intertwining his fingers and hanging from his hand; they formed – although she could not know or guess it – a chaplet brought from the Holy Land, each grain of which was wrought of camel-bone.

Perceiving her regard upon him, he slightly inclined his head in greeting, but his face remained as impassive as if carved of wood. He advanced towards her, his great stern eyes upon her, and she grew conscious of a faint uneasy quickening of her pulse, such as besets us at the approach of some creature of a species not known or understood. To her surprise he greeted her in English. He uttered commonplaces, but his deep, grave voice and sibilant Spanish accent seemed to lend them consequence. He expressed a hope that she had found a ship's quarters not too uncomfortable, that sleep had been possible to her in surroundings that must be unaccustomed, so that, waking refreshed, she had commended herself to the Holy Mother of God, the natural protectress of all virgins.

She realized that the apparent courteous hope was in reality a question, although perhaps she scarcely understood the depth to which it was meant to probe. Indeed, her active wits were already engaged on other matters. This man was a priest, and although his might be a creed superficially different from her own, yet in fundamentals it was essentially the same. Good and Evil wore the same aspect in Roman as in Lutheran eyes, and he was by his office and his habit a servant of the Good, an upholder of virtue, a champion of the oppressed. Had he known no English, he could not have availed her. He must have drawn his own conclusions touching her presence on that ship, or accept whatever tale Don Pedro told him. But the fact that she could appeal to him, tell her own story and be understood, seemed all at once to dispel her every qualm and open a clear way for her out of her present difficulties. Let him but know of the violence done her, of how she was placed, and his assistance must be won; he must stand her friend and protector, and he a man in authority who could enforce, even upon so great a gentleman as Don Pedro de Mendoza y Luna, the need to right this wrong.

Don Diego had blundered worse than he knew, or Don Pedro yet suspected, in bringing this Dominican as the ship's spiritual guide. The man's knowledge of English, which was the very ground upon which Don Diego had chosen him for a voyage to England, was the very ground upon which, had there been no other, he should have been left in Spain. But this was all outside her ladyship's knowledge. All that mattered was that he spoke her tongue and that he was here beside her to hear what she had to tell.

The colour flooded to her cheeks, a sparkle came to eyes that a moment since had been dull with dejection. Her first words were such as must commend her to him, and almost quiet the doubts concerning her that were stirring in his mind, doubts which his questioning greeting had desired to test.

146

"God must have sent you to me; God and that Holy Mother whom you pronounce the protectress of all maids in need. Be you her deputy by me. For I am sorely in need of protection."

She saw the stern eyes soften. Compassionate tenderness invested that ascetic countenance.

"I am an unworthy servant of the Lord and of those who call upon the Lord. What is your need, my sister?"

Briefly, with feverish speed, she told him that she had been ravished from her home and brought by violence aboard this ship, in which she was being carried to Spain in the power and at the mercy of Don Pedro de Mendoza.

He inclined his head. "I know," he said quietly.

"You know? You know?" There was almost horror in her voice. Was it possible that this priest was in the plot? Were the hopes vain to which his presence had but given birth? He knew, and yet bore himself with such indifference!

"I also know, if a man's words are to be believed, that Don Pedro means you honourably."

"What is that to the matter?" she cried out.

"Something. Something, surely, that his intentions concerning you are not villainous or sinful."

"Not villainous? Not sinful? To bear me off against my will! To coerce me!"

"It is a wrong, a grave and wicked wrong," Frey Luis admitted quietly. "Yet not so grave or so wicked as it might be, and as first I feared it was. I feared a mortal sin to imperil the salvation of his soul. And who voyages in ships should more than another preserve that state of grace in which to meet his Maker, since at any moment the perils of sea may summon him to that Dread Presence. But a wrong there is, as I perceive. You desire me to prevail upon Don Pedro to repair it. Content you, my sister. In my protection, under God's, whose servant I am, rest you assured that no evil shall befall you. Don Pedro either returns you to your home at once, or you shall be delivered from this coercion so soon as you touch Spanish soil."

She could have laughed in her exultation, so easy had it been to secure the frustration of all Don Pedro's measures. The voyage no longer had any peril to daunt her. The mantle of St Dominic protected her, and although she knew little, if anything, about that ardent, zealous saint who had preached the love of Christ with fire and sword and warred relentlessly upon all who did not think as he did, she felt that she would hold his name ever hereafter in reverence and love.

Frey Luis had passed his beads and breviary into his left hand. He raised now his right, with three fingers extended, and made the sign of the cross in the air over her golden head, a murmur of Latin on his lips.

To the Lady Margaret this was almost as the ritual of some incantation. Her wide-set, generous eyes dilated a little as she looked at him. Frey Luis read the question of that uncomprehending stare, observed that golden head held rigid, unbowed and unresponsive to his benediction, and his own eyes reflected a sudden doubt which mounted swiftly to conviction. Dismay overspread the austere face. This thing which Don Pedro had done went deeper than he could have dishonoured him by suspecting, it suddenly assumed proportions of wickedness and evil far exceeding any which he attached to the abduction in itself, indeed the last wickedness he would have believed of a nobleman of a family so renowned for piety as Don Pedro's, a family which had given Spain a Primate. This abducted woman, whom Don Pedro intended for his wife and the mother of his children, was a heretic.

Before that horrible discovery Frey Luis recoiled in body as in spirit. His lips tightened; his expression became masklike. He folded his hands within the sleeves of his white woollen habit, and without another word turned on his sandalled heel and moved slowly away to cogitate this horror.

Chapter 15

Scylla

So deeply perturbed by his discovery was Frey Luis that he required time to recover from the shock and to rehearse the measures by which he was to combat Satan for the imperilled soul of Don Pedro de Mendoza y Luna. The holy man prayed long and fervently for guidance and for strength. As one who sincerely regarded the world and its honours as trivial evanescences to be crossed on the path to eternity, he stood in no awe of the great, acknowledged no superiority in any nobility that was not rooted in zeal for the Faith. He would serve no king who was not himself a servant of God; acknowledged no king who did not acknowledge himself that. Worldly power, which himself he had spurned when he assumed the habit of St Dominic, became a contemptible mockery in his eyes, a thing of scorn, from the moment that it ceased to be employed first and foremost in the service of the Faith. It follows from all this, which was not without its unperceived leaven of arrogance and the deadly sin of pride, that Frey Luis was no respecter of persons or of rank. Yet whilst despising wordly rank, he must acknowledge it. It was necessary to reckon with it. Evil could be wrought by it. Because self-seeking men were sycophantic to it, great strength was often necessary so as to stand against it and thwart it where it addressed itself to unholy ends.

For this strength prayed Frey Luis, and it was not until the following afternoon that he felt himself sufficiently equipped and inspired for his struggle with the devil.

Don Pedro took the air – crisp and sharp, despite the sunlight – upon the poop. He was distressed and moody when Frey Luis approached him. But because it was some time before the Dominican's words showed whither he was travelling, Don Pedro offered no interruptions, betrayed no impatience.

Frey Luis went a long way round, so as completely to disguise his approaches; so as to say all that mattered, all that should germinate in the soul of Don Pedro, before Don Pedro, discerning the friar's real aim, should be tempted to set a term to his discourse. It amounted to little less than a sermon.

He began by speaking of Spain, of her glory first and then of her difficulties. Her glories he described as the mark of divine favour upon her. God made it manifest that the Spaniards were today his chosen people, and woe unto Spain should she ever grow negligent of the stupendous grace vouchsafed her.

Don Pedro permitted himself to wonder was the scattering of the Armada by the hosts of Heaven a manifestation of this grace.

The doubt inflamed Frey Luis. Not the hosts of Heaven, but the powers of darkness had been responsible for that. God had permitted it as a warning to a people against the deadly sin of pride – one of Satan's most artful snares – which might betray them into supposing that their glories were the result of their own puny endeavours. It was necessary to remind men, lest they perished, that without the favour of Heaven nothing was to be achieved on earth.

There were a dozen answers which suggested themselves to the logical mind of Don Pedro, who had first known doubt on that morning when he awakened in the cove below Trevanion Chase. But he offered none of them, knowing already how they would be met.

Frey Luis passed on to speak of his country's difficulties. The jealous enemies without, and the insidious enemies within; the latter inspired and sustained by the former. Because Spain, under God's favour and protection, was unconquerable in direct and honourable warfare, Satan sought to undermine the religious unity which rendered her invulnerable by insinuating sectarian disorders into her bosom. To wound her in her faith was to bleed her of her strength. The Jews, those enemies of the Cross, those armies of the powers of darkness, had been driven out. But the New Christians remained with their frequent Judaizings. Gone were those other legionaries of Hell, the followers of Mahomet. But the Moriscoes remained, and their frequent lapses into the abominations of Islam continued a defilement. And after all, the taint of Jew and Moor was in many a man of lineage. Not every nobleman of Spain was as clean of blood as Don Pedro de Mendoza y Luna. But not even clean blood was nowadays a sufficient safeguard, since it assured no immunity from the poison of heresy, a poison which, once introduced into the body, laboured there until it had destroyed it utterly. And there were signs of it, more than signs of it, in Spain already. Frey Luis became lugubrious. Valladolid was a hotbed of Lutheranism. Salamanca was little better than a heretical seminary. The disciples of Luther and Erasmus became daily bolder. Even a primate of Spain, Carranza, the Archbishop of Toledo, had been guilty of Lutheranizing in his catechism.

Upon this climax of exaggeration, Don Pedro interrupted him. "The archbishop was acquitted of the charge."

The Dominican's eyes flashed with holy wrath. "That acquittal shall be atoned for in Hell by those who betrayed their God in pronouncing it. For seventeen years Carranza lay in the prisons of the Holy Office, defending himself with sophistries which the Devil inspired in him for his self-preservation. He should have left them for the fire. In such matters there is no room for arguments or casuistries; whilst men talk, the evil grows; it grows even from their disputations. What is needed is that we extirpate these buboes of heretical pestilence, that we cauterize them once and for all with the purifying flame. To the fire with all these putrescences! And so, Amen!" He flung up one of his long arms in a gesture of denunciation almost terrifying in its remorseless vehemence.

"Amen, indeed!" Don Pedro echoed.

The Dominican's lean, feverish hand clawed the nobleman's arm in its black velvet sleeve. His eyes glowed with eagerness and saintly zeal.

"That is the response I expected from you, the response worthy of your nobility, of your clean blood and of the representative of the great house of Mendoza, which has laboured ever to the glory of God and of Spain."

"What other response could have been possible? I am, I hope, a faithful son of Mother Church."

"Not merely faithful, but active; a member of the Militia Christi. Are you not in some sort my brother, my spiritual brother in the great fraternity of St Dominic? Are you not a lay tertiary of the order, and so, consecrated to uphold the purity of the Faith and to expunge heresy wherever you shall find it?"

Don Pedro began to frown at so much vehemence. "Why do you question me, Frey Luis?"

"To test you, whom I find upon the brink of a precipice. To assure myself that your faith is strong enough to keep you from the vertigo that may hurl you down into the depths."

"I am on the brink of a precipice? I? You give me news, brother." And Don Pedro laughed with a flash of white teeth behind his black beard.

"You stand in danger of defiling the purity of your blood which hitherto has been without taint. You have announced to me that you will give your children a heretic for their mother."

Don Pedro understood, though, truth to tell, the thing took him by surprise. The fact was, although he dared not admit it to this zealot, that, swept headlong by the stream of passion, he had given no thought to this side of the matter.

For an instant he stood appalled. He was a devout and faithful son of the Church, as he had announced; and he was dismayed to discover how reckless he had been of matters which should have claimed his first attention. But the dismay was momentary. The same high confidence that he would win the Lady Margaret to be a willing bride assured him that he would have no difficulty in bringing her within the fold of the True Faith. He said so, and by the confident assurance entirely changed the current of the friar's thoughts. Frey Luis was uplifted like a man who suddenly perceives the light where all before him had been darkness.

"Blessed be God!" he exclaimed piously. "Woe me for the weakness of my own faith! I failed to see, my brother, that you were chosen to be the instrument of her salvation."

He enlarged upon his theme. In his view it justified all that Don Pedro had done, the very violence he had used in abducting this lady. Here was no question of any yielding to carnal lusts such as the friar had shuddered to his soul in contemplating. Don Pedro was snatching a brand from the burning, carrying off not so much a fair smooth body cast in the Satanic mould of loveliness for a man's corruption, but rather, a soul that was in peril of damnation. The friar would be his ally now in this worthy work. He would bear the light of the true faith to this damsel for whom such high temporal destinies were reserved. He would labour in the holy work of delivering her from the heretical abominations absorbed in the abominably heretical country of her birth, and by converting her to the true faith, render her a fit bride for the Count of Marcos, a fit mother for future Mendozas.

Even if Don Pedro had possessed the inclination he would not have dared to oppose Frey Luis in this. But it was what he himself desired, what, now that he came to consider it, he perceived must happen before he could dare to take Margaret to wife.

And so Frey Luis was granted charter to preach conversion to the Lady Margaret.

He went about it with an infinite caution, patience and zeal, labouring assiduously for three days to break down the earthworks which he clearly perceived to have been thrown up about her by Satan. But the more he laboured, the more did those Satanic ramparts grow to frustrate the gallant zeal of his attacks.

At first the Lady Margaret had been interested in his expositions. Perhaps, even because of her interest, she had come to interrupt him with questions. How did he know this? What was his authority for that? And when he answered her, behold her presenting him with embarrassing rejoinders straight from Scripture, begging him to reconcile this or that of his statements with these passages from Holy Writ.

To her it was an engrossing game, a heaven-sent pastime to beguile the tedium of those days upon that ship, to take her mind from distracting activities upon the past and the future. But to him it was an appalling torment. There was a simplicity about her which was devastating, a directness of question and a lucidity of statement that at moments reduced him to despair.

Frey Luis had never met her equal. This need not surprise us. His inquisitorial dealings had chiefly been concerned with Judaizers and relapsed Moriscoes. His knowledge of English had brought him into touch with some English and other mariners consigned for heresy to the prisons of the Holy Office. But they had been ignorant men, even when ship-masters, in religious matters. They had clung stubbornly to certain fundamental tenets of the heretical creed in which they had been reared; but they had attempted no argument or answers to the arguments which, in the performance of his holy duty, he had placed before them.

The Lady Margaret Trevanion's was a very different case. Here was a woman who had read and re-read the Scriptures, largely for lack of other reading matter, until she knew – whilst scarcely aware of it – a deal of them by heart. Add to this that she was gifted with a clear intelligence, a ready wit, and a high courage, and that she had been reared in the habit of expressing herself with the utmost frankness. These matters which Frey Luis came so assiduously to expound had never greatly exercised her mind in the past. Her father was not a religious man, and sentimentally his leanings had been rather to the old Romish faith. He had been careless of his daughter's religious training, and had left her to pursue it for herself. But if she had never yet exercised herself upon it in the past, she was ready enough to exercise herself upon it now, when in a sense she found herself challenged to do so. The ease with which she found herself embarked in polemical argument, the readiness with which quotations came to her hand as required, surprised her very self.

It more than surprised Frey Luis. It brought him to a raging despair. It proved to him how right were the Fathers of the Church to forbid the translation and diffusion of the sacred writings, and what a lure of Satan's it was to place those books in the hands of those who, because they could not understand them, must of necessity pervert their meaning. Thus, by the wiles of the Devil, the very means of salvation were transformed into instruments of corruption.

When he said so in furious denunciation, she laughed at him, laughed like a Delilah or a Jezebel, flaunting her white beauty, as it seemed to him, before his eyes as if to take him in the lure of it, as she had taken Don Pedro. He covered his face with his hands.

"Vade retro, Sathanas!' he cried aloud, whereat she but laughed the more.

"So, sir friar," she rallied him, "I am become Satan now, and I am to get behind you! You are ungallant, which is no doubt very proper in a priest, however distressing in a man. But behind you I will not get. I'll face you out, sir, until one of us goes down in defeat."

He uncovered his face to stare at her with eyes of horror. He took that rallying phrase in its literal sense. "Until one of us goes down in defeat?" he echoed. Then his voice soared passionately. "Until Satan triumphs, you mean! Woe me!" And on that he fled from the great cabin, where the atmosphere had grown stifling, to seek breath and sanity, on the open deck with the salt tang of the sea in his nostrils.

That happened on the third day of his efforts of conversion and it was fateful. Her words pursued him. "I'll face you out until one of us goes down in defeat." It was a threat; a threat of Satan's spoke through those fair, false lips. He perceived it now. Out here under God's sky, it came to him that he had stood in direct peril. He, the hunter, had begun to be the hunted. There were moments, as he now perceived, when his own faith had momentarily faltered under the specious arguments, the glib answers with which she had counter-assailed him; moments when he had stood in doubt of what actually was the teaching of the Church, bewildered by a sudden confrontation with some text of Scripture which seemed to give the lie to what he had last said. And this had happened to him, a man learned in these matters, at the hands of a woman, a girl, an untutored child! It was unthinkable, preposterous that she should be able to do this of her own wit. Whence had she the power? Whence? It must be that she was possessed, a subject of unholy inspiration.

The conviction grew, and something beside the thought of her polemics came to strengthen it. The image of her was solid before his eyes. He beheld her concrete, almost palpable, before him even now: the lissom form on the cushions of the sea-chest with the glowing horn panes of the stern windows behind her, her head thrown back in laughter, and lending her an air of wantonness; the red-gold hair that seemed at moments to flame in the sunlight, the blue eyes so full of a false alluring candour, the white throat, so fully revealed by the wanton cut of her corsage and the swelling curve of breast below, along which his eyes had unduly lingered. They lingered now upon the image of it all, even though he pressed his palms against his eyeballs as if to crush them, revolted, terrified to find that image evoking an unholy thrill in his starved virility.

"Vade retro, Sathanas!" he muttered again, and piteously from the depths of his soul cried out for help against the terrible lure of the flesh, so long and fiercely repressed and now rising up to destroy him. "Vade retro, Sathanas!"

A hand touched his shoulder. He started as if a red-hot iron had been pressed against him. Beside him, as he sat there on the hatch-coaming to which he had sunk stood the slight, elegant figure of Don Pedro observing him with a half-smile.

"With what devil do you wrestle, Frey Luis?"

Frey Luis looked up at him with haunted eyes. "That is what I desire to know," he answered. "Sit here beside me," he invited, and the great gentleman obeyed.

There was a silence, at the end of which the Dominican began to discourse. He spoke of witchcraft and demonology in a fevered manner and with a leaning to impure things – not necessarily in itself

156

impure. He expounded the origin and nature of the Devil; alluded to the many weapons and snares of which the Devil avails himself, and the dangers created by the illusions in which these are veiled. Antichrist, he asserted, was to be fathered by an incubus, even as the accursed heresiarch, Luther, had been fathered.

The discourse dragged on. It was obscure and Don Pedro wearied of it.

"What have I to do with all this?" he ventured.

The friar swung to him, and laid a hand heavily upon his shoulder. Solemnly he put a question.

"Would you prefer a crumb of ephemeral and poisoned pleasure to the banquet of infinite and everlasting bliss which is offered to you in Heaven?"

"God help me! Of course not."

"Then be warned in time, my brother."

"Of what?"

Frey Luis answered obliquely. "God hath set woman in the world to put man to the proof. Woe unto him that fails!"

"If you said it in Greek, I might understand you better," was the impatient answer.

"This woman… " the friar was beginning.

"If you mean the Lady Margaret Trevanion, you speak of her differently or not at all."

Don Pedro got up stiffly, breathing noisily through his nostrils. But Frey Luis was not to be abashed.

"Words are naught. It is the fact they express that signifies. This lady, my lord, is beyond conversion."

Don Pedro looked at him and fingered his beard. "Beyond such arts of it as yours, you mean."

"Beyond all arts. She is possessed."

"Possessed?"

"Of a devil. She had recourse to witchcraft. She… "

Leaning over him, Don Pedro hissed an interruption. "Silence, madman! Is your vanity so monstrous, your pride so egregious, that because you have not the wit to persuade her, you must assume the

157

Devil speak with her tongue? Why, what a paltry tale, and how often has it not served an incompetent man of God?"

The friar, however, untouched by offence, slowly shook his head. "There's more to it than that. God's grace has revealed to me that which I should have had the wit to perceive before with my earthly senses. For I hold the proof of it. The proof, do you hear? As you might hold it if she had not caught you in her spells, trammelled you in her evil web."

"No more!" Don Pedro stood stern and fierce. "You push presumption to amazing lengths, sir friar. Do not push it so far that in my just resentment I should forget the habit that you wear."

The friar rose, too, and stood close beside him, half a head taller, stern, indomitable in his holy zeal. "No threats will silence one who knows himself within his rights to speak, as I am."

"Are you so?" Don Pedro had dropped all outward signs of anger. He was his habitual, mocking self, mocking and something sinister. "Remember that I, too, have rights here on this ship, and these include the right to have you flung overboard if you become importunate."

Frey Luis recoiled, not in fear of the threat, but in horror of the spirit that prompted it.

"You say this to me? You threaten sacrilege, no less? You are so lost already that you would raise your hand against an anointed priest?"

"Begone!" Don Pedro bade him. "Go preach of Hell to those poor devils in the forecastle."

Frey Luis folded his hands under his scapulary, assuming an outward impassivity. "I have sought to warn you. But you will not be warned. Sodom and Gomorrah would not be warned. Beware their fate!"

"I am neither Sodom nor Gomorrah," was the biting answer. "I am Don Pedro de Mendoza y Luna, Count of Marcos and Grandee of Spain, and my word is paramount aboard this ship; my wish the only law upon these decks. Remember it unless you are prepared to take your chance of travelling home like Jonah."

For a moment Frey Luis stood considering him with inscrutable, hypnotic eyes. Then he raised his hands and drew the cowl over his head. There was almost a symbolism in the act, as if intended to express the completeness of his withdrawal.

Yet he went without malice of any kind in his piteous heart; for piteous he was to the core and marrow of him. He went to pray that the divine grace might descend upon Don Pedro de Mendoza y Luna to deliver him from the snares of an enchantress inspired by Satan to destroy his soul. That fact was now crystal-clear to Frey Luis Salcedo. As he had said, he held the proof of it.

Chapter 16

Charybdis

They cast anchor at evening two days later in the spacious bay at Santander, lying sheltered in its green amphitheatre of hills, with Mount Valera in the background thrusting up its detached mass from the range of the Sierras de Isar.

Those last two days aboard the *Demoiselle* had been days of profound uneasiness under a sullen superficial calm. Frey Luis had made no further attempt to approach the Lady Margaret, and there was something ominous and menacing in his very abstention, and in its implication that he had abandoned the hope of her conversion. Twice he attempted to re-open the subject with Don Pedro, and well might it have been for Don Pedro had he listened and so learned the precise peril in which he stood. But Don Pedro was at the end of his patience in several ways. The fundamental pride and haughtiness of his nature reminded him that he had tolerated from this conventual zealot more insolence already than self-respect permitted. Piety demanded in him a certain measure of submission; but there were limits to the strain to be imposed upon it and those limits had been overpassed by the presumptuous friar. Realizing it, Don Pedro became curt and rude with him, asserted his rank and nobility, and dismissed Frey Luis with threats of violence, which but served to confirm the Dominican in the terrible conclusions he had already drawn.

With the Lady Margaret Don Pedro was almost sullen now. Uneasiness began to stir in him. He began to fear the ultimate frustration of his hopes from her calm obduracy, from the firm manner in which she repelled his every advance with the constant reminder that he had by the ingratitude of his conduct made her regret the hospitality her house had afforded him. He would have reasoned her away from this. But she would not suffer him to do so. However he might twist and turn, she brought him ever back to the source.

"We have," she insisted, "a fact, a thing done, which nothing in the world could possibly excuse. Why labour, then, to seek what does not exist?"

Her firmness, the more formidable because of her unbroken outward calm, began to sow in his heart the seed of despair. He thought of what he was, of what he offered her. Enough, surely, to have contented any woman. Her obduracy was exasperating. He brooded over it. It festered in him, and began to warp and transmute his nature, which fundamentally was chivalrous.

The explosion came after those two days of sullen silences and sullen glances. It came when the anchor was being cast on that calm evening of October in the Bay of Santander.

She sat in the great cabin, her anxieties sharpened by the knowledge that the voyage was at an end and that she must gird herself for battle now upon some new ground which she did not yet perceive and for which she was unable to discover any weapons.

"We have arrived," he announced to her. He was pale, angry, his dark eyes aflash.

She weighed her words before she uttered them. "You mean that you have arrived, sir. For me this is not an arrival. It is a stage in the tiresome journey you have forced upon me."

He agreed, deliberately affecting to misunderstand her. "True. Tomorrow we continue on land. We have yet some leagues to go. But it is not far. In a few days now we shall be within my own walls at Oviedo."

"I trust not," said she with her outward imperturbability. Her confidence was in Frey Luis. Although for two days he had not approached her, although his latter visits had all been concerned with her conversion to the true faith, yet she trusted to his promise to protect her and to the fundamental virtue and goodness discernible in the man.

"You trust not?" Don Pedro was sneering. He approached her where she sat on the cushioned sea-chest under the tall stern windows. Seated thus, her face was little more than a white blur in the shadows. But what little daylight lingered was confronted by him, revealing his countenance and the wicked mockery that writhed on it.

This persistent cold opposition to his imperious will, this utter unresponsiveness to the love which might have made a saint of him, was converting him swiftly into a devil. He realized in that moment that the change had been steadily growing in those days on board the *Demoiselle*. Standing over her now he perceived that his love was all but transmuted into hate.

For her he would have made the last sacrifice. He would have laid down his life, he assured himself. And all the return he could awaken in her was this glacial scorn, this unchanging attitude of repulsion. His present impulse was to punish this obstinacy and this folly; to render her brutally aware of him; to possess her, merely so that she might learn his dominance; to break her in body and in soul.

"You trust not?" he repeated. "Upon what do you found this trust of yours?"

"Upon God," she answered him.

"God! The God of heretics? Will He move in your defence?"

"He moved in my people's," she reminded him, "when the invincible might of Spain was arrayed against them. Spain thought of England as you think of me. A dream from which there was a rude awakening. Your awakening, Don Pedro, may be as rude."

He swung away from her, wringing his hands, beating fist into palm in a gesture of exasperation. Then he was back again, his mood soft once more, his tone a lover's.

"We are uttering words that should never pass between us. If you will but be reasonable! It is naught but unreason blocks the way. Your obstinacy it is which denies you to me. You will not listen, however humbly I sue, because you have taken an obdurate resolve against it."

"You are modest, sir. You are assuming that you can win any woman who will listen to you."

"That is to corrupt my meaning. It is to forget all that I said to you when first you came on board… "

"When first you dragged me here, you mean."

He went on without heeding the correction. "I told you then of a force outside ourselves, of my persuasion that, as it drove me, so must it drive you if you would suffer yourself to be driven. Listen, Margaret!" He was down on one knee beside the sea-chest. "I love you, and you may trust my love to render your life glorious. There is no return for you. Even if I allowed you to go free, it is too late. You have been with me here a week on board this ship, under my hand. You see what must be assumed, that already can be repaired in no way save by marrying me. Let it be done now. There is a priest here who will… "

She interrupted him. "You speak of assumptions! I tell you, man, in England there is no one will assume anything against me when I shall have told my tale."

He rose, inflamed again with anger, casting all courtliness aside. "The assumption might be justified," he threatened. "Only the strength and quality of my love have made me hold my hand."

She came to her feet in a bound, breathing hard. "God! You dare say that to me! You knave! You gentleman!"

"Gentleman?" She heard his tinkling laugh. "Where have you lived not yet to have discovered that gentility is just a garment worn by a man? You may have me in that garment or without it. The choice is yours, madam. Nay! Listen! There is no need for further words. Very soon now you'll lie in my house at Oviedo. How you lie there is a matter for your own determining. But if you are wise you will lie there as my wife; you will marry me before we leave this ship."

On that he departed abruptly, slamming the cabin door so that the bulkheads trembled.

Shaking, outraged, mortified, she sank down again to the seat from which she had risen; and there for the first time she loosed her grip of her self-control, and gave way to tears of anger and of panic.

In that hour of her overwhelming need, a figure rose before her, the figure of Gervase, stalwart, laughing, clean-limbed, clean-souled, mirror to her now of all that a gentleman should be. And she had hurt him that she might trifle with this Spanish satyr, by foolish imprudences which gave this man the right to think that he had power to whistle her down the wind when he so chose. She had played with fire, and, by Heaven, the fire had licked out not merely to scorch her, but to consume and destroy her. Little fool that she had been, vain, empty-headed little fool to have found satisfaction in the attentions of one whom she conceived of consequence because he had seen the world and quaffed at many of life's cups. Heavy was the punishment of her heedlessness.

"Gervase! Gervase!" she called in a whisper to the surrounding gloom.

If only he were there, she would cast herself upon her knees before him, purge herself by confession to him of her wilful folly, and acknowledge the love for him which was the only love her life had ever known or would ever know.

Then her mind turned to Frey Luis, and she recovered her shaken courage in the confidence of his protection. Aboard the ship he had been powerless despite the authority of his sacerdotal office. But now that land was reached he could summon others to enforce that authority if Don Pedro should still attempt to withstand it.

Of this she had confirmation later, when locked in her own cabin she heard through the thin door Don Pedro talking to Duclerc whilst Pablillos was serving supper. She had excused herself when Don Pedro had come to summon her to table, and he had accepted her excuses without argument.

He spoke French with Duclerc, for all that the master was fluent enough in Spanish. But it was characteristic of the cultured Don Pedro that he must be addressing each man in his own language. He asked what kept Frey Luis and why he was not at table.

"Frey Luis went ashore an hour ago, monseigneur," was the answer.

"Did he so?" grumbled the Spaniard. "And without farewells? Why, then, a good riddance to the croaking raven."

The Lady Margaret's heart leapt within her. She guessed the errand upon which the friar was gone, and she was glad that Don Pedro should have no suspicion of it.

Her guess was correct enough in that Frey Luis had gone ashore on matters concerned with her salvation. But there was this difference, that it was not salvation in the sense in which she understood it.

The manner of it was made manifest early on the following morning. Her ladyship had risen betimes after a sleepless night of alternating hope and anxiety; she had dressed and gone on deck long before Don Pedro was astir, so that she might be ready for Frey Luis however early he should come. That he would come early she was assured; and again her assurance was justified, for early he came; and with him a boatload of gentlemen in black with swords at their sides, and some of them carrying partisans as well.

The Spanish sailors on the *Demoiselle* came crowding to the bulwarks to watch the approach of that barge and a murmur of dread and wonder ran through their ranks for they were under no misapprehension as to the character of the escort with which Frey Luis returned. These were alguaziles of the Inquisition, the pursuivants of the Holy Office, whose approach was not to be regarded with equanimity by any man, no matter how tranquil his conscience.

Duclerc, the master, hearing that murmur, beholding the excitement among his seamen, despatched a boy to the cabin to inform Don Pedro. The information brought that gentleman swiftly on deck. He came profoundly intrigued, but without anxiety. No doubt this was some formality of the port where foreign vessels were concerned, the result of some new inquisitorial enactment.

He emerged into the open, in the ship's waist, just as Frey Luis, having climbed the entrance ladder, lowered in obedience to his command, was setting foot on deck. At his heels came some six of the black-arrayed pursuivants.

Her ladyship, who had eagerly watched that approach from the heights of the poop, was in the act of descending the companion when Don Pedro came forth. He heard her blithe greeting of the friar called across the deck; he turned in time to see her smile of welcome, and the hand-wave of friendliness and understanding. His brows met; a doubt entered his mind. Was there treachery here at work? Was the priest in alliance with this girl to frustrate his ends concerning her? Was this presumptuous Dominican venturing to interfere in the affairs of the Count of Marcos?

Of the nature of this interference Don Pedro's doubts were brief. The priest's answer to her ladyship's welcome was also an answer to the question in Don Pedro's mind.

In response to that friendly hand-wave Frey Luis raised an arm to point her out to those who had followed him aboard. The rigidity of the movement and the grimness of his countenance lent the gesture a denunciatory character. He said some words to his followers rapidly, in Spanish; words which made Don Pedro catch his breath; words of command in response to which they moved forward promptly. Frey Luis stepped aside to observe. The seamen, having backed to the other quarter, stood ranged against the bulwarks and some in the ratlines, looking on with round eyes of awe.

Her ladyship faltered, paused in her advance, and sensing in all this something ominous and very different from what she had expected, frowned her perplexity. And then, abruptly, Don Pedro stepped between her and those advancing men in black, and by his challenge halted them.

"What's this?" he demanded. "What have you to do with this lady?"

Respect for his high rank gave them pause. One or two of them turned their heads to look for instruction to Frey Luis. It came, addressed to the nobleman.

"Stand aside, Lord Count!" The friar was stern and peremptory. "Do not presume to resist the Holy Office, or you will bring yourself, together with this woman, under its displeasure. At present there is no charge against you, who are but the victim of this woman's enchantments. See to it that you do not, yourself, provide one."

Don Pedro stared at him livid with passion. "Lord God!" he ejaculated, as the full measure of the peril to the Lady Margaret was suddenly unrolled before him. That mention of enchantments revealed it all to him, as if in a sudden flash of light. He remembered how the friar had spoken of witchcraft and demonology. He perceived now the application of that discourse, saw almost in detail the course that would be taken. Whether his rage was fed by this intent to rob him of a cherished possession, or whether it sprang from a sudden anguished realization of the horror to which his rashness had committed Margaret, it may be difficult at this point to determine. But his immediate action and all his subsequent conduct through the affair point to the nobler motive, to a belated forgetfulness of self in his concern for the woman whom I believe that he sincerely loved. His real offence against her was that he loved her too arrogantly; took too much for granted; but this was simply a natural expression of the inherent arrogance of this great gentleman of Spain, this spoilt darling of Fortune.

Certain it is that he was blinded now by fury, driven headlong to a rashness that must imperil his life and even – by his own lights – the salvation of his soul. And I prefer to think that he was so driven by his sudden and terrible concern for Margaret.

He advanced a step, very stiff and haughty, his bare head thrown back, his left hand resting heavily upon the pommel of his sword, so that the weapon was thrust horizontally behind him. He had completed his preparations for going ashore, and he was booted and armed for the journey to come, which may be in the circumstances fortunate or unfortunate, according to how you regard the sequel.

His blazing eyes met the calm, almost melancholy glance of Frey Luis. "You will depart this ship," said Don Pedro through his teeth, "and take your inquisitorial rabble with you before I have you all flung into the water."

Quietly Frey Luis admonished him. "You speak in anger, sir. I will forget your words. Once again I warn you against implicating yourself by resistance with this heretical witch whom it is our business to arrest. Be warned, Don Pedro!"

"Warned! You insolent friar, be you warned that there are presumptions from the consequences of which not even your sweat-reeking habit can protect you." Harshly, peremptorily, he raised his voice. "Don Diego!"

His intendant appeared from the other side of the companion. The man started forward at the call, livid and trembling visibly. Don Pedro's orders were brisk. There were muskets in the mainmast rack. There were men to handle them in plenty. Let this rabble be swept overboard at once.

Don Diego hesitated. Great was his awe of the Count, his master. But greater still his awe of the Church Militant, which could ride roughshod over nobility, over royalty itself. The seamen, too, were horror-stricken. Not one of them would move foot or hand to obey such a command if spoken by any below the rank of the king himself.

Lest they should be tempted to do so, Frey Luis spoke a word of warning sharply, and almost in the same breath commanded the pursuivants to take the woman in despite of any opposition that might be offered.

They advanced again. Don Pedro swept her into the gangway behind him, whilst himself he blocked the entrance to it. The Lady Margaret suffered this because she had not understood the altercation; she had perceived clearly enough in the friar's face and manner that whatever his intention it was not friendly to herself. She was bewildered, not knowing here who was her friend or who her foe; and she found no confidence inspiring her in these men in black with the white cross embroidered on their doublets who moved in obedience to the friar's commands.

Out flashed Don Pedro's sword, whilst his left hand plucked the heavy dagger from his hip.

"Sacrilege!" she heard the friar denounce the act, and understood the word.

"Stand!" raged Don Pedro to the pursuivants, who were standing already, halted by his naked weapons.

But they paused for no more than to draw their swords. This done they advanced again, calling upon him to yield, reminding him of the penalties to which this sacrilegious resistance was exposing him.

He answered them with furious mockery, with wild vituperation. Again he summoned Don Diego and the crew to stand beside him, and because they would not stir, but stood huddled like scared sheep, he called them dogs and cowards and by the foulest epithets that one man may cast upon another. Alone, then, his back protected by the gangway, whence Margaret, white and agitated, looked on in horror, he defied the alguaziles. He invited them to journey on his sword to the Paradise of their dreams or to the Hell of which Frey Luis had preached. He said blasphemous things which it would seem to those who heard them must doom him irrevocably when they came to be repeated to the Inquisitors of the Faith.

When at last they fell upon him, he stabbed one in the neck with his dagger and sheathed his sword in the bowels of another before they closed with him, bore him to the deck, knelt upon him and trussed him with leather thongs into a helpless human bundle.

They left him then to give their attention to the woman, to this heretical witch who had been the only original object of their quest.

Stiff and straight she stood as they advanced and laid rough hands upon her. They would have used violence to drag her forward, had she resisted; but so as to be spared this, she made haste to advance of her own free will.

"What does it mean?" she demanded of Frey Luis. "Is this the protection you afford a lady in distress, a maid who cast herself upon your pity, trusted to your priestly office? What does it mean, sir?"

The compassion of all the ages was in his great sombre eyes.

"My sister, you have been grievously misled. The heretical godlessness of your native land is answerable. But the poison has entered into you. Come with me, and you shall be made sound and whole. This poison shall be expurgated, so that you may come to be filled with grace, delivered from the abominable practices in which Satan the seducer has prompted you. In the bosom of the Faith you shall find infinite compassion. Have no fear, my sister."

To her senses all this was fantastic: the tall, lean friar with his gaunt face and smouldering pitiful eyes; the two black pursuivants, coarse and bearded, who stood on either side of her; the other two, between whom stood Don Pedro, gagged and bound, his doublet torn from neck to waist; the black, sprawling figure on the deck, in a puddle of blood from which a trickle was crawling snakewise towards the scuppers; the other on his knees, tended on by Diego, who was staunching the blood that flowed from the wound in his neck; the huddle of stricken, staring seamen in the background; the masts and spars and shrouds above, and before her, across the stretch of opalescent limpid water, a green hillside dotted with white houses set in gardens or amid terraced vineyards, a straggling town dominated by a great castle, all lying in the peaceful sparkle of the morning sun.

This was that fabulous land of Spain, the mistress of the world.

Chapter 17

The Holy Office

It would seem that all had been settled and predetermined by Frey Luis with the representatives of the Holy Office in Santander that morning before he returned to the *Demoiselle* to make his arrest. For at the mole, when they landed from the barge, the prisoners found horses and a mule-litter waiting in the charge of a small company of javelin-men. Here no time was lost. Under the eyes of a considerable gaping concourse of people of all conditions attracted hither by the presence of the apparitors of the Inquisition; the Lady Margaret was consigned to the litter; Don Pedro was set on horseback between two mounted aguaziles; the friar tucked up his gown to bestride a mule; the remainder of the company, numbering in all a full score, got to horse; and so they departed.

It had been determined that because the seat of the Asturian nobleman, Don Pedro de Mendoza y Luna, was in the neighbourhood of Oviedo, to Oviedo he should be sent together with the woman who was accused of having practised magic against him. The resources of the country were at the disposal of the Holy Office. Frequent relays of horses such as no other power in the kingdom, save the royal authority itself, could have commanded, were available to the apparitors. They travelled swiftly along the coast, with the ocean on their right and the mountains on their left. They left Santander in the early morning of Thursday, the 5th of October, setting foot ashore at almost the very hour in which at Greenwich Sir Gervase Crosby and Sir Oliver Tressilian were stepping aboard the *Rose of the World* to give chase. Such good speed did those horsemen make that by the afternoon of Sunday, dusty, jaded and saddle-worn, it is true, they brought up at the portals of the Holy House in Oviedo, having covered over a hundred miles in less than three days.

To the Lady Margaret, tossed and jolted in the litter, without knowledge of whither she was being taken or to what purpose, the journey was but a continuation of the nightmare begun upon the deck of the *Demoiselle* on Thursday morning. She afterwards confessed that for most of the time she was in a state of stupor, her reason numbed, her wits befogged. The only thing that she clearly perceived was that Don Pedro was caught with her in a snare for which his own presumptuous folly was responsible. Whatever her present danger at least it had removed her from all that Don Pedro had intended.

But in escaping the rock of Scylla she had been sucked into the whirlpool of Charybdis.

She would have questioned Frey Luis during those days of travel. But Frey Luis rigorously and studiously refrained from approaching her, even when they paused for food or rest or change of horses.

Don Pedro, now delivered of his gag and no longer pinioned, rode between his guards with Hell in his soul, as may well be imagined. His frame of mind needs no explaining. It could be one thing only; what it was.

Oviedo, however, did not prove the journey's end, as was supposed. One night only was spent there, and this to the Lady Margaret in conditions of discomfort such as she had never known. Don Pedro de Mendoza y Luna was the first among Asturian noblemen, and in the province of Oviedo, which contained his vast estates, he was accounted second in importance only to the king himself. To proceed against him in the very heart of a province in which he was of such weight and consequence would be a serious step entailing grave responsibilities and provoking perhaps even graver consequences. It was a responsibility which the inquisitors of

Oviedo desired in common prudence to avoid, if to avoid it were not inconsistent with their duty to the Holy Office. Nor was his temporal consequence the only consideration: Don Pedro commanded also spiritual and even inquisitorial influence by the fact that the Inquisitor, General Don de Quiroga, the Cardinal-Archbishop of Toledo, was his uncle. This rendered doubly grave the responsibility of dealing with his case. A brief consideration revealed not only the prudent, but actually the proper course to the inquisitors of Oviedo.

Don Pedro, and the woman responsible for his implication in the terrible charge which was levelled against her by Frey Luis Salcedo, should be sent for trial to Toledo, where he would be under the eye of the Inquisitor-General, his uncle. The reason for this decision, duly registered by the notary of tribunal at Oviedo, was to be discovered in his rank and in the particular nature of the offence.

Frey Luis, perceiving their motives and accounting them pusillanimous, sought to combat them, and to insist that in defiance of all perils and worldly considerations the matter should be dealt with here. But his arguments were swept aside, and on the morrow he was constrained to set out again with his prisoners upon the long journey south to Toledo.

Upon that journey a week was spent. They quitted the Asturias by the defiles of the Cantabrian Mountains, emerging upon the plains of old Castile, going by way of Valladolid and Segovia, then crossing the Sierra of Guadarrama and descending to the fertile valley of the Tagus. It was a journey that well might have afforded interest to an English lady had that English lady's interest not been already unpleasantly preoccupied by the pains and perils of her own situation and the gravest doubts of the future. Yet a hope she nourished based upon her English nationality. At Oviedo she had not been before any person of authority with whom she could lodge her claim for protection at the hands of the ambassador of France in the absence of any ambassador of England just then at the Escurial. But when formal action against her came to be taken, as she supposed to be the intention, of necessity she must be brought before some court, and then would be her opportunity.

This opportunity presented itself at Toledo on the day after her arrival there.

The prisoners were lodged in the Holy House, as the palace-prison of the Holy Office was always styled. A long, low, two-storied building in a narrow street near Santo Domingo el Antiguo, it did not materially differ in appearance from any other palace in Toledo, if we except the splendid Alcazar crowning the granite heights of the great city. It was almost windowless on the side of the street, as a result of the Moorish influence, as dominant in architecture as in every other factor of life in this city, where until less than ten years ago Arabic was as freely spoken in the streets as Spanish, and ceased to be spoken freely then only in obedience to the interdict against the use of the language.

The long, low white building presented to the world a countenance almost as blank and inscrutable as that of the inquisitors, who, behind its portals, laboured so zealously to maintain the purity of the Faith. Admission was gained by a wide Gothic doorway, closed by massive double gates of timber studded with great iron bosses. Above the doorway was hung a shield upon which was figured the green cross of the Holy Office, a cross of two rudely hewn, rudely trimmed boughs, from which some burgeoning twigs still sprouted; under this was to be read the motto *Exsurge Domine et judica cansam Tuam.* In one of the wings of the great door a smaller door or postern was practised. In the other, at a man's height, there was a Judas grille with its little shutter. Through this Gothic doorway you entered a vast stone hall, whence, on your immediate right, a wooden staircase ascended to the floor above; at the inner end and on the same side a stone-flagged corridor like a tunnel led away into the unknown; from this, on the left soon after entering it, stone steps led down into cellars, dungeons and other underground places. From the cool gloom of the great hall there was a view, through farther gates stoutly latticed in their upper halves, of the sunlit quadrangle about which the building stood, of green shrubs, of flowers, of vines carried upon a trellis of black beams that were supported by rough-hewn granite pillars, of a fig-tree shading a brick wall, with its windlass above, and beyond all this the fine Moorish tracery of the cloisters, where black-and-white Dominicans paced slowly in couples reciting the office of the day. A place of infinite peace and rest it seemed, faintly pervaded b y   a n   o d o u r of incense and of wax from the distant chapel.

Many an unfortunate Judaizer, relapsed Morisco or suspected heretic coming in terror of the apparitors who haled him thither, must upon entering the palace have felt some of his terror melting from him in the instinctive assurance that in such a place no evil could befall him, an impression to be confirmed presently by the benignity of his examiners. By this benignity the Lady Margaret was agreeably surprised on the morning after her arrival there, when she was fetched from the wretched cell with its straw pallet, wooden table and chair, where she had spent so miserable a night of sleeplessness and resentment.

Two familiars, lay brothers of St Dominic, conducted her to the small room where her examiners awaited her. It was on the right of the long corridor on the ground floor. Its windows opened upon the garden, but they were set so high that whilst admitting abundant light and air, no outlook was to be obtained from them.

In this austere room with its whitewashed walls sat the ecclesiastical court that was to make inquisition into her ladyship's case. At an oblong table of square deal, upon which there was a crucifix between two tall candles and a vellum-bound copy of the Gospels, sat three cowled figures: the presiding inquisitor, Frey Juan Arrenzuelo, with the Diocesan Ordinary on his right and the Fiscal Advocate on his left. At right angles with these, at the table's end, on their left, sat another Dominican, proclaimed, by his quills, his tablets and the inkstand of orange-root before him, the notary of the tribunal.

Beside the notary, on his left, sat one who did not rightly belong to the court, and whose place in the proceedings would normally have excluded him from open participation in them. This was the delator, Frey Luis Salcedo, admitted here partly because of the peculiar character of the case which would have rendered futile the concealment of his identity, partly because his excellent knowledge of the language of the accused rendered his presence as desirable to her as to the court itself.

A wooden bench ranged against the wall at the back and a stool set before the table completed the furniture of that bleak chamber.

The Lady Margaret introduced by her guarding familiars was a startlingly different figure from the cringing, panic-stricken prisoners whom the tribunal was accustomed to behold. Her demeanour was proud to the point of haughtiness. Her step was firm, she carried her head high, and between her fine brows there was a frown of impatience, of displeasure, almost of menace. Thus might a great lady frown upon impertinent underlings who obstructed her.

Her beauty, too, and the particular quality of it, was in itself a disturbing factor to these austere men. She still wore that gown of dark red velvet in which she had been carried off, with a farthingale, so narrow as to be no more than a suggestion of a farthingale, entirely failing to dissemble the supple slimness of her body. The corsage was cut low and square, revealing the snowy whiteness of her throat. Her exquisitely featured face was pale, it is true; the delicate tints had faded from it under weariness and stress. But from its pallor she seemed to gather an increased air of purity and virginity. If the lines of her mouth were resolute, they were of a resoluteness in dignity and good; if the glance of her blue eyes was steady it was a steadiness derived from a clear conscience and a proper pride.

The inquisitors considered her in silence for some seconds as she advanced. Then the cowled heads were lowered. It may be that her stateliness, her calm, her beauty and the aura of purity and worth in which she seemed to move made them tremble lest the contemplation of these outward and so often deceptive signs should cause them to weaken in the stern duty that lay before them. Only Frey Luis, his cowl thrown back from his tonsured head, continued steadily to regard her, a sombre wonder in his deep-set eyes. He was marvelling anew, no doubt, as he was presently to express it to the tribunal, that

Satan should be permitted so admirably and deceptively to empanoply his servants.

The familiar halted her before the table. Frey Juan uttered three words rapidly in Spanish, whereupon one of her guards stooped to thrust forward the stool, and made a sign to her to be seated. She looked questioningly at the Inquisitor, who bowed his head, whereupon composedly she sat down, folding her hands in her lap, and waited.

The familiars fell back at a sign from Frey Juan, who then leaned forward a little and considered her anew. Reflected light from those whitewashed walls dispelled the shadows cast about his face by the cowl. It was a lean, pallid face with solemn eyes and a wistful, sensitive mouth; a gentle, pitiful face; a face to command confidence and even affection. When he spoke his voice was low and level, gentle and persuasive. It went with his face, and, like it, possessed a rare quality of attractiveness. It was impossible to mistrust or fear a man with such a voice, at moments almost womanly in its tenderness, though always masculine in tone. The Diocesan Ordinary beside him was a shorter man, rubicund of countenance, with twinkling eyes and a humorous mouth. The Fiscal was stern-faced with deep lines in cheeks that sagged below the line of his jaw, giving him an almost doglike appearance.

The Inquisitor addressed her in English, which he spoke haltingly but without other difficulty. His knowledge of the language had led to his appointment to deal with the case. He began by asking her if she spoke Spanish or French, and when she had answered in the negative he sighed.

"Then I do what I can in your own tongue. Frey Luis Salcedo will help me if it is needful."

He might have been a physician whom she had come to consult about her health, or a Morisco merchant hoping to persuade her to make some purchases from among his Moorish wares. He proceeded, as the forms prescribed, to inquire her name, her age and her place of abode. Her replies were swiftly written down by the notary, spelled out to him by Frey Luis.

The Inquisitor passed on. "The informations we are given are that you have by misfortune been reared in the Lutheran heresy. Do you confess this?"

She smiled a little, which startled them all. It was not usual for an accused to smile in that place, especially when asked an incriminating question.

"Whether I confess it or not, sir, does not seem to me to be your concern."

It was a moment before Frey Juan recovered. Very gently then he addressed her: "It is our concern to safeguard the purity of the Faith and to suppress all that may imperil it."

"In Spain," she said. "But I am not in Spain from choice or of my own will. I have been brought here by force. I am here because of an outrage committed by a Spanish gentleman. The only concern with me of Spanish laws, whether civil or ecclesiastical, if administered with any pretence of justice, should be to right the wrong I have suffered, and to enable me to return home with the least delay. I cannot imagine myself before any Spanish court, civil or ecclesiastical, in any quality but that of an accuser and plaintiff suing for justice."

Frey Juan translated the sum of this to his fellow inquisitors. Amazement overspread their countenances in the moment of silence that followed before Frey Luis broke in: "Is more needed to establish my accusation? She stands upon forms of law, arguing with diabolical skill, like an experienced advocate. Heard any ever of a woman with the wit to do that? Observe her calm; her air of insolent contempt. Has any woman ever so confronted you? Can you doubt whence she derives her strength and whence her ready arguments?"

Frey Juan waved him into silence. "You are here as a witness, Frey Luis, not as an advocate for or against the accused. You shall speak, if you please, only to those matters upon which you may be questioned, only to the facts within your knowledge. Inferences from those facts, like judgement upon them, are for us."

Frey Luis bowed his head under the mildly delivered rebuke, and the Inquisitor passed on to answer her ladyship.

"Courts, secular and ecclesiastical, have their forms of law upon which it is lawful and proper to insist. Theirs it is to judge only of torts between man and man. But this Holy tribunal is above and apart, since its function is to judge of the torts man does to God. Here the ordinary forms of law do not weigh. We have our own forms, and we proceed, under God's guidance and by God's grace, as seems best to his holy service." He paused, then added, in his gentle voice – "I tell you this, my sister, so that you may dismiss any hope of sheltering yourself behind anything which may have only an accidental connection with your case."

Still there was no sign of dismay in those clear eyes. The frown of impatience between them grew more marked. "However contemptuous you may be of forms, and whatever the accusations you may hold against me, there yet remains a proper order of procedure, and this must compel you first to hear the accusation which I have to lodge, since the offence committed against me occurred before an offence for which it can be shown I am answerable. When you have heard this accusation, to the truth of which Frey Luis Salcedo there is a witness, and when you have redressed the wrong, whether or not you punish the offender, you will find that in redressing it all occasion for any charges against me will have disappeared. This because, as I understand you, my only offence lies in that being a Lutheran I am in Spain. I repeat that I did not come to Spain of my own will, and the righting of the wrong of which I complain will itself remove me from Spain, so that I shall cease to contaminate its saintly soil."

Frey Juan frowned and slowly shook his head. "Sister, you mock!" he sadly reproved her.

"Sometimes it is only by mockery that the truth may be rendered apparent." Then she raised her voice, and admonished them almost sternly. "Sirs, you are wasting time and abusing your powers. I am not a subject of the King of Spain, and I am not within his dominions of my own choice. England has no envoy at present in Madrid. But the envoy of France will serve my case, and I desire to appeal to him and to place myself under his protection. You cannot deny me this. You know it."

"Place yourself under God's protection, my sister. For there is no other protection can avail you now." Frey Juan grew more and more pitiful in manner, and sincerely, for he was profoundly touched to see this misguided creature using such vain pleas to battle against the holy toils in which she was taken. It was like watching the futile struggles of a netted bird, a thing to touch the heart of any compassionate man.

He conferred with his fellows; told them of her obduracy and perversity. The Fiscal Advocate thereafter spoke at length. The Ordinary added a word or two of approbation. Frey Juan inclined his head, and turned to her once more. The notary wrote briskly meanwhile.

"We are of opinion that to cut short and end all argument, we should take you upon your own ground. Your Lutheranism you have now admitted. Of this we may take a merciful view since it is an error in which you were reared. We may also, since mercy is our norm and guide, take a merciful view of your other errors since they are the more or less natural fruits of the first. But if you desire at our hands the mercy we are so ready to dispense, it is necessary that you earn it by a contrite spirit, and a full and frank confession of the sins of which you are accused."

She would have interrupted here; but his fine hand suddenly raised gave her pause. It would save time perhaps if she let him have his way and heard him out.

"The plea that you are not in Spain of your free will cannot avail you. You are in Spain as a result of the practices of which you are accused. So that the responsibility of your presence here lies as much with you as if of your own free will you had journeyed hither."

This moved her scorn and disgust. "I have heard my father say that there is no distortion of facts beyond the power of casuistical argument. I begin to perceive how shrewdly that was said."

"You do not ask of what you are accused?"

"Of carrying off Don Pedro de Mendoza," I suppose, she mocked him.

His countenance remained gently impassive. "It comes to that; it might be so expressed."

Her eyes grew round as she stared at him. Frey Luis was whispering swift interpretations to the notary, whose quill scratched briskly. For some moments it was the only sound. Then Frey Juan resumed: "You are accused of having exercised the damnable arts of sorcery against Don Pedro de Mendoza y Luna, of having bewitched him, so that, false to the faith of which he has ever been a valiant champion, false to his honour and his God, he proposed to take a heretic to wife. You are also accused of blasphemy, which is to be sought in the case of one who has abandoned herself to these diabolical practices. Do you confess your guilt?"

"Do I confess? Confess to being a witch?" It was too much for her fortitude even. She pressed her hand to her brow. "Lord! I begin to think myself in Bedlam!"

"What is that? Bedlam?" Frey Juan looked from her to Frey Luis, who explained the allusion.

Frey Juan shrugged, and continued as if she had not spoken. "So that if the accusation is true your plea that you are here because a gentleman of Spain has offended against you must fail. Your claim to appeal to the secular courts through the envoy of France or another must also fail. You are here because of an offence committed by you against a Spanish noble, entailing an infinitely greater offence against the Faith and the majesty of God which brings you within the jurisdiction of this holy tribunal. You will understand now how vain was your plea, since before any secular tribunal may hear your accusation against Don Pedro de Mendoza y Luna, it will be necessary that you clear yourself of the accusation against yourself."

She answered promptly, having by now recovered her self-command. "That should not be difficult, provided that there is any common sense in Spain. Who is my accuser? Is it Don Pedro? Does he shelter himself behind this grotesque falsehood to escape the consequences of his evil? Is it not clear to you that the testimony of such a man in such a case is not to be believed, that it would not be admissible before any tribunal having the flimsiest sense of justice?"

The Inquisitor did not answer until again he had interpreted her question, and taken the feeling of his coadjutors, and also, in this instance, of Frey Luis.

"All that," he said then, "is as clear to us as to you, and Don Pedro is not your accuser. The accusation rests upon independent testimony, and that of a man well qualified by his learning to draw conclusions." He paused a moment. "It is not the custom of this tribunal to disclose delators to an accused. But we depart from our rule, lest you should feel that you are receiving less than justice. Your accuser is Frey Luis Salcedo."

She turned her golden head to look at the friar where he sat beside the notary. Their glances met, and the stern, glowing eyes of the Dominican firmly bore the scorn of her clear regard. Slowly her glance returned to the wistful, compassionate face of Frey Juan.

"It was to Frey Luis that I appealed for protection at a time when I perceived myself to lie in the worst danger that may threaten a virtuous woman. Is that his evidence that I have practised witchcraft?"

The Inquisitor asked a question of his coadjutors. They bowed, the Fiscal rapping out a dozen words in his harsh voice, and turning as he did so to the notary. From among his papers, the notary selected a document which he handed to the Fiscal. The Fiscal glanced at it, and passed it on to Frey Juan.

"You shall hear the actual terms of the accusation," said the Inquisitor. "We show you every patience and consideration." He began to read.

And now her ladyship learnt how on the evening of her first being carried aboard the *Demoiselle*, Frey Luis had listened at the cabin door whilst Don Pedro had talked to her, and afterwards had written down what he had overheard, a deal of it in the actual words that Don Pedro had employed. The reading of the document revived her memories of that interview; what Frey Luis had set down corresponded with those memories. It was an accurate, a scrupulously accurate, report.

Amongst other of Don Pedro's sayings on that occasion to which her attention was now drawn, the following was particularly stressed by the beautifully modulated voice of the Inquisitor: "I did not ask to love you. I did not even desire it of my own volition. The desire was planted in me. It came I know not whence, a behest which there was no disobeying, compelling, overmastering."

That quotation closed the lengthy charge, seeming to supply the crowning proof and confirmation of the arguments by which Frey Luis proceeded with his accusation. In its beginnings this accusation almost appeared to be levelled at Don Pedro. It stated how he had boarded the ship which had gone to fetch him from England, bearing with him a woman whom it subsequently transpired he was abducting. Frey Luis alluded to Don Pedro's antecedents; the virtuous, honourable ways of his life; the piety which had ever marked his actions and led him to enrol himself as a lay tertiary of the Order of St Dominic, a member of the Militia Christi; the clean untainted blood that flowed in his veins. He pointed out his difficulty in believing that such a man should be spontaneously guilty of the offence which he found him in the act of committing. His relief to discover that Don Pedro included marriage in his intentions towards this woman was changed to stark horror when he discovered her to be a heretic. If it was difficult to believe that Don Pedro should have gone to such lengths of violence for the gratification of carnal lusts, it was impossible to believe that he should contemplate with equanimity the infinitely greater sin which was now disclosed. His replies to the remonstrances of Frey Luis showed that he had not given the matter a proper consideration or even ascertained what were the religious beliefs of the woman he was proposing to make his wife. This in itself betrayed a culpable negligence amounting in all the circumstances to a sin. He recognized it to the extent of permitting Frey Luis to proceed to preach conversion to this woman. But it appeared to Frey Luis that the permission was given, not out of such zeal for the Faith as men would have looked for in such a noble as Don Pedro, but merely out of expediency.

Followed in great detail an account of the friar's efforts at conversion, of their failure, of the blasphemous pleasantries and demoniacal arguments with which his endeavours were met by this heretical Englishwoman, who quoted Scripture freely and perverted it to her own ends as glibly as Satan was notoriously in the habit of doing.

It was then that he perceived the hellish source of her inspiration, and first conceived the true explanation of Don Pedro's conduct to lie in the fact that he was bewitched. This was now abundantly confirmed. There were Don Pedro's sacrilegious threats to himself in utter disregard of his sacred office and the habit which he wore; there was his violent resistance to the officers of the Inquisition at Santander and the sacrilegious shedding of blood before he was taken; but chiefly, and entirely conclusive, there was the admission of Don Pedro himself – in the words quoted – that in the matter of his unholy love for the prisoner he was driven, against his own will and desires, by a force outside of himself, whose source he did not know, whose impulse he had not the strength to resist.

What, asked Frey Luis in conclusion, could this force be, when all the circumstances were considered, but the agency of Satan, exercised by a woman who had abandoned herself to the exercise of those unholy arts? What purpose was here to be served but to introduce the corrupting poison of heresy into Spain through the bewitched person of Don Pedro and the offspring of this terrible union which he contemplated?

The reading ceased. The Inquisitor set down the last sheet before him, and his piteous eyes were levelled on her ladyship across the intervening table.

"You know now both your accuser and the precise terms of the accusation. Do you deny anything that is here set down?"

She was very still and white; there was no longer any challenge in her eyes or any shadow of smile upon her lips. She began to perceive something of the terrible toils which prejudice, superstition and fanatical reasoning had woven for her. But she made nevertheless a brave effort to defend herself.

"I deny none of the facts set down," she answered steadily. "They have been recorded with a scrupulous accuracy, such as I should have expected in a man of truth and honour. In fact they are as true as the reasoning from them is untrue, and as the deductions from them are false and fantastic."

Frey Luis translated, and the notary recorded her reply. Then Frey Juan took up the matter with her.

"To what force, other than the force here assumed, could Don Pedro possibly have been alluding in his words to you?"

"How should I know that? Don Pedro spoke in imagery, I think, seeking in fanciful terms to palliate his monstrous offence. His explanation was false, as false as are your inferences from it. It is all falsehood built on falsehood. Unreason growing from unreason. God of Mercy, it is all a nightmare! Maddening!"

Distress lent her a momentary vehemence of tone and even of gesture.

Still the Inquisitor showed only a saintly patience.

"But unless you had practised some such arts upon him, how are we to explain Don Pedro's betrayal of his honour, of his piety, of his duty and of all those things which birth and rearing are known to have rendered sacred to him? You may not know the history of the great house of Mendoza, a house unfailingly devoted to the service of God and the King, or you would understand how impossible all this would be to one of its members who had not gone mad."

On that she answered swiftly: "I do not say that he has not gone mad. Indeed, it seems the only explanation of his conduct. I have heard that men go mad for love. Perhaps – "

But the Inquisitor gently interrupted her. He was smiling wistfully.

"You are quick to make a point."

"Satan lends her all his subtlety," growled Frey Luis by way of interjection.

"You are quick to make a point," Frey Juan repeated, "and to seize on an explanation that will serve instead of the correct one. But… " He sighed and shook his head. "It is to waste time, my sister." He changed his tone. He leaned forward, setting his elbows on the table, and spoke with quiet persuasive earnestness.

"We who are to judge you," he said, "are also to help and serve you; and this is the greater of our functions towards you. The expiation of your offence is worthless unless it is sincere. And it cannot be sincere unless it is accompanied by an abjuration of the abominable arts to which the Devil has seduced you. For the Lutheran heresy which you practise we must pity rather than blame you, since this is the result of the error of your teachers. For the rest, we must also pity you, since but for the heretical teaching behind it, that would not have been possible to you. But if we are to render effective our pity, and employ it, as is our duty, to rescue your mind from error and your soul from the terrible peril of damnation, you, my sister, must co-operate with us by a full and frank confession of the offence with which you are charged."

"Confess?" she cried. "Confess to this abominable nonsense, to these false inferences?" She laughed short and mirthlessly. "I am to confess that the Lady Margaret Trevanion practices witchcraft? God help me, and God help you! You'll need more evidence, I think, than this before you can establish so grotesque a charge."

It was the Fiscal who, being informed of her words, delivered the reply that became his office, requesting Frey Luis to interpret it to her.

"The further evidence that we may need for your conviction we look to you to furnish us, and we conjure you to do it, so that your soul may be saved from everlasting hell. If contrition itself, if a sincere repentance of your faults will not suffice to draw confession from you, the Holy Office has means at its command that will lead the most recalcitrant to avow the truth."

She went cold with horror at those words so coldly uttered by Frey Luis. For a moment they robbed her of the power of speech. She was conscious of those three cowled forms immediately facing her, and the pitiful face of Frey Juan Arrenzuelo out of which two eyes regarded her with a compassion almost divine in its apparent limitlessness.

He raised a hand in dismissal of her. One of the familiars touched her shoulder. The audience was at an end – suspended, in the inquisitorial term.

Mechanically she rose, and knowing fear at last in fullest measure, she suffered herself to be led back along the chill dark corridor to her cell.

Chapter 18

Domini Canes

For two days the Lady Margaret was left to meditate in the solitude and discomfort of her prison. Her fears having been aroused by the parting words of the Fiscal Advocate, it was supposed that these might now be left to the work of sapping her resistance and obduracy.

Her meditations, however, took a turn which the inquisitors of the Faith were very far from expecting, and this she revealed when next she was brought to audience before them.

There had been a change meanwhile in the constitution of the court. Frey Juan de Arrenzuelo remained to preside, and the Diocesan Ordinary was the same rubicund and humorous-looking man whom last she had seen on the Inquisitor's right hand. But instead of the former Fiscal Advocate another had been found who understood English well and spoke it tolerably, a man this of terrifying aspect with a thin hawk-nose, a cruel, almost lipless mouth and close-set ungenerous eyes which looked as if no pitying glance had ever issued from them. The notary, too, had been changed, and his place was taken by another Dominican with sufficient knowledge of English to interpret for himself what might transpire in the course of the examination he was to record. Frey Luis was again present.

The audience was taken up by the Inquisitor at the point where it was last suspended. He began by once more entreating the accused to enable the court to use her with clemency by a full and frank confession of her sin.

If, on the one hand, the Lady Margaret had been weakened by fear and by distress, on the other she had been strengthened by indignation at the discovery which she believed that her meditations had brought her. To this indignation she now gave the full expression which she had prepared.

"Would it not better become your priestly office to depart from subterfuge?" she asked Frey Juan. "Since you claim to stand for the truth in all things, were it not better that you allow the truth to raise its head?"

"The truth! What truth?"

"Since you ask me, I will tell you. It is always possible, however improbable, that it may have escaped you. Men sometimes overlook the thing under their very feet. Don Pedro de Mendoza y Luna is a Grandee of Spain, a very great gentleman in this great kingdom. His actions are those of a villain, for which the civil courts – the secular courts, you call them – should punish him. They are also such as to render his faith suspect. Besides, as I understand it, he has committed sacrilege in threatening violence to a priest and sacrilegious murder in shedding the blood of men employed by the Holy Office. For these well-attested offences your courts of the Inquisition should punish him. There would appear to be no escape for him. But because he is a great gentleman… "

She was interrupted by the notary, who had been writing feverishly in his endeavour to keep pace with her. "Not so fast, my sister!"

Deliberately she paused, to give him time. Indeed, she desired as ardently as did he and every member of the court that her words should be recorded. Then she resumed more slowly:

"But, because he is a great gentleman, and there are inconveniences in punishing a great gentleman, who commands, no doubt, high influence, it becomes necessary to shift the blame, to find a scapegoat. It becomes necessary to discover that he was not responsible for his villainies; temporal or spiritual, that he was in fact bewitched at the time by an English heretic whose wicked and perverse will plunged him into this course for the purpose of destroying him in this world and the next."

This time it was the Fiscal Advocate who interrupted her, his voice rasping harshly.

"You increase your infamy by a suggestion so infamous."

The mild Inquisitor raised a hand to silence him. "Do not interrupt her," he begged.

"I have done, sirs," she announced. "The thing is clear, as clear and simple as it is pitiful, mean and cruel. If you persist in it, you will have to answer for it sooner or later. Be sure of that. God will not permit such wickedness to go unpunished. Nor, do I think, will man!"

Frey Juan waited until the notary had ceased to write. His compassionate eyes pondered her very solemnly.

"It is perhaps natural, reared as you have been, and ignorant as you are of us and of our sincerity, that you should attribute to us motives so worldly and so unworthy. Therefore, we do not resent it, or allow it to weigh against you. But we deny it. There is no thought in our minds to spare any man, however high-placed, who shall have offended against God. Princes of the royal blood have done penances for offences of which the Holy Office has convicted them without hesitation or fear of their power and influence. We are above such things. We will go to the fire ourselves sooner than fail in our sacred duties. Take my assurance of that, my sister, and return to your cell, further to meditate upon the matter, and I pray that God's grace may help you to a worthier view. It is clear that your mood is not yet such as would enable us profitably to continue our endeavours on your behalf."

But she would not be dismissed. She begged to be heard a moment yet in her own defence.

"What can you have to add, my sister?" wondered Frey Juan. "What can you have to urge against the evidence of the facts?" Nevertheless he waved back the familiars who had already advanced for the purpose of removing her.

"The evidence is not one of facts, but of inferences drawn from facts. No one can prove this witchcraft with which you so fantastically charge me by the direct evidence of having seen me distilling philtres, or murmuring incantations, or raising devils, or doing any of those things which witches are notoriously reputed to do. From certain effects observed in one who to my distress and dismay has been associated with me, and because this person is a great gentleman towards whom it is desired to practise leniency, inferences are drawn to inculpate me and at the same time to exculpate him. Commonest justice, then, should admit inferences to be similarly drawn in my defence."

"If they can so be drawn," Frey Juan admitted.

"They can, as I shall hope to show."

Her firmness, her candour, her dignity were not without effect upon the Inquisitor. In themselves these things seemed almost, by the evidence of character contained in them, to rebut the charge of sorcery. But Frey Juan reminded himself that appearances can be terribly deceptive, that an air of purity and sanctity is the favourite travesty used by Satan for his evil ends. He allowed her to proceed because the rules of the tribunal expressly prescribed that an accused should be encouraged to talk, since thus frequently many matters that must otherwise remain hidden were inadvertently disclosed. Calmly she posed the first of the questions she had considered and prepared in the solitude of her cell.

"If it is true that I used the arts of sorcery upon Don Pedro with the object of inducing him to take me to wife and the further object of luring him into the ways of Lutheranism which you account the ways of damnation, why did I not keep him in England, where I could in perfect safety have carried out my evil designs?"

Frey Juan turned to the Fiscal, inviting him to answer her, as his duty was. A contemptuous smile curled the man's thin lips. "Worldly considerations would suffice to influence you there. The Count of Marcos is a gentleman of great position and wealth, which you would naturally desire to share. The position would be forfeited, the wealth confiscated, once it were known that he remained in England as a result of a heretical marriage. For that offence he would have been sentenced to the fire. Because contumaciously absent he would have been burnt in effigy, to be burnt in his proper person later and without further trial at any time when he should come within reach of the arm of the Holy Inquisition." He smiled again, satisfied with the completeness of his reply, and fell silent.

"You are answered," Frey Juan informed her.

She had gone white in her dismay. "You account this piling of absurdity upon absurdity an answer?" It was a cry almost of despair. Then she recovered. "Very well," she said. "Let us test elsewhere this net which you have drawn about me. Have I your leave to interrogate my accuser?"

Frey Juan questioned with his eyes first the Diocesan, then the Fiscal. The first by a shrug and a grunt implied that the matter was of no great consequence. The second assented sharply in his rasping voice.

"Why not? Let her question by all means – *ut clavus clavo retundatur.*"

Permitted, then, she turned her gaze full upon Frey Luis, where he sat beside the industriously writing notary.

"Amongst all that you overheard when you listened at the cabin door to Don Pedro's talk with me, you heard him, whilst urging me to become his wife, inform me that there was a priest on board the ship who would marry us at once?"

"It is set down in my memorial," he answered shortly, his great eyes almost malevolent.

"Do you remember what answer I returned him?"

"You returned him no answer," said Frey Luis emphatically.

"But if I had bewitched him for the purpose of becoming his wife, should I have left such a proposal as that unanswered?"

"Silences are not to be construed as negatives," the Fiscal cut in.

She looked at the priestly advocate, and a wan smile momentarily flitted across her face.

"Let us by all means come to speech, then." And once more she turned to Frey Luis. "On the following morning when first I met you on deck, what did I say to you ?"

Frey Luis made a gesture of impatience, turning to the presiding Inquisitor.

"The answer to this is already in my memorial. I have there set down that she informed me that she had been brought aboard by force, that Don Pedro sought to coerce her into marriage, and she appealed to me for protection."

"If I had bewitched Don Pedro so as to induce him to marry me, should I have made such a complaint or should I have appealed to anyone – particularly to a priest – for protection?"

Frey Luis delivered his answer violently, the malevolence deepening in his eyes. "Have I anywhere said that you bewitched him to the end that he should marry you? How should I know the purpose of such as you? I say only that you bewitched him, else it is impossible that a God-fearing pious son of Mother Church could have thought of marriage with a heretic, that he could have threatened sacrilegious violence to a priest, or have sacrilegiously shed the blood of men discharging the sacred functions of apparitors of the Holy Office."

"If all this proves him to have been bewitched – as well it may, for I do not understand these things – how does it prove that I bewitched him?"

"How?" echoed Frey Luis, and remained staring at her with glowing eyes until prodded into answering by the Inquisitor.

"Ay. Answer that, Frey Luis," said Frey Juan in a tone which, although quiet, startled his assessors.

The truth is that – as he was subsequently to confess – a doubt had been set astir in the mind of Frey Juan Arrenzuelo. It was a vague doubt which had been started by her assertion that the whole accusation against her was made with the object of rendering her a scapegoat for the offences of Don Pedro de Mendoza y Luna. It was upon the utterance of this accusation that he had sought to dismiss her, so that before proceeding with her examination he might have leisure to make an examination of conscience and assure himself completely that there was no ground for the thing she imputed, be it in himself or in her accuser. Since then, however, her firm demeanour, which it seemed impossible to associate with any but a quiet conscience, and the strong inferential arguments contained in her questions, had served to increase his doubt.

So now he insisted upon an answer from Frey Luis to a question which he suddenly perceived that the memorial itself, to have been complete, should have raised and answered.

The Dominican's reply now took the shape of counter-questions. But he addressed himself, to the court. He found it impossible to support the glance of those clear, challenging eyes of hers. "Is it upon this alone that I base my accusation of witchcraft? Have I not set forth in detail the satanical subtlety of the answers with which she met my endeavours to convert her to the true faith? I have not dared confess, but I confess it now and cast myself upon the mercy of this sacred tribunal, that there were moments when I was in danger of coming under her infernal spells, moments when I, myself, began to doubt of truths in Holy Writ, so subtly did she pervert their meaning. It was then I knew her for a servant of the Evil One; when she mocked me and the holy words I spoke with wicked, wanton laughter." Passion inflamed him, and lent a warmth of rhetoric to his denunciation, by which his hearers were impressed. "It is not upon this thing or upon that that my conviction rests, the solemn conviction upon which I have based my accusation; but upon the aggregate of all, a sum utterly overwhelming in its terrible total." He stood tense and taut, his great dark eyes looking now straight before him into infinity, seeming to them a man inspired. "I have set down what I have clearly seen with the eyes of my soul by the Heavenly light vouchsafed them."

Abruptly he sat down, and took his head in his hands, trembling from head to foot. At the last moment his courage had failed him. He had not dared to add that to him the crowning proof of her evil arts lay in the spell which she had cast over him, to assail him in the very stronghold of his hitherto invulnerable chastity. He dared not tell them of the haunting vision of her white throat and curving breast

which had first assailed him as he sat on the hatch-coamings of the
Demoiselle, and which had constantly tormented him since then, so
much so that more than once he had faltered in his duty as her
accuser, had actually considered neglecting it on the morning that he
landed at Santander, had since been tempted to fling down the pen,
to deny the truth which he had written, and to imperil his immortal
soul by lies to save her lovely body from the fire to which in justice
it was inevitably doomed. Because her beauty assailed his senses with
all the power of some pungent overmastering perfume, because he
writhed in longing for the sight of her and in agony for the thought
of the just doom that must overtake her, he could entertain no single
doubt of her guilt. That her spells could so beat down the ramparts
of purity which years of self-denial and piety had built so solidly
about his soul was to him the crowning proof of the abominations
which she practised, of the arts by which she went to work to
weaken him whose duty it was to destroy her. Not until that fair
body, which Satan used as a lure for the perdition of men's souls,
should have been broken by the tormentor and finally reduced to
ashes at the stake would Frey Luis account performed the duty
which his conscience imposed upon him.

He heard Frey Juan quietly asking her if she was answered, and
he heard her firm reply.

"I have heard a whirl of meaningless words, protestations of
convictions of Frey Luis' own, which can hardly be accounted proof
of anything. He says that I argued with subtlety in matters of religion.
I argued out of such teaching in these matters as I have received. Is
that proof of witchcraft? Then every Lutheran, it follows, is a
witch?"

This time Frey Juan made no rejoinder. He dismissed her,
announcing the audience suspended.

But when she had been removed by the familiars, he turned to
Frey Luis. To ease the disquietude of his conscience, he now
subjected Frey Luis to an examination so minute and searching that
in the end the Fiscal Advocate remonstrated with him that in his
hands the accuser seemed to have become the accused.

Frey Juan met the remonstrance with a stern reminder. "It is not merely lawful, but desirable, to examine a delator closely; especially when, as in this instance, there is no evidence other than his own."

"There is the evidence of the facts," the Fiscal replied, "the evidence of words used by Don Pedro, which the woman admits herself to have been correctly reported, and there is what Don Pedro himself cannot deny."

"And," ventured Frey Luis, with the fierce vehemence of righteous exasperation, "there is her own heresy which she has admitted. To a heretic all things are possible."

"But because all things are possible," he was quietly answered, "we are not to convict a heretic of all things beside heresy, unless we have abundant proof."

"To ease your mind, Frey Juan, were it not best to put her to the question at once?" suggested the Fiscal Advocate. And Frey Luis, swept by his emotions, made echo to that.

"The question, ay! The question! Let torture wring the truth from her evil stubbornness. Thus shall you have the confirmation that you need for sentence."

Frey Juan's countenance was stern; all compassion, all wistfulness had departed from his eyes. He turned them almost angrily upon the Fiscal.

"To ease my mind?" he echoed. "Do I sit here in this seat of judgement to ease my mind? What is my ease of mind, what my torment of mind, compared with the service of the Faith? The truth of these matters shall be reached in the end, however long we labour to extract it. But we shall extract it for the greater honour and glory of God and not for my ease of mind or the ease of mind of any living man." He rose abruptly, leaving the Fiscal Advocate silenced and abashed. Frey Luis would have interrupted again. But he was sternly reminded that he was not a member of that court, nor entitled to speak there save when bidden as a witness.

In the silence that followed, Frey Juan took up the notes which the notary had made. He read them carefully. "Let copies be sent to the Inquisitor-General this evening, as he has required."

Now, the Inquisitor-General of Castile, Gaspar de Quiroga, Cardinal-Archbishop of Toledo's special interest in this case was sprung from the fact that Don Pedro de Mendoza y Luna, as we know, was his own nephew, his only sister's child cherished by him in the place of the son which his vows denied him. This fact, notorious throughout Spain, it was which had rendered the Inquisitors of Oviedo fearful of dealing with Don Pedro's case and had brought them to the decision of referring it to Toledo, where it could be under the eye of the Inquisitor-General himself.

The Cardinal was profoundly distressed and perturbed. Whatever the outcome, and however much of the blame a scapegoat might be made to bear, the fact remained that Don Pedro had grievously offended. It would be held that he could not have so offended had he not lapsed from grace by some action of his own, and for this it was impossible that he should escape punishment. Some heavy penance he would certainly have to perform to satisfy the requirements of a tribunal which had not hesitated in its time to impose penances upon princes of the blood. Short of that it would be said that his uncle made an unworthy use of his mighty and sacred office to favour his own relatives and to relieve them of the payment of their just dues. Obstacles enough were placed already in the path of the Inquisitor-General by a King who with difficulty curbed his jealousy by any usurpation of power in his dominions, by a Pope who could hardly be said to approve of the lengths to which the Holy Office carried its ardour in Spain, and by the Jesuits who missed few opportunities of marking their resentment of the interferences and even persecutions which they had suffered at the hands of their Inquisition.

Nor would Don Pedro by his conduct, whether before the court appointed to examine him or in the private audiences to which his uncle summoned him from the prison of the Holy House where he was meanwhile confined, do anything to lighten the task before the Inquisitor-General.

He laughed to furious scorn the charge of witchcraft levelled against Margaret, refused utterly to avail himself of the escape which such an accusation against her offered him, denounced himself for a scoundrel in his dealings with her, and regarded his present difficulties as the natural and proper punishment which he had brought upon himself. He would accept it, he announced, with fortitude and resignation but for the knowledge that his own villainy and the stupid bigotry of his judges had implicated Margaret with him and placed her in a position of danger, of the full terrors of which she would herself be scarcely aware as yet.

To his uncle in private and, what was infinitely worse, to the Inquisitors deputed by his uncle to examine him in the court over which Frey Juan de Arrenzueio presided, he persisted in the assertion that because of his rank and his relationship with the Inquisitor-General it was sought to spare him the consequences of his acts by a trumped-up tale of his having been bewitched. The Lady Margaret, he assured his judges, hectoring them boldly and angrily, had practised against him no magic but the magic of her beauty, her virtue and her charm. If these were arts of sorcery, then half the young women in the world might be sent to the stake, for at some time or other and against some man or other they had all exercised them.

It was mad enough to have Don Pedro thus insisting upon incriminating himself, arid saying no word that helped forward the incrimination of the heretical woman who was at the root of all this distressing business. To insist, almost as if attempting to persuade him, that his very words and demeanour were but proofs that the sorcery was still working briskly in his veins, was merely to render him ribald and offensive in his exasperation. He called the inquisitors dolts, asses in stupidity and mules in obstinacy, and did not even hesitate to tell them on one occasion that he believed it was they who were possessed of devils, so infernally did they corrupt all things to their own predetermined ends, so damnably did they corrupt truth into falsehood.

"The truth to you, sirs, is what you desire to think it is, not what every sane evidence may reveal it. You desire no evidence save that which will confirm your egregious preconceptions. There is no animal in the world so hot on a false scent and so persistent as you Dominicans. Domini canes!" Deliberately he broke the word into two, and saw by their resentful eyes that they had caught the insult he intended. He repeated it again and yet again, rendering it each time more clearly an invective, and finally translating it into Spanish for them to make quite sure that his meaning did not elude them. "Dogs of the Lord! Hounds of God! That is what you call yourselves. I wonder what God calls you?"

The audience was immediately suspended, and word was sent to Cardinal Quiroga of his nephew's extravagant words and indecent conduct, which left little doubt now in the mind of any of his examiners that he was indeed the victim of arts of witchcraft. But Frey Juan now added a note to the effect that however persuaded they might be of this, yet the evidence was hardly sufficient to justify sentence of the woman Margaret Trevanion upon the charge of sorcery, wherefore he submitted to the Inquisitor-General that this accusation against her should be abandoned, and that the court should proceed upon the charge of heresy alone. If she was indeed a witch, she would still suffer for it in suffering for the offence which was provable against her. A grand *Auto de Fé* was preparing in Toledo for the following Thursday, the 26th of October – Frey Juan wrote on Thursday the 19th – and the charge of heresy could be disposed of so that the accused should suffer then, whilst Don Pedro should at the same time purge his offence by some penance in that *Auto* which the Inquisitors would determine and lay before his eminence for approval.

Chapter 19

Philip II

At the very hour in which the Inquisitor-General in Toledo was considering the vexatious matters contained in Frey Juan de Arrenzuelo's communication, Sir Gervase Crosby was seeking audience of King Philip II at the Escurial.

Fifteen days had been spent between Greenwich and Madrid, fifteen days of ageing torment, during which impatience at the slowness of their progress had almost made him mad. Whilst his Margaret in her peril was so instantly needing him, he found himself crawling like a slug across the spaces of the earth to reach her. The voyage was a nightmare. It had the effect of transmuting the buoyant, lighthearted lad into a man who was stern of countenance and of heart, with a sternness which was never thereafter quite to leave him.

They came at last into the bay of Santander, six days after the Demoiselle had cast anchor there. Contrary winds had delayed them. In making the port of Santander they had no thought of following in the track of the vessel in which her ladyship had been carried off. They made it because it was the first port of consequence and the most convenient whence to continue the journey to Madrid, which was Sir Gervase's goal. Idle to seek to ascertain whither the Lady Margaret had been taken; idle to attempt to follow her until armed with those powers which he hoped to wring from the King of Spain.

Therefore it was the King of Spain, that fabulously mighty prince, whom he must seek in the first instance.

The *Rose of the World* flew no flag to announce her nationality as she came to anchor in those Spanish waters. If Sir Oliver Tressilian was fearless, he was also prudent. He would face whatever perils might be thrust upon him. But he would not go about the world inviting peril by any unnecessary jactancy.

Yet the lack of a flag had much the same effect to have been expected from the display of one belonging to a hostile nation. Within an hour of casting anchor in the bay, two great black barges came alongside the Rose of the World. They were filled with men in steel caps and shimmering corselets, armed with pikes and musketoons, and the first of them bore the Regidor of Santander in person, who came to inquire the nationality and business of this vessel, which with a row of cannon thrusting their noses from her open ports had much the appearance of a fighting craft.

Sir Oliver ordered the ladder to be lowered, and invited the Regidor to come aboard, nor made any objection when six soldiers followed him as a guard of honour.

To the King's representative in Santander, a short pompous gentleman inclining although still young to corpulence, Sir Gervase made known in the execrable but comprehensible Spanish which he had been at pains to learn during his voyage with Drake, that he was a courier from the Queen of England with letters for King Philip of Spain. In confirmation of this he displayed the package with its royal seals and royal superscription.

This earned him black looks together with courteous words from the Regidor, Don Pablo de Lamarejo. Royal messengers he knew were sacred, even when they happened to be English and heretics ripe for damnation, and deserving on that and other accounts no mercy or even consideration from any God-fearing man. He supposed that the vessel and crew employed to bring the messenger were to lie under the same protecting aegis of international custom, and he even undertook, in response to Sir Oliver's request, to send out supplies of fresh water and provisions.

Sir Gervase went ashore alone in the Regidor's barge. He had requested to land a couple of men of his own to accompany him as servants. But the Regidor, with the utmost outward suavity, had insisted upon supplying Sir Gervase with a couple of Spaniards for the purpose, who would be so much more useful to him by virtue of their knowledge of the country and the language. Sir Gervase perfectly understood the further intention which was that they should act as his guards. Whilst the Regidor did not in any way dare to hinder him, at the same time he deemed it prudent to take such measures as should make this Queen's messenger virtually a prisoner during his sojourn in Spain or until the King's majesty should expressly decree otherwise.

This to Sir Gervase was a matter of no account. So that he reached the King with the least delay, he cared not in what circumstances he reached him. They could have carried him to Madrid bound hand and foot had they so chosen.

Sir Oliver Tressilian was to remain at Santander to await his return. Should he not have returned within exactly one month, nor sent any message, Sir Oliver was to assume failure and go home to report it to the Queen. On that understanding the friends parted, and Sir Gervase, whose countenance, pallid under its sunburn, was become almost that of a Spaniard in colour and in gravity, set out for Madrid with his two alguaziles who pretended to be grooms. They made as good speed as the mountainous country and the infrequent change of horses would permit. They travelled by way of Burgos, famous as having been the birthplace of the Cid, and of Roman Segovia on its rocky summit with its Flavian aqueduct. But for these and other marvels of man and of nature Sir Gervase had no thought or care. The eyes of his soul were set feverishly ahead, towards that Madrid where he should find an end to his torturing suspense, and perhaps – if God were very good to him – find healing for his despair.

Six days did that land journey consume. And even then it was not ended. The King was at the Escurial, that vast monastery palace on the slopes of the Guadarrama Mountains lately completed for him by artists and craftsmen whom he had hampered at every turn by the intrusion of his own abominable tastes and opinions in matters of architecture and decoration.

It was late evening when Gervase and his companions reached the capital, and so they were forced to lie there until the morrow. Thus the circle of a full week on Spanish soil had been completed before Sir Gervase beheld the enormous palace which contained the monarch of half the world. Grey, austere, forbidding stood that edifice, built, it was said, upon the plan of the gridiron upon which St Lawrence suffered martyrdom. The skies were themselves grey that morning and may have heightened the illusion which made the granite mass seem almost a part of the Guadarrama Mountains that were its background, made it appear to have been planted there by nature rather than by man.

Afterwards, in retrospect, that noontide seemed to him a dream, leaving vague and misty impressions. There was a great courtyard, where magnificently-equipped soldiers paraded; a wide staircase of granite by which an officer to whom he announced his errand conducted him to a long vaulted gallery, whose small windows overlooked the quadrangle of the royal wing. Here a throng moved and hummed: courtiers in rich black, captains in steel, prelates in purple and in scarlet, and monks in brown, in grey, in white and in black.

They stood in groups or sauntered there, and the subdued murmur of their voices filled the place. They looked askance at this tall young man with his haggard eyes and cheeks that were grown swarthy under a mane of crisp auburn hair, outlandishly dressed in clothes that were stained by travel and with long boots on which the dust lay thickly.

But it was soon seen that he had some greater claim to audience than any of those who had been waiting there since Mass, for without delay came an usher to sweep him from that gallery, and to conduct him by way of an anteroom, where he was relieved of his weapons, into the royal presence. Sir Gervase found himself in a small chamber of a monastic severity, where his nostrils were assailed by the nauseous smell of medicinal unguents. The walls were whitewashed and without decoration beyond that supplied by a single picture representing an infernal zodiac made up of the whirling, flaming figures of demons and of damned.

In the room's middle stood a square table of dark oak, plain and unadorned, such as might be seen in any abbot's refectory. It bore a little heap of parchments, an inkstand and some quills.

In a Gothic wooden chair of monastic plainness, beside this table, his right elbow resting upon the edge of it, sat the greatest monarch of his day, the lord of half the world. To behold him was to experience in extreme measure the shock which the incongruous must ever produce. It is probably common to all men to idealize the wielders of royal power and royal dignity, to confound in imagination the man with the office which he holds. The great title this man bore, the great dominions over which his word was law, so fired men's fancy that the very name of Philip II conjured a vision of superhuman magnificence, of quasi-divine splendour.

Instead of some such creation of his fancy, Sir Gervase beheld a small, sickly, shrivelled old man, with a bulging forehead and pale blue, almost colourless, eyes set fairly close to a pinched, aquiline nose. The mouth was repulsive, with its under jaw thrusting grotesquely forward, its pallid lips, which gaped perpetually to reveal a ruin of teeth. A tuft of straggling fulvid beard sprouted from his elongated chin, a thin bristle of moustache made an untidy fringe above. His hair, once thick and golden, hung now in thin streaks that were of the colour of ashes.

He sat with his left leg, which was gouty and swathed, stretched across a cushioned stool. He was dressed entirely in black, and for only ornament wore the collar and insignia of the Golden Fleece about his narrow ruff. Quill in hand, he was busily annotating a document, and in this occupation continued for some moments after Sir Gervase's admission, entirely ignoring his presence. At length he passed the document to a slim man in black who stood on his left, This was Santoyo, his valet, who received it, and dusted the wet writing with sand, whilst the King, still ignoring Gervase's presence, took up another parchment from the pile at his elbow and proceeded to deal with it in the same way.

In the background, against the wall, two writing-tables were ranged, and at each of these sat a secretary, writing busily. It was to one of these, a little hairy black-bearded fellow, that the valet delivered the document he had received from the royal hand.

Behind the King, very tall and straight, stood a middle-aged man in the black habit and long mantle of a Jesuit. This, as Sir Gervase was presently to discover, was Father Allen, who might be regarded as the ambassador at the Escurial of the English Catholics, and who stood high in the esteem of King Philip. In the deep embrasure of one of the two windows by which the chamber was abundantly lighted stood Frey Diego de Chaves, Prior of Santa Cruz, a heavily-built man of jovial countenance.

The royal pen scratched and spluttered on the margin of the document. Sir Gervase waited as immovable and patient as the officer who had conducted him, who remained a few paces behind him now. As he waited he continued in increasing wonder to consider this mean, insignificant embodiment of the hereditary principle, and there surged in his mind the image of some unclean spider seated in the very heart of his great web.

At last the second document was passed to Santoyo, and the ice-cold eyes under that bulging brow flashed a fleeting furtive glance upon the stalwart, dignified gentleman who stood so patiently before him. The pallid lips moved, and from between them issued a voice, low of pitch, dead-level of tone and very rapid of speech. This utterance, which so commonly exasperated foreign envoys by its elusiveness, sounded like nothing so much as the heavy hum of an insect in that quiet room. His Majesty had spoken in Spanish. As ill-educated and unlettered as he was cruel, pusillanimous and debauched, this lord of half the world spoke no language but his own, could read no language but his own, save only a little schoolboy's Latin.

Sir Gervase had a knowledge of Spanish sufficient for ordinary purposes. But of the King's speech he had caught no single word. He stood undecided a moment until Father Allen, acting as interpreter, revealed his own English origin.

"His Majesty says, sir, that he understands you to be the bearer of letters from the Queen of England."

Sir Gervase plucked the sealed package from the bosom of his doublet and advanced to proffer it.

"Kneel, sir!" the Jesuit commanded, sharp and sternly.

Sir Gervase obeyed, going down on one knee before the monarch.

Philip of Spain put forth a hand that was like the hand of a corpse. It was of the colour and transparency of wax. He took the package, seemed to weigh it a moment whilst he read the superscription in the unmistakable writing of Elizabeth of England. Then he turned it over and considered the seals: His lips writhed into a sneer, and again there came from him that rapid dead-level murmur of speech, the import of which this time eluded all present.

At last with a half-shrug he broke the seals, spread the sheet before him, and read.

Sir Gervase, who had risen again and stepped back, watched the royal countenance with anxious, straining interest. He saw the frown gradually descend to the root of that predatory nose, saw the lips writhe again, and the hand that held the sheet tremble violently as if suddenly palsied. If he thought and hoped that this reflected fear, he was soon disillusioned. The King spoke again, and this time, for all the rapidity of his utterance, rage lent a power to his voice to make it audible throughout the chamber. Sir Gervase heard his words clearly and understood them as clearly.

"The insolent bastard heretic!" was what he said, and saying it, crumpled the offending letter in his lean hand as he would have crumpled the writer could that same hand have encompassed her.

The scratching of the secretaries' pens was suddenly suspended. Santoyo, at his master's elbow, Father Allen behind his chair, and Frey Diego in the window embrasure, stood immovable and appeared to have ceased to breathe. A deathly stillness followed that explosion of royal wrath from a prince who rarely suffered any outward sign of emotion to escape him.

At the end of a long pause, in which he resumed his icy composure, the King spoke again. "But is it possible that I am mistaken; that I do not understand; that I misinterpret?" He smoothed the crumpled sheet again. "Allen, do you read it for me; translate it to me," he commanded. "Let me lie under no error."

The Jesuit took the letter, and as he read currently translated its message into Spanish in a voice of increasing horror.

Thus was it that Sir Gervase became acquainted with the precise tenor of the Queen's message.

Elizabeth of England had in her time written many letters that her counsellors must have accounted terrible; but never a letter more terrible than this one. It was terrible in its very brevity and lucidity, considering the message it conveyed. She had chosen to write in Latin, and in this she informed her brother-in-law, King Philip the Second of Spain and First of Portugal, that a subject of his, a gentleman of his nobility, named Don Pedro de Mendoza y Luna, who, being shipwrecked upon her shores, had received shelter and comfort in an English house, had repaid the hospitality by forcibly carrying off the daughter of that house, the Lady Margaret Trevanian. The bearer would give His Majesty further details of this if he desired them. She passed on to remind the Majesty of Spain that in her prison of the Tower of London lay under her hand the Spanish Admiral Don Pedro Valdez and seven noble Spanish gentlemen, besides others taken with him on the Andalusian flagship; and she warned His Majesty, taking God to witness, that unless the Lady Margaret Trevanian were returned safe and scatheless to her home, and unless the bearer of this letter, Sir Gervase Crosby, and his companions, who were going to Spain so as to serve as escort to the lady, were afforded safe-conduct and offered no least injury of any sort, she would send her brother, King Philip, the heads of Don Pedro Valdez and his seven noble companions; and this in despite of all usages of war and practices of nations that he might urge.

Utter silence followed the reading for a moment. Then the King broke it by a laugh, a short, horrible cackle of scorn.

"I read aright, it seems." Then, in another tone, raising his voice to an unusual pitch: "How long, O Lord, will you suffer this Jezebel?" he cried out.

"How long, indeed!" echoed Father Allen.

In the window-embrasure Frey Diego seemed turned to stone. His florid countenance had become grey.

King Philip sat huddled, musing. Presently he made a gesture of contempt. "This," he said, "is a puerile insolence! An idle threat! Such a thing could not be. Her own barbarous people would not permit such a barbarity. It is an attempt to frighten me with shadows. But I, Philip of Spain, do not start at shadows."

"Your Majesty will find it no shadow when those eight heads are delivered to you."

It was Gervase who had spoken, with a temerity that spread consternation in the room.

The King looked at him and looked away again. It was not in King Philip's power to look any man steadily in the face.

"You spoke, I think?" he said softly. "Who bade you speak?"

"I spoke what seemed necessary," said Gervase, unintimidated.

"What seemed necessary, eh? So that necessity is the excuse? I am learning, sir. I am learning. I never weary of learning. There are some other things you might tell me since you are so eager to be heard." The menace of his cold rapid voice and his dead reptilian gaze were terrible. They seemed to suggest endless resources and utter remorselessness in their employment. He half-turned his head, to summon one of the secretaries. "Rodriguez! Your tablets. Note me his replies." Then he glanced at Sir Gervase again. "You have companions, this letter tells me. Where are those companions?"

"At Santander, awaiting my return on board the ship that brought me."

"And if you do not return?"

"If I am not on board by the thirteenth of November, they sail for England to report to Her Majesty that you prefer to receive the heads of your eight gentlemen rather than administer in your own realm the justice which decency demands."

The King sucked in his breath. From behind him Father Alien admonished this daring man in English.

"Sir, bethink you to whom you speak! I warn you in your own interests."

The King made a gesture to silence him. "What is the name of the ship that is waiting in Santander?"

There was contemptuous defiance in the readiness with which Sir Gervase answered.

"The *Rose of the World* out of the Fal River. She is commanded by Sir Oliver Tressilian, an intrepid gentleman who understands the art of sea fighting. She carries twenty guns and a good watch is kept on board."

The King smiled at the veiled threat. Its insolence was of a piece with the rest. "We may test the intrepidity of this gentleman."

"It has been tested already, Your Majesty, and by your own subjects. It is likely if they test it again that they will do so to their own cost as heretofore. But if it should happen that the *Rose of the World* is prevented from sailing and is not home by Christmas, the heads will come to you for a New Year's gift."

Thus in rough, ungrammatical but perfectly comprehensible Spanish did Sir Gervase bait the lord of half the world. It inflamed his rage that this almost inhuman prince should be concerned here only with the hurt to his own dignity and vanity, and should give no thought to the misdeed of Don Pedro de Mendoza, and the horrible suffering caused an innocent lady.

But now, having drawn forth what knowledge he required, King Philip changed his tone.

"As for you, you English dog, who match in insolence the evil woman who sent you on this audacious errand, you, too, have something to learn before we finally dismiss you." He raised a quivering hand. "Take him away, and keep him fast until I need him again."

"My God!" cried Gervase in horror, as the officer's hand closed upon his shoulder. And because of his tone, and of a movement that he made, the officer's grip tightened, and he plucked a dagger from his girdle. But Gervase, heedless of this, was appealing in his own tongue to Father Allen.

"You, sir, who are English, and who seem to have influence here, can you remain indifferent when an English woman, a noble English lady, has been carried off in this manner by a Spanish satyr?"

"Sir," the Jesuit coldly answered him, "you have done your cause a poor service by your manner."

The officer pulled him forcibly back. "Let us go!" he said.

But still Sir Gervase protested. He appealed now in Spanish to the King. "I am a messenger, and my person should be sacred."

The King sneered at him. "A messenger? Impudent buffoon!" And by a cold wave of the hand he put an end to the matter.

Raging, but impotent, Sir Gervase went. From the doorway, over his shoulder whilst the officer was forcibly thrusting him out, he called back to the Majesty of Spain.

"Eight noble Spanish heads, remember! Eight heads which your own hands will have cut off!"

At last he was outside, and men were being summoned to take charge of him.

Chapter 20

The King's Conscience

You have beheld an unusual spectacle. That of King Philip II of Spain acting upon impulse and under the sway of passion. It was conduct very far from his habit. Patience was the one considerable – perhaps the only – virtue in his character, and to his constant exercise of it he owed such greatness as he had won.

"God and Time and I are one," was his calm boast, and sometimes he asserted that, like God, he moved against his enemies with leaden feet, but smote with iron hands.

It was not by any means the only matter in which he perceived a likeness between God and himself, but it is the only one with which at the moment we need be concerned. For here, for once, you behold him departing from it, yielding to an impulse of rage provoked by the outrageous tone of that message from the detestable Elizabeth.

This letter, with its cold threat of perpetrating an abomination revolting to all equity and humanity, he must regard as an impudent attempt to intimidate and coerce him. And further to incense him there had been added to the incredible insolence of the letter the even more incredible insolence of its bearer.

As he presently informed Father Allen, it was as if, having slapped his face with that impudent communication, she had entrusted its delivery to a messenger who was to administer a kick on his own behalf. In all his august career he could not remember to have had a

211

man stand before his face with such contumely and so little awe of his quasi-divinity. Is it any wonder that this demi-god, accustomed only to incense, should have found his nostrils irritated by that dose of pepper, and that under this irritation he should have come so human as to sneeze?

He was certainly the wrong man with whom such liberties could be taken, and of all moments in his life the present was certainly the moment in which his temper could least brook them. At another time he might have sustained his patience by the conviction of a heavy reckoning to be presented to the arrogant bastard who usurped the throne of England; he might have smiled at these stings of a gnat which in his own good time his mighty hand should crush. But now, in the season of his humiliation, his great fleet dispersed and shattered, with scarcely a noble house in Spain that did not mourn a son, his strength so exhausted that it would hardly be in his own lifetime that the King of Spain would recover sufficiently to make himself feared again upon the seas, he was denied even this consolation. To the shattering blow delivered to his consequence in the world were added now such personal insults as these, which he could punish only by petty vengeances upon worthless underlings.

He bethought him of other letters which Elizabeth of England had written him, defiant, mocking letters, now bittersweet, now caustically sarcastic. He had smiled his patient, cruel smile as he read them. He could afford to smile then, in his assurance that the day of reckoning would surely come. But now that by some incomprehensible malignity of fortune he was cheated of that assurance, now that the day of reckoning was overpast, having brought him only shame and failure, he could smile no longer at her insults, could bear them no longer with the dignified calm that becomes a demi-god.

But if weakened, he was not yet so weak that he could with impunity be mocked, coerced and threatened...

"She shall learn," he said to Father Allen, "that the King of Spain is not to be moved by threats. This insolent dog who was here and those others with him on that ship at Santander, heretics all, like her pestilent heretical self, are the concern of the Holy Office." He turned to the bulky figure in the window-embrasure. "Frey Diego, this becomes your affair."

Frey Diego de Chaves stirred at last to life again, and moved slowly forward. His dark eyes under bushy grey eyebrows were preternaturally solemn. He delivered himself now of some commonsense in a deep rich voice.

"It is not Your Majesty who is threatened so much as those unfortunate gentlemen who have served you well, and who languish now in an English prison awaiting the ransoms that are being sent from Spain."

The King blinked his pale eyes. Sullenly, impatiently, he corrected the Prior's statement.

"They are being threatened only in their lives. I am threatened in my dignity and honour, which are the dignity and honour of Spain."

Frey Diego had come to lean heavily upon the heavy oaken table. "Will the honour of Spain be safe if she suffers this threat to be executed upon her sons?"

The King gave him one of his furtive glances; whereupon the Dominican continued: "The nobility of Spain has been bled white in this disastrous enterprise against England. Can Your Majesty afford to add to the blood that has been already shed that of so great and valuable a servant as Valdez, the greatest of your surviving captains of the sea, that of Ortiz, of the Marquis of Fuensalida, of Don Ramon Chaves, of – "

"Your brother, eh?" the King snapped to interrupt him. "Behold your impulse! A family concern."

"True," said the friar gravely. "But is it not a family concern also for Your Majesty? Does not all Spain compose the family of the King, and are not her nobles the first-born of that family? This insolent Englishman who was lately here and his shipmates at Santander, what are they to set in the balance against those Spanish gentlemen in London? You may fling them to the Holy Office for heretics, as is your right, indeed almost your duty to the Faith, but how will that compensate for the eight noble heads – eight truncated, bleeding heads – which the Queen of England will cast into Your Majesty's lap?"

His Majesty started visibly, appalled by the vivid phrase. It was as if he beheld those bleeding heads in his lap already. But he recovered instantly.

"Enough!" he rapped. "I do not yield to threats." But the source of his strength of spirit was revealed by what he added: "They are threats which that woman will not dare to execute. It would earn her the execration of the whole world." He swung to the Jesuit. "Am I not right, Allen?"

The Englishman avoided a direct answer. "You are dealing, Majesty, with a Godless, headstrong woman, a female antichrist without regard for any laws of God or man."

"But this!" cried the King, clinging to the belief in what he hoped.

"Execrable as it would be, it is no more execrable than the murder of the Queen of Scots. That, too, was a deed that all the world believed she would never dare."

Here was a blow to the faith he built on Elizabeth's fear of the world's judgement. It brought him to doubt whether, indeed, he might not be building upon sand. It was a doubt that angered him, That he should yield to that detestable woman's threats was a draught too bitter for his lips. He could not, would not, swallow it, however men might seek to press the cup upon him. He said so harshly, and upon that dismissed both the Jesuit and the Dominican.

But when they were gone he found it impossible to resume, as he had intended, work upon those documents awaiting his attention. He sat there, shivering with anger as he read again the offensive letter or recalled again the offensive bearing of the messenger.

At long last his mind came to the matter which had provoked the threat. In his wrath at the effect, he had hitherto neglected to cast so much as a glance upon the cause. He pondered it now. What tale was this? Was it even true? The *Concepcion* which Don Pedro de Mendoza had commanded had been definitely reported lost with all hands.

How, then, came Don Pedro alive? The letter itself told him. He had been sheltered in an English household. He had escaped, then. And according further to this letter, he had returned to Spain bringing with him the daughter of the house in question. But if so, how came it that there was no word of this return, that Don Pedro had not come to report himself and pay his duty to his King?

One man might know: The Cardinal-Archbishop of Toledo, who was Don Pedro's uncle.

His Majesty summoned the secretary Rodriguez, and dictated a brief command to the Primate to wait upon him instantly at the Escurial. The Cardinal might enlighten him upon this, and at the same time he would take order with him as Inquisitor-General for dealing with these other English heretics now lying in his power.

A courier was instantly dispatched, with orders to ride all night and spare neither himself nor horseflesh.

On that the King sought to dismiss the matter for the present from his mind, to be resumed anon in consultation with the Inquisitor-General. But the matter would not be dismissed. The image excited by the vivid phrase of Frey Diego de Chaves persisted. Ever and anon as the King looked into his lap he beheld there a little heap of bleeding, truncated heads. One of them showed him the stern features of the brave Valdez, who had served him so well, and might but for this have lived to serve him better; the glazed eyes of the Marquis of Fuensalida looked up at him with undying reproach, as did the others. He had let those heads fall so that he might preserve his dignity. But how had he preserved it? If the act should bring execration upon Elizabeth who had executed it, what must it bring upon him who might have averted it but would not? He covered his reptilian eyes with his corpse-like hands in a futile attempt to shut out a vision that lay within his brain. Obstinately his purpose hardened before an opposition arising, as he accounted it, from a weakness in his nature. He would not yield.

Late on the following evening, whilst the King was at supper, eating, as he did all things, alone, Cardinal Quiroga was announced.

He bade him in at once, and only momentarily interrupted his consumption of pastry to greet the Primate.

From this interview he derived at last great comfort and assurance. Not only was Don Pedro in the prison of the Inquisition, but so was the woman he had carried off from England. She was accused of heresy and witchcraft. It was the exercise of her arts upon Don Pedro which had plunged him into offences against the Faith. He was to expiate these offences by doing penance in the great *Auto de Fé* which was to be held in Toledo on the following Thursday. In that same *Auto* the woman would be abandoned to the secular arm to be burnt as a witch, together with some others whom the Cardinal enumerated. He expressed a hope in passing that His Majesty would grace the *Auto* by his royal presence.

The King took a fresh piece of pastry from the gold dish, crammed it into his royal mouth, licked his fingers, and asked a question. What was the evidence of witchcraft against this woman?

The Inquisitor-General, familiar now with the particulars of a case which so closely concerned his nephew, returned a full and detailed answer.

The King sat back and half-closed his eyes. His lips smiled a little. He was extremely satisfied. The ground was cut from under his feet. His duty to the Faith made it impossible for him to yield to the demands of Elizabeth. Aforetime and successfully when protests had been addressed to him from England on behalf of seamen who had fallen into the hands of the Inquisition, he had replied that it was idle to appeal to him for anything that lay outside the province of the secular power in Spain. In matters of the Faith, in the province of God, he had no power to interfere with the proceedings of the Holy Office to which he might himself be amenable did he offend against religion. And this was no piece of hypocrisy. It was entirely sincere. As sincere as was now his thankfulness that if those noble Spanish heads must fall as a consequence, none could reproach him with it. The whole world should hear his answer to the Queen of England; that not by him, but by the Holy Office, had judgement been passed upon crimes against the Faith; if meanly to avenge this upon guiltless gentlemen she took their innocent lives, there being against them no charge to warrant putting them to death, the responsibility for that dark deed must lie upon her evil soul as surely as it must earn her the contempt and reprobation of the world.

And since his duty to the Faith, whose foremost champion he was, now bound his hands, he need fear no more the vision of those bloody heads in his lap.

Of all this, however, he said nothing to Quiroga. He thanked His Eminence for information which he had been driven to seek, because a rumour had reached him that Don Pedro de Mendoza was alive, and so dismissed him.

That night the King of Spain slept peacefully as do men whose consciences are tranquil.

Chapter 21

The Cardinal's Conscience

After Vespers on Sunday which the Cardinal-Archbishop had returned to celebrate in person in Toledo, having for the purpose quitted the Escurial at dawn and travelled at a speed possible only to royal or inquisitorial personages. His Eminence took up the papers concerned with the case of his errant nephew. He recalled that when the royal messenger had arrived to summon him to the Escurial he had been on the point of sending for the Inquisitor Arrenzuelo so as to discuss with him certain points which remained obscure.

Having refreshed his memory upon those points, which were contained in the appended note from Arrenzuelo, having indeed given them now an attention – prompted by his recent interview with the King – which they had not at first received, the Inquisitor-General found himself assailed by something of the uneasiness in which Frey Juan wrote. It appeared to him that they were here upon the edge of complexities which Arrenzuelo himself had failed to appreciate. He sent for him at once, and Frey Juan was prompt and even eager to obey the summons.

Honest and God-fearing, Frey Juan de Arrenzuelo never hesitated frankly and fully to express the doubts by which he was assailed, once the Inquisitor-General had invited him to do so.

He began by confessing that all might well be as Frey Luis Salcedo so cogently reasoned in his accusation. But in his conscience he could not account the accusation of witchcraft proven. Because, for Don Pedro's sake, he desired to account it proven he must practise the greater vigilance over his judgement. It was so perilously easy to believe what one desired to believe. The acts and words from which Frey Luis made his deductions, although clearly of the utmost gravity in the aggregate, might nevertheless be susceptible of interpretations quite other than those which he placed upon them.

It might well be, for instance, as Don Pedro himself insisted, that the only magic the woman had used had been the magic which Nature places in the hands of every woman. God had placed women in the world to test men's fortitude. Don Pedro might have succumbed; and, succumbing, have grown unmindful of all those guides of conduct proper to a God-fearing man. In his desire to make this woman his wife he had neglected to ascertain that she was a Lutheran. This in itself was serious. But, after all, Don Pedro had immediately perceived its seriousness when pointed out to him, and had been ready, even eager, that the woman should be converted to the true faith. The words he had used to her, where he spoke of forces outside himself which had driven him to love her, words to which Frey Luis attached so much importance, might also be no more than the fantastic vapourings of a lovelorn man. Frey Juan did not say that any of this was so. He merely displayed the doubts which had come to afflict him on this question of sorcery. He concluded with the statement that the woman was of an unusual and commanding beauty, such as had often driven men to extravagances of conduct.

Cardinal Quiroga, a tall, handsome, vigorous man of fifty, imposing in his scarlet robes, sat stern and thoughtful, his hands clasping and unclasping the carved arms of his great chair. They were beautiful hands, and it was said that to preserve their beauty of texture he wore, whilst sleeping, mittens that were rubbed in lamb's fat. He looked at the tall Dominican who stood before him in his black-and-white habit, his pallid face, in every line of which self-abnegation had set its imprint, as thoughtful as the Cardinal's own. His Eminence spoke slowly.

"I perceive the difficulty. I suspected it before you came; which, indeed, was the reason why I sent for you. Nothing that you have said has done anything but increase it. Do you offer no counsel?"

They looked into each other's eyes. Frey Juan made a little gesture of helplessness, slightly raising his shoulders.

"I seek the path of duty. It seems to me almost that it must lie in abandoning this charge of sorcery of which we have no clear irrefutable evidence. Both the prisoner and your nephew himself meet the charge by accusing us of having invented it so as to shelter Don Pedro from the consequences of having slain an officer of the Holy Office."

"Since that is not true, why need it perturb you?"

"It perturbs me that, if really innocent of sorcery, the woman is justified in believing it true. There remains against her the offence of heresy, which must be purged. But I desire her conversion and the salvation of her soul, and how shall we accomplish this if we are discredited in her eyes by her conviction that we proceed as we do out of ignoble worldly motives?"

The Cardinal bowed his head. "You probe deeply, Frey Juan."

"Is my duty less, Eminence?"

"But, if this charge of sorcery is abandoned, what then of my nephew? He has committed a sacrilege, other sins apart. For that a heavy expiation is required – his very life is forfeit – unless it can be shown that responsibility for his actions lies elsewhere."

Frey Juan stiffened. "Are we to fall into the very offence of which already this woman accuses us?" he cried. "Are we to justify her accusation?"

That brought the Cardinal to his feet. He stood as tall as Frey Juan, confronting the sudden sternness of the Dominican, a flush upon his cheeks, a kindling of anger in his dark eyes.

"What do you presume to conclude?" he demanded. "Could I have said what I have said in the assumption that my nephew is guilty? Am I not entitled, by every act of his past life, to assume him innocent of intentional evil, and to believe that he must, indeed, have been bewitched? That is what, in my conscience, I do believe," he insisted. "But because we lack the means fully to establish this thing, is Don Pedro de Mendoza to be left to suffer infamy, death and the confiscation of his estates?"

If Frey Juan remained unconvinced of the Cardinal's sincerity and freedom from nepotism, he was willing charitably to believe that his affection for his nephew made him build assumptions into convictions.

He perceived the dilemma: but he could do no more than briefly recapitulate the situation.

"The actual facts upon which Frey Luis has built his accusation are admitted by the prisoner. What she does not admit – what, indeed, her arguments go some way to dispel – are the inferences drawn from them by Frey Luis. These inferences are undoubtedly cogent, plausible and well-reasoned. Yet, as the evidence stands, and without independent confirmation, it does not permit us to sentence the accused. I do not see," he ended gloomily, "whence this confirmation is to be obtained."

"Whence but from the prisoner herself!" exclaimed the Cardinal, in the tone of a man who states the obvious.

Frey Juan shook his head. "That, I am persuaded, she will never yield."

Quiroga looked him in the face again, and his eyes narrowed.

"You have not yet proceeded to the question," he softly reminded him.

Frey Juan spread his hands. He spoke in a tone of self-accusation. "If I have not employed it, although urged to it already by my assessors, it is because of my fear, my firm persuasion, that it must fail."

"Fail?"

The amazement of the exclamation was eloquent indeed. It provoked a wistful little smile from the Dominican.

"You have not seen this woman, Eminence. You have had no opportunity of judging the strength of her spirit, the toughness of her fibre, the determination of her nature. If the truth sustains her – as well it may, remember, in this matter of witchcraft – I do not believe that if the tormentors were slowly to rend her limb from limb, an incriminating admission would be wrung from her. I say this upon long and deep consideration, Eminence. My office has taught me something of humanity. There are men and women in whom mental exaltation produces a detachment of the spirit which renders them unconscious of the flesh, and therefore, insensible to pain. Such a woman do I judge this one to be. If innocent of sorcery, consciousness of her innocence would produce in her such an exaltation."

He paused before concluding: "If we are to persist in the accusation of sorcery, we may have to come to the audience of torment before the end is reached. But, if we come to it, and fail in spite of it, as I believe we shall, what will then be the position of Don Pedro de Mendoza?"

The Inquisitor-General sat down again, heavily. He sank his chin to his breast, and muttered through his teeth. "Devil take the fool for having placed himself in this position!" More vehemently he added: "And Devil take this Frey Luis Salcedo for yielding to his excessive zeal!"

"Frey Luis acted in accordance with his lights and without regard to anything but his duty to his habit. He was within his rights, Eminence."

"But something rash, I think. Yourself you have come to perceive it and to be troubled by it. An accusation of this nature should never have been brought until I had been consulted. Witchcraft is a charge never easy to establish."

"Yet had the accusation not been lodged, Eminence, in what case must Don Pedro have found himself?"

The Cardinal raised his hands, and let them fall back resoundingly and heavily upon the arms of his chair. "Yes, yes! So we swing – backwards and forwards – in this matter. We are in a circle which we cannot break. Either this woman is convicted of having bewitched my nephew, or else Don Pedro is guilty of an offence for which the Holy Office prescribes the penalty of death with confiscation of his possessions; and you tell me that you do not believe the woman can be so convicted."

"That is my firm persuasion."

The Cardinal heaved himself up slowly, a deep frown of perplexity between his fine, thoughtful, wide-set eyes. He paced slowly the length of the room and back, his chin sunk upon his breast, and for some moments there was no sound there beyond the soft fall of his slippered feet upon the wood mosaics of the floor, the rustle of his trailing gown of scarlet silk.

At length he came to stand once more before the Dominican. He looked at him with eyes that did not seem to see him, so introspective was their gaze. His fine hand, on which a great sapphire glowed sombrely, toyed absently with the broad jewelled cross that hung upon his breast.

His full lips parted at last. He spoke very quietly and slowly.

"There is, I think, a way out of this difficulty, after all. I hesitate even now to urge its adoption, because it might appear to some to be not quite a legitimate way according to the laws that govern us." He broke off to ask a question. "Is it a truth, Frey Juan, that the end may justify the means?"

"The Jesuits assert it," answered the Dominican uneasily.

"Here is a case that may serve to show that they are sometimes right. Consider me now this nephew of mine. He is a man who has served God and the Faith as loyally as he has served his King. As much in the service of one as the other did he sail upon the ship which he commanded. He is a tertiary of the Order of St Dominic, and a man of devout and God-fearing nature. Remembering all this, are we not justified of the persuasion that it would have been impossible for him to have committed the offences against the Faith with which he is now charged unless he had been the victim of some aberration? Whether this aberration was the result of black arts employed against him, according to the arguments of Frey Luis Salcedo, or whether, as you seem to consider a possible alternative, it results from the simple and normal magic of Nature in such cases, we may be able to determine later. At the moment, all that we can determine is that the aberration exists. Of this, you, who have examined him and the English woman, entertain, like myself, no doubt?"

"No doubt whatever," answered Frey Juan promptly and truthfully.

"In that case, there would be no violence to our consciences or our duty if we were in this instance to reverse the normal order of procedure. The proper course is naturally that we first sift the charge against the woman, so as to establish clearly the grounds upon which Don Pedro is to be sentenced. But since in our own minds and consciences these grounds are firmly established already, might we not, ignoring the forms of law, proceed at once to sentence Don Pedro upon the indictment as drawn up by Frey Luis Salcedo? Upon that, which presumes that he was bewitched and not responsible for his deeds, the Holy Office will be appeased by imposing a penance *de leviter*, but public, to be performed at next Thursday's *Auto de Fé*. Thus he will be purged of his sin before we finally proceed against the woman. If, then, the charge of witchcraft should fail for lack of confirmation, and only the charge of heresy remain upon which to sentence her, at least it will be too late to reopen the case against Don Pedro."

The Cardinal paused, his eyes closely scanning the face of his subordinate inquisitor.

Frey Juan remained gravely impassive. It was a moment before he spoke.

"I, too, had thought of that," he said slowly.

The Cardinal's glance quickened. His hand fell upon the Dominican's shoulder and gripped it. "You had! Why then… " He left his question there.

But Frey Juan shook his head, and sighed. "It is never too late in questions of the Faith to reopen a case against an accused, if it is shown that there was more against him than appeared at the trial in which he was sentenced."

"Why, that I know. But here… Who is there would dream of reopening it?"

Frey Juan hesitated before answering. "There are other consciences than ours, Eminence. An enemy of Don Pedro's might be moved by his conscience to see him expiate to the full his offence against the Faith. A successor of mine or yours, Eminence, perusing the records, might perceive the irregularity and be moved to correct it."

"Those risks we could take without loss of sleep."

"Those, perhaps, yes... But there is yet another. There is the delator, Frey Luis Salcedo."

The Cardinal stared at him. "Frey Luis Salcedo? But it is he who argues and insists upon the witchcraft!" He removed his hand from the Dominican's shoulder as he spoke.

"I say it without hostility to him, Eminence! His zeal is greater than his discretion. He is of a terrible singleness of aim, and in this matter he has shown a tenacity and persistence which have led me to remind him that hatred, even when springing from righteousness, can be a mortal sin. If I know him at all, be will be driven to frenzy if the accusation of witchcraft is not established. He is intolerant of all doubts in the matter; violent in asserting his conviction and in insisting upon the cogency of his arguments. If, the witchcraft being presumed, we penance Don Pedro *de leviter*, Frey Luis will be the first to raise an outcry and denounce that penancing as a mockery should the witchcraft not subsequently be proven against the woman."

The Cardinal, a human man after all, not to be blamed by any reasonable person for his efforts on his nephew's behalf, flushed now with anger.

"But for what does he count, then, this man, in your tribunal? He is but a witness there, without powers or voice of any kind."

"He has the voice of a delator, and the voice of a delator is the one voice which the Holy Office has no power to silence. The Fiscal Advocate has been on his side in what arguments we have had, and I think that even the Diocesan Ordinary is becoming impatient with my endeavours to hold the scales level. In their opinion, I am too tender of a heretic."

The Inquisitor-General looked into the fine ascetic face of his subordinate.

"You think that Frey Luis might become vindictive?"

"That is what I have hesitated to say. But since Your Eminence has used the word, I confess that it is what is in my mind. If the woman is sentenced only as a heretic, he may take vengeance upon those whom he regards as having frustrated him by seeking in turn to frustrate them where Don Pedro is concerned; by demanding that Don Pedro be tried again, and sentenced for deeds which will then be beyond condonation."

Cardinal Quiroga was reduced to exasperation. He could only cry out again that they were held within a circle so that in whatever direction they moved they encountered ever the same points. He became, on the subject of his nephew and his folly, as nearly blasphemous as was possible to a prelate in the presence of a subordinate. Finally he urged that they should stake everything upon the question and its efficacy in wringing the requisite admission of guilt from the woman.

Frey Juan bowed his head. "If Your Eminence commands it, as is your right," he said. "But I solemnly warn you that it is a stake upon which Don Pedro will lose all."

This the Inquisitor-General perceived was but to recommence the arguments, to make another turn round that exasperating circle. Abruptly he dismissed Frey Juan.

"I must consider," he announced. "It is all before me now. I shall pray for guidance, and do you do the same, Frey Juan. Go with God!"

Chapter 22

The Royal Confessor

With the full facts of the sequel before us in intimate detail (for even where these details depend upon inference the indications are too clear to admit of error) it may be permissible to point out – as has been pointed out so repeatedly already – that the most trivial causes may be pregnant of the most terrible and even tragical effects.

Grotesque though it may seem, it is hardly too much to conclude that if King Philip of Spain had been less gluttonously addicted to pastry, the fortunes of the Lady Margaret Trevanion, whom he had never seen and whose name, heard but once, he did not even remember, would have run a totally different course.

On that Sunday night, at the Escurial, the lord of half the world indulged that gluttony of his to a more than normal degree. In the early hours of Monday morning he awoke in a cold sweat of terror with a cramp in the pit of his stomach produced, as he believed even after awakening, by the weight upon it of the bleeding heads of eight gentlemen of Spain.

He sat up in his great carved bed with a scream which brought Santoyo instantly to his side. The valet found him straining frantically to thrust with both hands that imagined bloody heap from his royal lap.

There were cordials and sedatives at hand prescribed for the use of this sickly, valetudinarian monarch, and practice had rendered

Santoyo expert in the administration of them. Quickly he mixed a dose. The King drank it, lay down again in response to the valet's solicitudinous advice, and, partially soothed, remained thereafter gently moaning.

The valet sent for the physician. The latter, when he came, probing by questions to discover the cause of this sudden indisposition, came upon the pastry, and shrugged his shoulders in despair. He had remonstrated about it before with the King, and had been vituperated for his pains and dubbed an incompetent, ignorant ass. It was not worth his while to risk the loss of the King's confidence by venturing again to tell him the truth.

He took counsel with Santoyo. The sleek, shrewd Andalusian valet suggested that it might be a matter for the King's confessor. Santoyo had picked up a good deal of theology in King Philip's service, and he was aware that gluttony was one of the seven deadly sins. Restraint might be imposed upon His Majesty if it were delicately pointed out to him that these excesses were of spiritual as well as physical injury; in other words, that in ruining his digestion he also damned his soul.

The physician, something of a cynic, as such men must be who have so wide and so intimate an acquaintance of their fellows, wondered from which of the other six deadly sins the King had ever been made to abstain by fear of damnation. In fact, he rather regarded His Majesty as an expert in the practice of the deadly sins, immunity from the consequences of which he no doubt ensured himself by the perfervidness of his devotions.

Santoyo, however, was much more practical. "A deadly sin that brings no evil material sequel to the satisfaction afforded by committing it is one thing. A deadly sin that gives you the stomach-ache is quite another."

The physician was constrained to acknowledge that the valet was the greater philosopher, and left the matter in his hands. Later in the course of that Monday, Santoyo sought Frey Diego de Chaves, and told him what had passed; he gave him details of the King's indigestion, its probable cause and peculiar manifestation.

Santoyo was flattered by the unusual and lively interest which the royal confessor displayed. He knew himself the best valet in Spain, and much else besides; but he now gathered from Frey Diego's warm commendation of his zeal and conclusions that he was also a considerable theologian.

He was not aware of the distress of mind in which he had found the Prior of Santa Cruz, or of how opportunely the matter came to his need. Ramon de Chaves, the Prior's elder brother, and the head of that distinguished family to which the Prior was himself an ornament, was one of the eight gentlemen in the Tower of London whose heads were placed in jeopardy by what Frey Diego accounted the fierce inhumanity of the Queen of England and the proud obstinacy of the King of Spain. When Santoyo found him he had been mentally torn between philosophic reflections upon the peril and futility of serving princes and practical considerations of how he might so move the King as to abstract his brother's head from the English axe.

The advent of Santoyo with his tale was like an answer to the prayers which last night he had addressed to Heaven. It opened out before him a way by which he might approach the King in the matter, without appearing to be actuated by any considerations of serving his own family. He was too well acquainted with the King's dark nature to entertain any hopes of moving him by entreaties.

The difficulty lay in the fact that the King usually confessed himself on Fridays, and this was Monday. The Prior had also informed himself – again out of fraternal solicitude – that there was to be an *Auto de Fé* in Toledo on Thursday, when the Englishwoman who was at the root of all this bother was to be burnt as a witch or a heretic, or both; and he knew that once this happened, whatever else might happen, nothing could save his brother's head from the sawdust.

Thus you have the interesting situation of the Inquisitor-General, moved to nepotism, on the one hand, and the Prior of Santa Cruz, also an Inquisitor of the Faith, moved by brotherly love, on the other, both seeking a scheme by which to frustrate the ends of the Holy Office.

229

The Prior, betraying to the valet solicitude only for the condition of the King, left it to him to induce His Majesty to send for him at the earliest moment. To reward his affection and fidelity to the King, to mark his appreciation of Santoyo's zeal in matters of religion, and to encourage its continuance, the Prior made him a handsome present, gave him his blessing, and so dismissed him. Thereafter Frey Diego awaited the royal summons with some confidence.

Santoyo went to work astutely, postponing all operations until the King should afford him a clear opening.

Philip II had been at his eternal labours of annotating documents in that monastic room in which he worked. These Santoyo had taken from him, dusted with pounce where necessary, and passed on to the secretaries, as usual, closely watching his royal master the while.

Came a moment when the King paused in his labours, sighed and passed a hand wearily across his pallid brow. Presently he stretched out his hand to take another document from the pile on the oak table at his elbow. It resisted him. He turned his head, and found Santoyo's hand pinning down the heap of parchments, Santoyo's eyes gravely upon him.

The heavy insect-like drone of the royal voice sounded in the room. "What is it? What do you do?"

"Has not Your Majesty laboured enough for today? You will remember that you were indisposed in the night. Your Majesty shows signs of weariness."

This was an unusual interference, almost an impertinence on the part of Santoyo. The King's pale cold eye looked up at him, to drop again immediately. Not even the glance of his valet could this man support.

"Of weariness?" he hummed. "I?" But the suggestion did its work upon that sickly and enfeebled body. He removed his hand from the parchments and, reclining in his chair, closed his eyes, so as to concentrate upon himself, and discover whether his valet might not be right. He found himself weary, indeed, he thought. He opened his eyes again.

"Santoyo, what did Gutierrez say of my condition?"

"He seemed to think that it arose from too much pastry… "

"Who told him that I ate pastry?"

"He asked me what you had eaten, Majesty."

"And so, to hide his ignorance, he fastened upon that. The ass! The unspeakable ass!"

"I told him, Majesty, that he was clearly wrong."

"So, so! You told him he was wrong. Behold you turned doctor now, Santoyo!"

"It scarcely needed a doctor to perceive what ailed Your Majesty. As I told Master Gutierrez, the unrest came not from your stomach, Majesty, but from your spirit."

"Tush, fool! What do you know of my spirit?"

"What I gathered from Your Majesty's words when you were stricken in the night." And he went on quickly: "Frey Diego de Chaves said something here on Friday which preyed upon your mind, Majesty. It would need the Prior of Santa Cruz to heal the wound he opened, to restore you the quiet that Your Majesty's spirit needs."

Now this was a disturbing reminder. It brought back the vivid phrase which had haunted the King ever since. At the time it showed the King the shrewdness of Santoyo's diagnosis. He muttered something utterly inaudible, then rousing himself, again put forth his hand to resume his labours. This time Santoyo dared not hinder him. But whilst he annotated the document he had taken, Santoyo, behind his back, was guilty of shuffling the waiting heap so that a sheet which had been at the bottom of the pile was now uppermost and was next to be taken by the King.

In this Santoyo revealed his shrewdness even more signally. Well aware of what was troubling the royal mind, of the mingled rage and fear and obstinacy provoked by the Queen of England's letter, he concluded that these emotions must be fed if His Majesty was to seek relief of them at the hands of the Prior of Santa Cruz, as Santoyo was conspiring that he should.

The letter which he had now judged it suitable to bring to the top of the pile – on the principle of striking the iron whilst it was hot –

was from the Duke of Medina-Sidonia, who had led the disastrous adventure against England. It was a letter which had arrived that morning, most opportunely.

The old Duke wrote humbly from his retirement to inform King Philip that he had sold one of his farms to raise the heavy sum required by England for the ransom of the gallant admiral Pedro Valdez. It was a small enough act, the duke protested, imploring His Majesty to behold an earnest of his love and loyalty in this sacrifice made to restore to Spain the services of the first of her surviving admirals.

The letter fluttered from the royal fingers gone suddenly nerveless. He sank back in his wooden monastic chair, closed his eyes and groaned; then opened them again and raged.

"Infidel! Bastard! Excommunicated heretic! Indemoniated she-wolf!"

Santoyo was leaning over him in solicitude. "Majesty!" he murmured.

"I am ill, Santoyo," droned the dull voice. "You are right! I'll work no more. Give me your arm."

Supported by a stick on one side, and leaning heavily on Santoyo on the other, he hobbled from the room. Santoyo craftily introduced again the name of Frey Diego de Chaves, suggested mildly that perhaps His Majesty required spiritual advice. His Majesty bade him be silent, and he dared not insist.

But that night again King Philip's sleep was troubled and this time there was no pastry to account for it – at least, not directly. Perhaps it was that the terrible images excited by the indigestion of Sunday night left their memories in his brain, so that they recurred now without extraneous stimulus; and undoubtedly they were assisted to recur by the thought of that letter from Medina-Sidonia announcing the dispatch of the ransom of that gallant Valdez, whose head was ever the foremost in that imagined in the royal lap, whose head must fall lest Elizabeth of England should be able to announce with a laugh that she had coerced Philip of Spain.

Another twenty-four hours of such haunting as this, and at last, on Wednesday morning, after yet another night of broken sleep, the King capitulated to the repeated suggestion of his valet that he should see his confessor. It may be that at the back of his mind, if only subconsciously, there was the thought of the *Auto de Fé* on the morrow and the knowledge that if he delayed another twenty-four hours it would be too late for action of any kind.

"In God's name!" he cried at last, to Santoyo's insistence. "Let Frey Diego come. Since he raised these ghosts, let him come and exorcize them."

The Prior of Santa Cruz did not keep the King waiting. He had been watching the passage of the hours in a mounting fever of panic. He had reached that point where, whether the King sent for him or not, he would use his position as keeper of the royal conscience to thrust himself upon the King and make a last effort by intercession, by reasoning, by bullying at need, to save his brother's head. But since the King sent for him, even at this late hour, all was well. He would lay aside those weapons of despair until others failed.

Calm and self-contained looked the portly man as be entered the royal bedroom and, having dismissed Santoyo and closed the door, approached the great carved bed in that austere room, flooded now with the sunshine of the autumn morning.

He drew up a stool, sat down, and after some platitudes on the score of the royal health and in answer to the royal complaints he invited the King to confess himself, and so ease his soul of any troublesome burden which might be retarding the healing of his flesh.

Philip confessed himself. Frey Diego probed the royal conscience with questions here and there. As a surgeon dissects and lays bare the recesses of the body, so did the Prior of Santa Cruz now dissect and lay bare some of the horrible recesses of King Philip's soul.

When it was done, and before he passed to the awaited absolution, Frey Diego diagnosed the royal condition.

"It is so plain, my son," he said, in the paternal tone of his office. "In this distemper which afflicts you, two deadly sins are co-operating.

You will not be healed until you cast them out. Neglect to do so will destroy you here and hereafter. The indigestion resulting from the sin of gluttony let loose against you tormenting visions resulting from the sin of pride. Beware of pride, my son, the first and deadliest of the sins. Through pride was Lucifer cast out of his high place in Heaven. But for pride there would have been no devil, no tempter and no sin. It is Satan's great gift to man. A mantle so light that a man may wear it without consciousness that it sits upon his shoulders, whilst in the folds of it are sheltered all the evils that labour for man's eternal damnation."

"Jesu!" droned the King. "All my life I have studied humility… "

The confessor interrupted him where the man would not have dared. "The visions that you tell me have haunted you these nights, whence come they, think you?"

"Whence? From regret, from fear, from love for those gentlemen of mine, whom that evil heretic in England is to butcher."

"Unless you banished the pride which prevents you from putting forth your hand to save them."

"What? Am I the King of Spain, and shall I bow my neck to that insolent demand?"

"Unless the deadly sin of pride insists that you carry your head erect whilst eight noble lives are immolated on the altar of pride."

The King writhed as if in physical pain. Suddenly he rallied, perceiving something that had been overlooked, something in which he fancied that he must find salvation.

"I can do nothing if I would. The matter is out of my hands. I am but King of Spain. I do not rule the Holy Office. I do not presume to meddle in the Kingdom of God. I do not presume, I say: I, whom you accuse of pride."

But the Prior of Santa Cruz smiled pityingly as his eyes momentarily met the King's furtive glance. "Will you cheat God with such a subterfuge? Do you think God is to be cheated? Can you conceal from Him what is in your heart? If the good of Spain, valid reasons of State, demand that you should stay the hand of the Inquisition, is your Inquisitor-General to deny you? Has no King of

Spain ever intervened? Be honest with your God, King Philip. Behold already one of the evils which I warned you lurk within pride's mantle. Cast off that mantle, my son. It is a garment of damnation."

The King looked at him and away again. There was agony in those pale eyes – the agony of pride.

"It is unthinkable," he droned. "Must I humble myself – "

"Out of your own mouth, my son!" Frey Diego cried in a voice like a trumpet call, and rose, his arm flung out in denunciation. "Out of your own mouth! Must you humble yourself, you ask? Ay, must you, or God will humble you in the end. There is no other escape for you from these ghosts. These bleeding heads grin at you now from your lap. They grin so while they are still firm upon the shoulders of living men; men who have loved you and served you and ventured their lives in your service and in Spain's. What will they look like when they shall indeed have fallen, because your pride would not stay the axe of the executioner? Will that lay those ghosts, do you think, or will it bring them gibbering about you until you are driven mad, assuring you that, like another Lucifer, by your pride have you forfeited your place in Heaven, by your pride doomed yourself to an eternity of torment."

"Cease!" cried the King, writhing in his great bed, and thus convinced, appalled to perceive under the Prior's fiery indication the pit on the edge of which he stood, he capitulated. He would rend his pride; he would bow his neck; he would submit to the insolent demand of that heretical woman,

"Thus," said the Prior in a gentle, soothing voice, applying an unguent now that the irritant had done its work, "shall you lay up treasure in Heaven, my son."

Chapter 23

The Auto de Fé

Having been driven by the spiritually minatory persuasions of his confessor into that immolation of his monstrous pride, King Philip, in prey to a reaction common enough in such cases, displayed a feverish, anxious haste to perform in the eleventh hour what three days ago might have been done in dignified leisure.

An hour or so before noon on that Wednesday, Sir Gervase Crosby was hailed from the underground stone chamber of the Escurial in which he had been imprisoned. Such had been his angry distress at his failure to save Margaret that it is to be doubted if through these interminable days of maddeningly impotent conjecture he had given a thought to the fate in store for himself.

He was brought now, not before the King, who could not bear the humiliation of announcing his surrender to this man, whose bones he had hoped to have broken in the torture-chamber of the Inquisition, but before the little hirsute gentleman he had seen at work in the royal closet on the occasion of his audience. This was the secretary, Rodriguez, who, himself, had penned at the King's dictation the letter to the Inquisitor-General of Castile, which His Majesty had signed and sealed, the letter which the secretary now proffered to Sir Gervase.

In curt terms and with great dignity of manner the little man informed Sir Gervase of the situation in a formal speech which sounded like a lesson learnt by heart.

236

"His Majesty the King of Spain, having further considered the matter of the letter from the Queen of England, has decided to comply with the request in it. He has reached this decision in spite of the gross terms employed by Her Majesty, and unintimidated by threats which he is persuaded that she would not dare in any case to execute. He has been moved solely by a justice inclining to clemency, having ascertained that a wrong had been done by a subject of his own which for the honour of Spain it behoves him to right."

It was at this stage that he displayed the sealed package which he held.

"The woman, whose surrender is demanded, is a prisoner of the Holy Office, charged not only with heresy, but with witchcraft exercised against Don Pedro de Mendoza y Luna, whereby he was so far seduced from his duty to his God and his honour that he carried her off and brought her here to Spain. She lies at present in the prison of the Holy House at Toledo, having been in the hands of the Inquisitors of the Faith from the moment that she landed on Spanish soil. So far, as we believe, no harm or hurt has come to her beyond the inconvenience of detention. But she is under sentence to suffer in the *Auto de Fé* which is to be held tomorrow in Toledo, wherefore you are enjoined by His Majesty to make all speed in bearing this letter to Don Gaspar de Quiroga, Cardinal-Archbishop of Toledo and Inquisitor-General of the Faith. This letter commands him to deliver into your hands the person of the Lady Margaret Trevanion, and you are further accorded, by His Majesty's gracious clemency, fourteen days in which to leave Spain, taking this woman with you. Should you still be within His Majesty's dominions after the expiry of that term the consequences will be of the utmost gravity."

Sir Gervase took the proffered letter in a hand that trembled. Relief was blending with fresh dreadful anxiety to unman him. He knew the distance to Toledo, perceived how short was the time and how the slightest mischance even now that this miracle had happened might render him too late.

But the King was now as anxious as he was that there should be no mischance. He was further informed by the Secretary Rodriguez that a suitable escort would be provided for him as far as Toledo, and that the relays of horse maintained by the royal post would be at his disposal. Finally, he was handed a brief document, also bearing the royal arms and signature, commanding all dutiful subjects of the King of Spain to assist him and his companions in his journey from Toledo to Santander and warning them that who hindered him did so at his peril. Upon that the secretary dismissed him with an enjoinder to set out at once, and not to delay.

He was conducted to the courtyard by the officer who had fetched him from his prison. Here he was delivered into the care of another officer, who waited there with six mounted men and a spare horse. His weapons were restored to him, and riding beside the officer at the head of that little escort, he quitted the gloomy palace of the Escurial and galloped away from the granite mass of the Guadarrama Mountains towards Villalba. Here, turning south, they rode at speed down the narrow valley through which the River Guadarrama winds its way to the mighty Tagus. But the road was rough, often no better than a mule-track, and delays were frequent and inevitable, with the result that it was nightfall before they reached Brunete, where fresh horses would be available.

Still forty miles from Toledo, and informed that the *Auto de Fé* would be held in the forenoon, Sir Gervase was racked by a desperate anxiety, which would not permit him to take here even the hour's rest which the officer had advised as they approached the place. The fellow, a slim youngster of about Sir Gervase's own age, showed himself courteous and considerate, but he was a Catalan and spoke with an accent that rendered him almost incomprehensible to the Englishman, whose imperfect knowledge of Spanish was confined to pure Castilian.

At Brunete, however, a set-back awaited them. Three fresh horses only were available. Normally a dozen were stabled there. But a courier from the Inquisitor-General to the Council of State in Madrid had passed that way at noon, travelling with an escort, and had made a heavy draught upon the royal post.

The young officer, whose name was Nuno Lopez, a man of a New-Christian family, in whose blood there was a Moorish taint, accepted the situation with the placid Saracen fatalism of his forebears. He shrugged.

"*No hay que hacer*," he announced. "There is nothing to be done."

You conceive Sir Gervase's exasperation at this calm finality. "Nothing to be done?" he cried. "Something is to be done to get me to Toledo by sunrise."

"That is impossible." Don Nuno was imperturbable. Perhaps he was glad to have so good a reason for not spending a night in the saddle. "In six hours' time – by midnight, perhaps – the horses left here by the Grand Inquisitor's courier may be in case to travel. But they will hardly travel fast."

Sir Gervase sensed rather than understood Don Nuno's meaning. He answered very slowly and emphatically so that Don Nuno might have no difficulty in understanding him.

"There are three fresh horses here; enough for you and me and one of your men. Let us take these at once, and go."

Standing in the yellow light that streamed from the open door of the post-house to mingle with the fading October daylight, Don Nuno smiled tolerantly as he shook his head.

"It would not be safe. There are brigands in these hills."

But to this Sir Gervase had a ready answer. "Oh, if you're afraid of brigands, saddle me one of the fresh horses, and I'll ride on alone."

The officer no longer smiled. He had drawn himself up stiffly, and above his tightened mouth his moustachios appeared to bristle. For a moment Sir Gervase thought the fellow was going to strike him. Then the Catalan spun round on his heel, and to his men, dismounted and standing in line at their horses' heads, he spat out in a rasping, angry voice, orders which to Sir Gervase were utterly incomprehensible.

Within five minutes the three fresh horses were waiting and one of Don Nuno's troopers with them. Meanwhile, Don Nuno had provided himself with supper, consisting of a piece of bread and an onion. He washed this down with a draught of rough Andalusian wine, and climbed into the saddle.

"*Vamos!*" he peremptorily commanded.

Sir Gervase mounted, and the three men trotted out of the village, and resumed their journey.

As they rode, the officer found it necessary to ease his mind. Addressing his companion uncompromisingly as "Sir English Dog" – *Señor perro de inglez* – he informed him that he had said something which hurt his honour and which must be corrected between them as soon as occasion served.

Sir Gervase had no desire to find himself with a quarrel on his hands. Nightmare enough was provided already by this ride through the dark against time and to a destination bristling with unknown difficulties. He swallowed his vexation, ignored the insult in the form of address, and apologized for any offence he might have given.

"It will not serve," said the Catalan. "You have placed me under the necessity of proving my courage."

"You are proving it now," Sir Gervase reassured him. "This was all the proof I desired of you. I knew you would afford it, which was why I demanded it. Forgive the subterfuge which would have been wasted on any but a brave man."

The Catalan made out with difficulty his meaning, and was mollified.

"Well, well," he grumbled. "For the present we will leave it there. But later on a little more may be necessary."

"As you please. Meanwhile, in God's name, let us remain friends."

They rode amain through that lonely valley, where an almost full moon was casting inky fantastic shadows and turning the gurgling stream whose course they followed into a ribbon of rippling silver. It grew very cold. The wind came icily from the Sierra to the north and Don Nuno and his man wrapped themselves tightly in their cloaks for protection. Sir Gervase had no cloak, not even a jerkin over his velvet doublet. But he was insensible to the cold as to any other physical sensation. He was conscious of nothing beyond a lump in his throat cast up there, it seemed, by the anxiety consuming his soul.

An hour or so after midnight his horse put its foot in a hole in the road and came down heavily. It was a moment before Sir Gervase could raise himself from where he had been flung. Beyond some bruises, he had suffered no hurt, but he was still half-stunned, as in the moonlight he watched Don Nuno running his hand over the fetlock of the quivering beast which had meanwhile also risen.

The officer announced in a voice of relief that there was no harm done. But a moment or two later it was found that the horse was lame, and could not be ridden farther.

They were, Don Nuno announced, near the village of Chozas de Can. It could not be more than a couple of miles away. The trooper surrendered his mount to Sir Gervase and, taking the reins of the lamed horse, trudged along beside it whilst the other two moved with him at that slow walking pace, Sir Gervase's giddiness from his fall dispelled by mounting anxiety at the loss of time involved in this snail's crawl.

It took them an hour to reach Chozas de Can. They knocked up a tavern in the village "in the King's name". But horses there were none to be had. So the trooper was left there, and Sir Gervase and Nuno Lopez now pushed on alone.

They were within twenty-five miles of Toledo, and only some twelve or thirteen miles from Villamiel, where fresh horses awaited them for the last swift stage of the journey. But, however swift might be that last stage when they came to it, the present one was little swifter than had been the progress since the laming of Sir Gervase's horse. The moon had set, and in that narrow valley-road the darkness was almost palpable. They advanced at little more than a walking pace, until the autumn dawn enabled them to move more briskly, and thus came at last to Villamiel, just after seven o'clock, with still fifteen miles to go.

The officer emphatically announced himself hungry, and as emphatically asserted that he would go no farther until his fast was

RAFAEL SABATINI

broken. Sir Gervase asked him at what hour exactly the *Auto* was held.

"The procession from the Holy House usually sets out between eight and nine."

It was an answer that turned Sir Gervase's anxiety to frenzy. He would not wait an instant beyond the time necessary for the saddling of a fresh horse. Don Nuno, hungry and weary, having been in the saddle now for over eighteen hours with little food and no sleep, was out of temper. The Englishman's demands appeared to him unreasonable in that mood. An altercation arose between them. It might have been protracted but for the sudden coming of the fresh horse which Sir Gervase had so peremptorily commanded.

Sir Gervase flung away from the angry officer, and vaulted into the saddle.

"Follow me at your leisure, sir, when you have broken your fast," he shouted to him as he rode off.

Nor did he look behind him for all the din that he could hear the Spaniard making in calling to him. He rode now at a breakneck pace through an empty village – for almost every inhabitant had left it to attend the show in Toledo – swung to the left over the narrow old bridge across the river, and then turned south again towards his destination.

Afterwards he could remember nothing of that ride. Jaded by nights of broken slumber culminating in this last night spent in the saddle, racked by maddening fears that even now he might arrive too late, he was conscious of nothing until suddenly, at about nine o'clock, he beheld before him and a little below him the great city of Toledo, contained within its circle of Moorish fortifications. Above the burnt-red tiles of the roofs surged the vast grey mass of the Cathedral of this Spanish Rome, and dominating all from its eminence above the city on the far eastward side stood the noble palace of the Alcazar, aglow in the morning sunlight.

At breakneck speed Gervase rode down the hill from whose summit he obtained his first glimpse of that terrible city of his goal, then up again to the heights of that great rampart of granite upon which the city stood, a rampart encircled on three sides of its precipitous base by the broad, deep, swirling waters of the pellucid Tagus.

As he advanced now he overtook straggling groups of countryfolk on foot, on horseback, on mules and donkeys, and even in ox-wains, all making for the city, and all of them very obviously dressed in their best. As he approached the Visagra Gate the stragglers had become a multitude, with all the shouting and confusion resulting from their being detained there by the guard which would admit only those on foot. It was then that Sir Gervase understood the meaning of this concourse. The *Auto de Fé* was the attraction drawing the people of the surrounding countryside to Toledo, and these were the late-comers, meeting the fate of late-comers.

He thrust impatiently through them, trusting to his safe conduct to ensure him exception to the delaying rule. He announced himself as a royal messenger to the officer of the gate, who eyed him mistrustfully. He displayed his letter to the Inquisitor-General with its royal seals and thrust his safe conduct under the man's nose.

The officer was impressed and became courteous. But he was not to be shaken in the matter of the horse. He gave reasons, rapidly, why it could not enter. Gervase, not understanding these, insisted that there was not a moment to lose, since the orders he carried were concerned with the *Auto de Fé*, which was already being held.

The officer stared impatiently; but perceiving that he had to deal with a foreigner, explained himself now very slowly and clearly.

"You would lose more time if you attempted to take your horse into the city. You would not ride a mile in an hour. The streets are choked with people from here to the Zocodover. Leave your horse with us. It will be waiting for you when you return."

Gervase dismounted, understanding at last that there was nothing else to be done. He inquired of the officer the shortest way to the Archiepiscopal Palace. The man directed him to the Cathedral, advising him to inquire again when he had got as far as that.

He passed under the barrel vaulting and the portcullis of that great Arab gate, and so entered the city. At first progress was easy, and he fancied that the guard with the officiousness of his kind had made difficulties where none existed. But presently, in a measure, as he advanced through those narrow, crooked streets still stamped with the character of their Saracen builders, he found the wayfarers increasing to the proportions of a crowd. Soon, as he continued to advance, the crowd became an almost solid press, in which presently he found himself wedged, and compelled to move with it as relentlessly as if he were being swept along by a torrent. Desperately he protested, and attempted to clear himself a way, announcing himself a royal messenger. The general noise drowned his puny voice, leaving it audible only to those immediately about him in that noisome, reeking press. These eyed him with mistrust. His foreign accent and unkempt appearance earned him only contempt and derision. If his clothes were those of a gentleman, they were now so travel-stained that their nature was no longer to be discerned, whilst his countenance, on which the dust had caked, with its stubble of auburn beard and its haggard, red-rimmed, blood-injected eyes, was by no means in case to inspire confidence. The human stream swept him along the narrow street into a broader one, and on to a point where this entered a vast open space. In the middle of this space he beheld an enormous scaffold, enclosed on three sides, and flanked on two of these by tiers of benches.

The stream swept him to the left and thrust him against a wall. For a moment he was content to remain there that he might draw breath. He began to be conscious of a terrible and alarming lassitude, the natural result of sleeplessness, lack of food, anxiety and exertion almost transcending the limits of human endurance. His left knee was pressed hard against a projection in the wall. Heaving a little space about him, he saw that he had brought up against what he supposed to be a mounting-block some two feet high. Instinctively, to gain ease and air, he climbed upon it, and found himself now raised clear above that sea of human heads, and so placed that none could press upon him, breathe in his face or thrust elbows into his flanks. In prey to his increasing lassitude, he was content to remain there a moment, and snatch a brief rest from battling with that human tide.

The street at the corner of which he had come to rest was packed with people save in the middle, where a space was kept clear by a barricade of wood, guarded at intervals by men-at-arms in black, wearing corselet and steel cap and leaning upon their short halberts. This barricade was continued across the square to the wide steps of the great scaffold, which Gervase now considered more attentively.

On the left stood a pulpit, and immediately facing it in the middle of the scaffold a cage of wood and iron within which there was a seat. At the scaffold's far end, midway between the tiers, an altar had been raised. It was draped in purple and surmounted by a veiled cross between tall gilded candlesticks. To the left of this there was a miniature pavilion surmounted by a gilded dome, from which curtained draperies of purple, fringed with gold, descended to the ground. On the dais within this was placed a great gilded throne-like chair flanked by a lesser one on either side. Above, at the meeting-point of the draperies, two escutcheons were affixed, one bearing the green cross of the Inquisition, the other the arms of Spain.

About that vast scaffold the people seethed and writhed in perpetual movement, resembling some monstrous ant heap, sending up a rolling murmur that was like the sound of waves upon a shore, into which was blended intermittently the note of a bell that was being tolled funereally.

Of the houses overlooking the square, and of those in the street, as far as his glance could carry, Gervase saw that every window was thronged, as indeed was every roof. The balconies were all draped in black, and black he observed were the garments of every person of consideration, man or woman, in all that concourse.

A moment thus, to become conscious of all this, and then the meaning of it recurred to startle him into action. That dreadful bell was tolling for his Margaret, amongst others; this droning heap of pestilential human insects was assembled here for the spectacle of her martyrdom, which had begun already and which would certainly be consummated unless he bestirred himself.

He made a vigorous attempt to descend from that mounting-block, sought to thrust back those who stood immediately before it, so as to clear a way for himself. But they, being so wedged by others that they could not stir, answered him with fiercely virulent Spanish vituperations, and threats of how they would deal with him if he persisted in incommoding them. What did he want? Was he not better placed, and had he not a better view than they? Let him be content with that and not seek to thrust himself nearer to the front or it would be the worse for him.

The noise they made, the shrill voice of a woman in particular, drew the attention among others of four black alguaziles who stood on the steps of a house close by. But as there was nothing unusual in the character of the altercation, those apparitors of the Holy Office, who were there to preserve order where possible, and perhaps to spy for sympathizers with the penanced when they should appear, would hardly have bestirred themselves had it not been for one comparatively trivial detail. Scanning the man responsible for that turmoil, one of them observed that he was armed; sword and dagger hung from the carriages of his belt. Now the bearing of arms in the street during the holding of an *Auto de Fé* was a flagrant offence against the laws of the Holy Office, punishable by a term of rigorous imprisonment. The apparitors conferred a moment, and accounted it their duty to take action.

They called for room, and by a miracle room was made for them. The awe in which men stood of the liveries of the Holy Office was enough to make them accept the risk of being crushed to death rather than remain indifferent before such a demand. Two by two the sturdy black figures advanced until they stood before Sir Gervase. Using their staves with a brutal callousness, such as no secular soldiers would have dared employ in so dense a throng, they cleared a little space before the mounting-block. Their action provoked not so much as a murmur from any of the sufferers. They were empanoplied as much against reproof as against resistance by the spiritual armour of their office.

246

Sir Gervase found himself contemptuously challenged by one who appeared to be their leader, a burly, swarthy fellow, whose cheeks were blue from the razor. In an accent which made the rascal stare, Sir Gervase informed him that he was the bearer of a letter from the King of Spain to the Inquisitor-General, which it was the utmost urgency he should deliver without a moment's delay.

The man grinned contemptuously, in which his fellows followed his example.

"By my faith, you look like a royal messenger!" he sneered.

The grins became laughs, in which several bystanders joined. When a man in authority condescends to jest, however poorly, every clown within hearing will flatter him by a guffaw.

Sir Gervase thrust sealed package and safe-conduct under the mocker's eyes. The fellow mocked no more. He even overlooked the serious matter of the weapons Sir Gervase was wearing. He thrust back his hat to scratch his head, and so presumably stimulate the brain within it to activity. He half-turned and looked across the press of people. He took counsel with his three companions; finally he made up his mind.

"The procession to the *Auto* started half an hour ago from the Holy House," he informed Sir Gervase. "His Eminence is with the procession. Impossible to approach him now. You must wait in any case until he returns to the palace. Then we will escort you to him."

Distraught, Sir Gervase flung back at him that the matter could not wait. The letter was concerned with this very *Auto*. The apparitor became stolid, as men do to defend themselves from hopeless unreason. He conveyed that he was a very clever fellow, but not quite omnipotent; and nothing less than omnipotence would enable anyone to approach His Eminence at present or until the *Auto* was over. As he finished a cry went up from the multitude, and a sudden heave ran through it, stirring its surface as when a ripple runs over water.

The apparitor looked down the long street, Sir Gervase looked with him, and caught in the clear sunlight a distant glint of arms. The cry all about him was: "They come! They come!" and by this he knew that what he beheld was the head of the vanguard of the dread procession.

He plagued the apparitor now with anxious questions, touching this scaffold and the various parts of it. When he betrayed the fact that he supposed the condemned would suffer there, he provoked a smile and a question as to his origin which had left him so ignorant in matters of universal knowledge. But he also elicited the information that the place of execution was outside the walls of the city. This scaffold was for the announcement of the offences, for the Mass and the sermon of the Faith. How should he suppose it a place of execution, seeing that the Holy Office shed no blood?

This was news to Sir Gervase. He ventured to question its accuracy. The alguazile afforded him the enlightenment of which an outlandish barbarian appeared to stand in need. Here the Holy Office publicly penanced those who were guilty of pardonable offences against the Faith and publicly cast out from the Church those who refused to be reconciled or who, by relapsing into an infidelity from which they had formerly been rescued, placed themselves beyond the reach of pardon. In casting them out the Holy Office abandoned them to the secular arm, whose duty to the Faith involved the obligation of putting them to death. But it was not, he repeated, the Holy Office which did this, as Sir Gervase had so foolishly supposed, for the Holy Office, he further repeated, could shed no blood.

It was a nice distinction over which at a remote distance of space or time a man might smile. But in the grim theatre of the event no smile was possible.

The procession drew nearer. Sir Gervase looked about him in his distraction, to right, to left, ahead and up at the balconies of the houses under which he stood, as if seeking somewhere a way of escape, a way of reaching the Inquisitor-General. As he looked upwards his eyes met those of a girl leaning from an iron balcony, from which was hung a cloth of black velvet, edged with silver. She was one of a half-dozen women who stood there to behold the show, a slight wisp of a creature, olive-skinned, with brilliant lips, and eyes

like two black jewels. She had been considering, it must be supposed
with approval, the Englishman's stalwart inches and bared auburn
head. The disfiguring grime and stubble she could hardly discern at
that distance. The attitude towards him of the apparitors may further
have marked him for a person of consequence.

As their eyes met in that momentary flash, she let fall, as if by
accident, a rose. It brushed his cheek in falling, but to the beauty's
chagrin, went entirely unheeded by him in his preoccupation of
spirit.

Slowly and solemnly the procession was entering the square. At
its head marched the soldiers of the Faith, a regiment of javelin-men
in funereal livery, relieved by the gleam of their morions and the flash
of the partisans they shouldered. Gravely, looking neither to right
nor to left, they passed towards the scaffold about the base of which
they were to range themselves.

Next came a dozen surpliced choristers intoning the Miserere as
they slowly advanced into the square. They were followed after a
little pause by a Dominican bearing the sable banner of the
Inquisition, charged with the green cross between an olive branch
and a naked sword, the emblems of mercy and of justice. On his left
walked the Provincial of the Dominicans, on his right the Prior of
Our Lady of Alcantra, each attended by three monks. Then came a
body of lay tertiaries of the Order of St Dominic, members of the
Confraternity of St Peter the Martyr, walking two by two, with
the cross of St Dominic embroidered in silver upon their mantles.
After them, on horseback, also two by two, came some fifty nobles
of Castile to give worldly pomp to the procession. Their horses were
caparisoned in sable velvet; they themselves were all in black, though
it was a black relieved by the gleam of gold chains and the sparkle of
jewels. So solemnly and slowly did they pass, sitting on their horses
in such rigid immobility, that they presented the appearance of a
troop of funereal equestrian statues.

The crowd had fallen into an awe-stricken silence, in which the
beat of iron-shod hoofs rang out in rhythm, as it seemed, with the

doleful receding chant of the choristers. Over all went still the tolling of that passing-bell from the Cathedral.

The Andalusian sunshine beat down from a sky as clear as blue enamel. It was reflected vividly from the white walls of the houses that served as background for this black phantasmagoria. To Gervase there was a moment in which it all became not merely incredible, but unreal. It did not exist. Nothing existed, not even his own limp weary body leaning there against the wall. He was simply a mind into which he had brought absurd conceptions of a world of independent beings of imagined shapes and attributes and habits. None of these things about him had any concrete existence, they were simply ideas with which he had peopled a dream.

The moment of detachment passed. He was aroused from it by a sudden rustle and movement in the throng, which was behaving as a field of corn behaves when a sudden gust of wind sweeps over it. Men and women were failing on their knees in a continuous movement proceeding from the right. So odd was this continuity that it almost seemed as if each unit of that throng in kneeling touched his neighbour and so drove him down whilst he, in his turn, did the like by the person next to him.

An imposing scarlet figure advanced upon a milk-white mule, whose scarlet trappings, fringed with gold, trailed along the dusty ground. Coming abruptly thus after the black gloom of the long lines of figures that had preceded him, he seemed of a startling vividness. Save for the violet amice of the Inquisitor which he wore, he was all flame from the point of his velvet shoes to the crown of his broad-brimmed hat. A cloud of pages and halberdiers attended him. He rode very stiff and straight and stern, his right hand raised its thumb and two fingers erect to bless the people.

Thus, at comparatively close quarters, Gervase beheld the man to whom his letter was addressed, the Cardinal-Archbishop of Toledo, the Pope of Spain, the President of the Supreme Council and Inquisitor-General of Castile.

He passed, and with a reversing of the movement that had heralded his approach the crowd came gradually erect again.

Informed of his identity, Gervase importuned the alguazile to make a way for him, so that he might at once deliver his letter.

"Patience!" he was admonished. "While the procession passes that will be impossible. Afterwards, we shall see."

Uproar broke out now, shouts, execrations, epithets of infamy. The noise came rolling up the street to infect those in the square as the foremost victims came into view. They were flanked on each side by guarding pikemen, and each was accompanied by a Dominican, crucifix in hand. There were some fifty of them, bareheaded, barefoot, and almost naked under the zamarra, the penitential sack of coarse yellow serge, streaked by a single arm of a St Andrew's cross. In his hand each carried an unlighted taper of yellow wax, to be lighted presently at the altar when the penitent's reconciliation should have been pronounced. There were tottering old men and feeble old women, stalwart lads and weeping girls, and all of them staggered onwards in their cassocks of infamy with lowered heads, their eyes upon the ground, crushed under their load of shame, terrified by the execrations hurled at them as they passed.

The haggard eyes of Sir Gervase scanned their ranks. Knowing nothing of the distinctions made and indicated by the signs upon the zamarra, he did not realize that there were penitents who, guilty of comparatively light offences, went to be reconciled and pardoned with the imposition of penances of varying severity. Suddenly his glance alighted upon a countenance he knew; a narrow handsome face with a peaked black beard and fine eyes which, looking straight before him, reflected now something of the agony within his soul.

Sir Gervase sucked in his breath. The scene before him was momentarily blotted out. In its place he beheld an arbour set above a rose-garden, and seated there a very elegant, mocking gentleman with a lute in his lap, a lute which Sir Gervase dashed to the ground. He heard again the level, mocking voice:

"You do not like music, eh, Sir Gervase?"

Then the scene melted into another: A sweep of lawn shaded by a quickset hedge, by which a golden-headed girl was standing. This same gentleman bowing to him with a false urbanity, and proffering him the hilt of a sword. Again that same pleasant voice: "Enough for today. Tomorrow I will show you how the estramaçon is to be met and turned."

He was back again in the Zocodover at Toledo. The figure which had raised these visions was abreast of him. He craned to look, and caught something of the agony in the man's face, conceived something of what it must cost him to be thus paraded, was taken even with pity for him, imagining that he went to his death.

The penitents passed, and in their wake stalked another posse of soldiers of the Faith.

Then, borne aloft, dangling from long green poles, their limbs jerked hither and thither as in the movements of some idiotic dance, or as if with the spasmodic twitchings of the hanged, came a half-dozen full-sized effigies in grotesque caricature of life. These figures of straw were arrayed in yellow zamarras smeared with tongues of fire and with horrid images of devils and dragons, and they were crowned by the coroza, the yellow mitre of the condemned. On their faces of waxed linen were figured bituminous eyes and scarlet idiotic lips. Grotesque and horrible, they passed. They were the effigies of contumaciously absent offenders which were to be burnt, pending the capture of the originals, and of others who, after death, had been discovered guilty of heresy; of these followed now the poor earthly remains. Porters came staggering under the exhumed coffins which were to be given to the flames jointly with the effigies.

The baying of the mob, which had died down after the passing of the penitents, now rose again with an increased ferocity. Gervase saw women crossing themselves and men craning forward with an interest grown overwhelming.

"*Los relapsos!*" was the cry, meaningless to him.

On they came, those poor wretches who had relapsed and for whom there was no reconciliation, and those who were in the same case because obstinate in their heresy. There were but six of them; but all six were doomed to the fire. They advanced singly, each one between two Dominicans, who were still exhorting these unfortunates to repent and win at least the mercy of strangulation before being burnt in fires which otherwise must be but a prelude to eternal flames.

But the crowd, less pitiful, entirely pitiless, indeed, in its perfervid devotion to the most pitiful of all religions, roared foul abuse, demoniac mockery, ordures of insult at those anguished wretches who were passing to the flames.

The first of them was a stalwart aged Jew; a misguided fellow who, perhaps for the sake of temporal profit – so as to overcome the barriers so calculatedly erected against the worldly advancement of the Israelite, so as to earn the right to continue in the land in which his forefathers had been established for centuries before the crucifixion – had accepted baptism and embraced Christianity. Later, his conscience stirring against this apostasy from the Mosaic Law, he had secretly relapsed into Judaism, to be discovered, hailed before the dread tribunal of the Faith, tortured into confession and then condemned. He dragged himself painfully along in his hideous livery of infamy, his yellow zamarra and coroza bedaubed with flames and devils. A band of iron, passed about his neck, held a wooden apple in his mouth to gag him. But his eyes remained eloquent of scorn as he flashed them upon the howling bestial Christian mob.

He was followed by one even more pitiful. A young Morisco girl of ravishing beauty stepped along with light and tripping movements of her graceful limbs; she seemed almost to be treading a measure as she came. Her long black hair, escaped from her yellow mitre, hung about her shoulders like a mantle. And as she went, she paused ever and anon, and leaning a hand upon the shoulder of the gaunt Dominican beside her, she would throw back her body and laugh with the wild abandoned joy of a drunken woman. Her mind had given way.

Next came a terror-stricken youth who was half-carried along by his guards, a dazed half-swooning woman, and two men in middle life so broken by torture that they could hardly crawl.

After these followed another double file of monks, and after them again a military rearguard akin to that which had headed the procession. But the details now entirely escaped Gervase. He had suddenly realized that Margaret was not among the condemned. Relief at this, and renewed anxiety springing from his ignorance of her real condition, shut out the scene around him.

Anon he remembered a glimpse of the great scaffold, the Inquisitor-General in the tribune; the condemned ranged on the tiers to the right, the effigies dangling above the topmost places; the nobles and clergy on the benches opposite; a Dominican preaching from the pulpit facing the condemned.

The remainder of the *Auto* was afterwards a confused dream-memory: the ritual of the Mass, the chanting of choristers, and the clouds of incense rising above the altar surmounted by its great green cross; then the figure of the Notary standing to read from a long scroll, his voice inaudible at the distance at which Gervase was placed; the movement of the apparitors, bringing the condemned from their benches and surrendering them to the corregidor and his men – the representatives of the secular arm – who waited at the foot of the great scaffold to mount them on donkeys, and so hurry them away under guard, each with a Dominican in attendance; the howls of execration from the mob; and, lastly, the stately return of that procession by the way it had come.

As it passed, the human torrent broke the dam that had so long confined it; the barricades, no longer guarded, yielding to pressure, were broken down and swept away, and the crowd swirled in on both sides and filled the street.

The alguazile touched Sir Gervase on the arm. "Come," he said.

Chapter 24

Recognition

The *Auto de Fé* was over. The reconciled had been reconducted to the Holy House, where, upon the morrow, measures would be taken for the enforcement of the penances to which they were sentenced. The condemned had been hurried away to the meadows by the river, beyond the walls. There, at La Dehesa, beside the swirling Tagus, in view of the smiling countryside beyond the river, that lovely peaceful amphitheatre enclosed by hills, a great white cross had been reared as the symbol of mercy. About it were the stakes, the faggots piled, and there, *Christi nomine invocato*, the work of the Faith was brought to an end in smoke and ashes. The crowd had followed to attend the closing scene of that great show, and was again kept within bounds by a stout barricade by men-at-arms. But the majority of those who had taken active part in the *Auto* had returned with the reconciled to the Holy House.

The Cardinal-Archbishop was back in his palace, disrobing, his mind at peace at last so far as his nephew was concerned. The course which he had advocated to Frey Juan Arrenzuelo had in the end been adopted. Don Pedro had been sentenced upon the depositions of Frey Luis. He was condemned to pay a fine of a thousand ducats into the treasury of the Holy Office and to attend Mass barefoot, clad only in his shirt, and with a rope about his neck, every day for a month in the Cathedral of Toledo, at the end of which his offence would be accounted purged and absolution and reinstatement would follow.

The case against the woman might now proceed strictly in accordance with inquisitorial duty and inquisitorial practice, and either as a witch or merely as a heretic, she would undoubtedly he burnt when they came to hold the next *Auto de Fé*. That, thought the Cardinal, was no longer a matter of sufficient importance to cause him any preoccupation.

But in this conclusion he was proved hasty. Within half an hour of his return to the palace Frey Juan Arrenzuelo came in agitation to seek him.

He brought news that already Frey Luis Salcedo was protesting openly against the order observed, which he denounced as an illegality. The sentence upon Don Pedro, Frey Luis was asserting, had been based upon matters which must remain presumptions until established by the condemnation of the woman as a witch. He desired to know, demanded to know, what course would be adopted if torture should fail to wring from the woman the necessary admission of her necromantic practices.

Arrenzuelo had sought to pacify him with the reminder that he might well wait until the situation which he feared arose; at present all his protests were in the realm of speculation.

"The realm of speculation!" Frey Luis had laughed. "Was it not in the realm of speculation that sentence was passed upon Don Pedro, so as to enable him to escape the graver punishment which may yet be his due?"

He had said this in the presence of a considerable audience in the Holy House, and it was impossible not to perceive the threat which he implied, and also the fact that his zeal and vehemence had impressed many of those who overheard him into sympathy with his views.

The Cardinal was deeply annoyed. But he was wise enough to put aside annoyance which could not serve him in dealing with one who was supported by right. He considered deeply for some moments, saying no word to betray his real chagrin.

At last he permitted himself a smile of much gentleness and some craft.

"Word comes to me from Segovia that the Inquisitor of the Faith there is so ill that a successor must be appointed. I shall confer the appointment on Frey Luis Salcedo today. His zeal and rigid honesty would seem eminently to qualify him. He shall leave for Segovia at once."

But the suggestion in which the Cardinal conceived that he had found the solution of his difficulty had the effect of visibly terrifying Frey Juan.

"He will see in that an attempt to remove an awkward testifier to the truth, an attempt to bribe him into silence. He will become a devastating flame of righteous anger nothing afterwards will quench."

The Cardinal perceived the truth of this, and stared blankly. All, then, was to be rendered vain by this impetuous friar unless torture should wring the requisite confession from the woman. That was now his only hope.

A secretary entered, unbidden, at that moment. Irritably the Cardinal waved him away.

"Not now! Not now! You interrupt us."

"On the King's business, Eminence." And in answer to the Cardinal's change of countenance, the secretary informed him that alguaziles of the Holy Office had brought in a man who excused himself for bearing arms in such a place at such a time on the ground that he was a messenger from the King with a letter for the Inquisitor-General, which he was to deliver in person.

Still travel-stained, haggard, and unshaven, Sir Gervase was introduced, a man worn almost to the last strain of endurance. His eyes, blood-injected from sleeplessness, seemed to have receded into his head; they shone with an unnatural glassy brightness amid the dark shadows that surrounded them. He lurched in his step as he now advanced.

The Cardinal, a humane man, observed these signs. "You have ridden hard, sir," he said, between question and assertion.

Sir Gervase bowed, and presented his letter. The Cardinal took it.

"Give him a seat, Pablo. He is in no case to stand."

Gratefully the Englishman slid into the chair to which the Cardinal waved him and which the secretary advanced invitingly.

His Eminence broke the royal seal. As he read, the cloud of care lifted from his brow. The eyes which he raised to look across the top of the royal parchment at Frey Juan were alight with relief, almost with laughter.

"Heaven, I think, has intervened," he said, and passed the sheet to the Dominican. "The woman is abstracted from the care of the Holy Office by royal command. She need preoccupy us no further."

But Frey Juan Arrenzuelo frowned as he read. The woman might not be a witch, but she was still a heretic and a soul to be saved, and he resented this royal intervention in what he accounted the affairs of God. At another time the Inquisitor-General would have shared that just resentment, and would not have relinquished this heretic without a struggle and a stern reminder to His Majesty that he intervened at his peril in matters of the Faith. But at present the command came so opportunely to solve all difficulties, to rescue the Inquisitor-General even from a possible accusation of nepotism, that, as he pondered it, His Eminence smiled. Before that smile, so placid and beatific, Frey Juan bowed his head, and stifled the protests which were rising to his lips.

"If you will confirm this, Eminence, in your quality as Inquisitor-General of the Faith, the prisoner shall be surrendered."

Subtly thus he reminded Cardinal Quiroga that the King transcended his royal and strictly secular authority. Cardinal Quiroga, very grateful for that royal presumption, dictated at once his confirmation to the secretary, signed it, and delivered it to the Inquisitor that he might attach it to the royal letter.

Then he turned his glance again upon Sir Gervase. "Who are you, sir, into whose charge the prisoner is to be consigned?"

Sir Gervase got to his feet and answered him. He gave his name and announced that he had followed from England with a letter from the Queen.

"An Englishman?" said His Eminence, raising his brows. Here, no doubt was another heretic, he thought. But he shrugged. After all, the matter was out of his hands, and he was very glad to be rid of it. He had no reason for anything but thankfulness towards this hard-worn messenger.

He offered him refreshment, of which he appeared to stand so sorely in need, whilst the prisoner was being brought from the Holy House. When inquisitorial duty permitted it, there was no more humane gentleman in Spain than this Cardinal-Archbishop of Toledo. Gervase accepted gratefully, having heard Frey Juan dismissed with instructions to send the prisoner at once to the Palace, and Frey Juan's reply that it should be done within the hour, so soon as the necessary formalities were satisfied and record made of the command concerning her.

Two familiars of the Holy Office conducted her from her cell. She imagined that she was being led to another of the exasperating audiences that made a mockery of justice. Instead, she found herself conducted across the great hall to the double doors that opened upon the street. The postern was set wide for her by one of the familiars, and she was waved out by the other, who followed.

Before the door stood a mule-litter, which he motioned her to enter. She looked about her, hesitating a moment. People were streaming through this as through other streets in numbers, dispersing after the consummation of the *Auto*. She desired to know what was intended by her. The novelty of the proceedings filled her with a fresh uneasiness. But having no Spanish it was impossible to ask questions. Being a woman, single-handed, weak and helpless, it was even more idle to attempt resistance. She must wait to ascertain; meanwhile command such patience as still remained in her.

She entered the litter, the leather curtains were closely drawn, and the mules went off briskly, guided by the man who rode the foremost, and escorted by some others which she had seen drawn up alongside and whose hoofs she now heard clattering beside her.

At last the little cavalcade came to a standstill, the curtains parted again, and she was desired to alight. She found herself before an imposing building in the great square, across which fell now the shadow of the vast Cathedral.

In that shadow the air was chill, and she shivered as she stood there. Then the same familiars ushered her through double gates of wrought iron bearing great gilded escutcheons, each surmounted by a cardinal's hat with its array of tassels. Under a deep archway they came into a quadrangle where the ground was inlaid with mosaics and in the middle of which a fountain played. Across this, at another door guarded by two splendid men-at-arms in steel and scarlet, familiars consigned her to a waiting chamberlain in black who bore a wand and about whose neck a chain was hung.

The mystery of it deepened. Had she fallen asleep in her cell, and was she dreaming?

This sleek black gentleman signed to her to follow him, and the familiars were left behind. They ascended a wide marble staircase flanked by a massive balustrade, rising from a hall that was hung with costly tapestries which Spain had no doubt filched from Flanders. They passed between two further men-at-arms, standing like statues at the stair-head, and along a corridor, until the chamberlain halted at a door. He opened it, signed to her to enter, bowed as she passed him, and closed the door upon her when she had crossed the threshold.

Understanding nothing, she found herself in a small plain room. Its windows looked out across the courtyard through which she had passed to the opposite wall, whose white surface was aglow in the last rays of the setting sun. A tall-backed chair was standing by a table that was topped with red velvet. Out of this chair a man rose now to startle her.

He turned to face her, and the incredible became the impossible; even when he spoke her name, spoke it on a sob, and came lurching towards her with out-held hands, her brain refused to be seduced by this illusion. And then she was in his arms, she felt them coiled about her, and this ghost – this untidy, grimy, unshaven ghost – was kissing her hair, her eyes, her very lips. He was no ghost, then. He was real. The thought brought her a new terror. She thrust back from him as far as his embrace allowed.

"Gervase! What are you doing here, Gervase?"

"I've come for you," he answered simply.

"You've come for me?" she repeated the words as if they had no meaning.

A smile crossed the man's weary face. His fingers fumbled at the breast of his doublet. "I had your note," he said.

"My note?"

"The note you sent me to Arwenack, asking me to come to you. See. Here it is." He drew it forth, a very soiled and crumpled scrap. "When I got to Trevanion Chase, you'd gone. So…so I followed; and I'm here to take you home."

"To take me home? Home?" She could almost inhale the perfume of the moors.

"Yes. All is arranged. This Cardinal is very good… The escort waits. We go… Santander and there Tressilian stays for us with his ship… All arranged."

His senses were swimming, he staggered as he held her, might indeed have fallen but for his hold of her. And then she said words which revived and renewed his strength as not even the Cardinal's wine had been able to do.

"Gervase! You wonderful, wonderful Gervase!" Her arms tightened about his neck as if she would have choked him.

"I knew you would find it out one day," he said weakly.

Rafael Sabatini

Captain Blood

Captain Blood is the much-loved story of a physician and gentleman turned pirate.

Peter Blood, wrongfully accused and sentenced to death, narrowly escapes his fate and finds himself in the company of buccaneers. Embarking on his new life with remarkable skill and bravery, Blood becomes the 'Robin Hood' of the Spanish seas. This is swashbuckling adventure at its best.

The Gates of Doom

'Depend above all on Pauncefort', announced King James; 'his loyalty is dependable as steel. He is with us body and soul and to the last penny of his fortune.' So when Pauncefort does indeed face bankruptcy after the collapse of the South Sea Company, the king's supreme confidence now seems rather foolish. And as Pauncefort's thoughts turn to gambling, moneylenders and even marriage to recover his debts, will he be able to remain true to the end? And what part will his friend and confidante, Captain Gaynor, play in his destiny?

'A clever story, well and amusingly told' – *The Times*

Rafael Sabatini

The Lost King

The Lost King tells the story of Louis XVII – the French royal who officially died at the age of ten but, as legend has it, escaped to foreign lands where he lived to an old age. Sabatini breathes life into these age-old myths, creating a story of passion, revenge and betrayal. He tells of how the young child escaped to Switzerland from where he plotted his triumphant return to claim the throne of France.

'...the hypnotic spell of a novel which for sheer suspense, deserves to be ranked with Sabatini's best' – *New York Times*

Scaramouche

When a young cleric is wrongfully killed, his friend, André-Louis, vows to avenge his death. André's mission takes him to the very heart of the French Revolution where he finds the only way to survive is to assume a new identity. And so is born Scaramouche – a brave and remarkable hero of the finest order and a classic and much-loved tale in the greatest swashbuckling tradition.

'Mr Sabatini's novel of the French Revolution has all the colour and lively incident which we expect in his work' – *Observer*

Rafael Sabatini

The Sea Hawk

Sir Oliver, a typical English gentleman, is accused of murder, kidnapped off the Cornish coast, and dragged into life as a Barbary corsair. However Sir Oliver rises to the challenge and proves a worthy hero for this much-admired novel. Religious conflict, melodrama, romance and intrigue combine to create a masterly and highly successful story, perhaps best-known for its many film adaptations.

The Shame of Motley

The Court of Pesaro has a certain fool – one Lazzaro Biancomonte of Biancomonte. *The Shame of Motley* is Lazzaro's story, presented with all the vivid colour and dramatic characterisation that has become Sabatini's hallmark.

'Mr Sabatini could not be conventional or commonplace if he tried'
– *Standard*